THE BOOK OF EVIDENCE

JOHN BANVILLE was born in Wexford, Ireland, in 1945. His first book, *Long Lankin*, was published in 1970. His other books are *Nightspawn*, *Birchwood*, *Doctor Copernicus* (which won the James Tait Black Memorial Prize in 1976), *Kepler* (which was awarded the *Guardian* Fiction Prize in 1981), *The Newton Letter* (which was filmed for Channel 4), *Mefisto*, *Ghosts*, *Athena* and *The Untouchable*. John Banville is the literary editor of the *Irish Times* and lives in Dublin with his wife and two sons.

JOHN BANVILLE

The BOOK *of* EVIDENCE

PICADOR

First published 1989 by Martin Secker & Warburg Limited

This edition published 1998 by Picador
an imprint of Pan Macmillan Ltd
Pan Macmillan, 20 New Wharf Road, London N1 9RR
Basingstoke and Oxford
Associated companies throughout the world
www.panmacmillan.com

ISBN 0 330 37187 8

7 9 8

A CIP catalogue record for this book is available from
the British Library.

Printed and bound in Great Britain by
Mackays of Chatham plc, Chatham, Kent

I

MY LORD, when you ask me to tell the court in my own words, this is what I shall say. I am kept locked up here like some exotic animal, last survivor of a species they had thought extinct. They should let in people to view me, the girl-eater, svelte and dangerous, padding to and fro in my cage, my terrible green glance flickering past the bars, give them something to dream about, tucked up cosy in their beds of a night. After my capture they clawed at each other to get a look at me. They would have paid money for the privilege, I believe. They shouted abuse, and shook their fists at me, showing their teeth. It was unreal, somehow, frightening yet comic, the sight of them there, milling on the pavement like film extras, young men in cheap raincoats, and women with shopping bags, and one or two silent, grizzled characters who just stood, fixed on me hungrily, haggard with envy. Then a guard threw a blanket over my head and bundled me into a squad car. I laughed. There was something irresistibly funny in the way reality, banal as ever, was fulfilling my worst fantasies.

By the way, that blanket. Did they bring it specially, or do they always keep one handy in the boot? Such questions trouble me now, I brood on them. What an

3

interesting figure I must have cut, glimpsed there, sitting up in the back like a sort of mummy, as the car sped through the wet, sunlit streets, bleating importantly.

Then this place. It was the noise that impressed me first of all. A terrible racket, yells and whistles, hoots of laughter, arguments, sobs. But there are moments of stillness, too, as if a great fear, or a great sadness, has fallen suddenly, striking us all speechless. The air stands motionless in the corridors, like stagnant water. It is laced with a faint stink of carbolic, which bespeaks the charnel-house. In the beginning I fancied it was me, I mean I thought this smell was mine, my contribution. Perhaps it is? The daylight too is strange, even outside, in the yard, as if something has happened to it, as if something has been done to it, before it is allowed to reach us. It has an acid, lemony cast, and comes in two intensities: either it is not enough to see by or it sears the sight. Of the various kinds of darkness I shall not speak.

My cell. My cell is. Why go on with this.

Remand prisoners are assigned the best cells. This is as it should be. After all, I might be found innocent. Oh, I mustn't laugh, it hurts too much, I get a terrible twinge, as if something were pressing on my heart – the burden of my guilt, I suppose. I have a table and what they call an easy chair. There is even a television set, though I rarely watch it, now that my case is *sub judice* and there is nothing about me on the news. The sanitation facilities leave something to be desired. Slopping out: how apt, these terms. I must see if I can get a catamite, or do I mean a neophyte? Some young fellow, nimble and willing, and not too fastidious. That shouldn't be difficult. I must see if I can get a dictionary, too.

Above all I object to the smell of semen everywhere. The place reeks of it.

4

I confess I had hopelessly romantic expectations of how things would be in here. Somehow I pictured myself a sort of celebrity, kept apart from the other prisoners in a special wing, where I would receive parties of grave, important people and hold forth to them about the great issues of the day, impressing the men and charming the ladies. What insight! they would cry. What breadth! We were told you were a beast, cold-blooded, cruel, but now that we have seen you, have heard you, why – ! And there am I, striking an elegant pose, my ascetic profile lifted to the light in the barred window, fingering a scented handkerchief and faintly smirking, Jean-Jacques the cultured killer.

Not like that, not like that at all. But not like other clichés either. Where are the mess-hall riots, the mass break-outs, that kind of thing, so familiar from the silver screen? What of the scene in the exercise yard in which the stoolie is done to death with a shiv while a pair of blue-jawed heavyweights stage a diversionary fight? When are the gang-bangs going to start? The fact is, in here is like out there, only more so. We are obsessed with physical comfort. The place is always overheated, we might be in an incubator, yet there are endless complaints of draughts and sudden chills and frozen feet at night. Food is important too, we pick over our plates of mush, sniffing and sighing, as if we were a convention of gourmets. After a parcel delivery word goes round like wildfire. *Psst! She's sent him a battenberg! Homemade!* It's just like school, really, the mixture of misery and cosiness, the numbed longing, the noise, and everywhere, always, that particular smelly grey warm male fug.

It was different, I'm told, when the politicals were here. They used to goose-step up and down the corridors, barking at each other in bad Irish, causing much merriment among the ordinary criminals. But then they all went on hunger strike or something, and were moved away to a place of their own, and life returned to normal.

Why are we so compliant? Is it the stuff they are said to put in our tea to dull the libido? Or is it the drugs. Your honour, I know that no one, not even the prosecution, likes a squealer, but I think it is my duty to apprise the court of the brisk trade in proscribed substances which is carried on in this institution. There are screws, I mean warders, involved in it, I can supply their numbers if I am guaranteed protection. Anything can be had, uppers and downers, tranqs, horse, crack, you name it – not that you, of course, your worship, are likely to be familiar with these terms from the lower depths, I have only learned them myself since coming here. As you would imagine, it is mainly the young men who indulge. One recognises them, stumbling along the gangways like somnambulists, with that little, wistful, stunned smile of the truly zonked. There are some, however, who do not smile, who seem indeed as if they will never smile again. They are the lost ones, the goners. They stand gazing off, with a blank, preoccupied expression, the way that injured animals look away from us, mutely, as if we are mere phantoms to them, whose pain is taking place in a different world from ours.

But no, it's not just the drugs. Something essential has gone, the stuffing has been knocked out of us. We are not exactly men any more. Old lags, fellows who have committed some really impressive crimes, sashay about the place like dowagers, pale, soft, pigeon-chested, big in the beam. They squabble over library books, some of them even knit. The young too have their hobbies, they sidle up to me in the recreation room, their calf eyes fairly brimming, and shyly display their handiwork. If I have to admire one more ship in a bottle I shall scream. Still, they

6

are so sad, so vulnerable, these muggers, these rapists, these baby-batterers. When I think of them I always picture, I'm not sure why, that strip of stubbly grass and one tree that I can glimpse from my window if I press my cheek against the bars and peer down diagonally past the wire and the wall.

Stand up, please, place your hand here, state your name clearly. Frederick Charles St John Vanderveld Montgomery. Do you swear to tell the truth, the whole truth and nothing but the truth? Don't make me laugh. I want straight away to call my first witness. My wife. Daphne. Yes, that was, is, her name. For some reason people have always found it faintly comic. I think it matches very well her damp, dark, myopic beauty. I see her, my lady of the laurels, reclining in a sun-dazed glade, a little vexed, looking away with a small frown, while some minor god in the shape of a faun, with a reed pipe, prances and capers, vainly playing his heart out for her. It was that abstracted, mildly dissatisfied air which first drew my attention to her. She was not nice, she was not good. She suited me. Perhaps I was already thinking of a time to come when I would need to be pardoned – by someone, anyone – and who better to do that than one of my own kind.

When I say she was not good I do not mean she was wicked, or corrupt. The flaws in her were nothing compared with the jagged cracks that run athwart my soul. The most one could accuse her of was a sort of moral laziness. There were things she could not be bothered to do, no matter what imperatives propelled them to her jaded attention. She neglected our son, not because she was not fond of him, in her way, but simply because his needs did not really interest her. I would catch her, sitting on a

7

chair, looking at him with a remote expression in her eyes, as if she were trying to remember who or what precisely he was, and how he had come to be there, rolling on the floor at her feet in one of his own many messes. Daphne! I would murmur, for Christ's sake! and as often as not she would look at me then in the same way, with the same blank, curiously absent gaze.

I notice that I seem unable to stop speaking of her in the past tense. It feels right, somehow. Yet she often visits me. The first time she came she asked what it was like in here. Oh, my dear! I said, the noise! – and the people! She just nodded a little and smiled wanly, and looked about her idly at the other visitors. We understand each other, you see.

In southern climes her indolence was transformed into a kind of voluptuous languor. There is a particular room I remember, with green shutters and a narrow bed and a Van Gogh chair, and a Mediterranean noon pulsing outside in the white streets. Ibiza? Ischia? Mykonos perhaps? Always an island, please note that, clerk, it may mean something. Daphne could get out of her clothes with magical swiftness, with just a sort of shrug, as if skirt, blouse, pants, everything, were all of a piece. She is a big woman, not fat, not heavy, even, but yet weighty, and beautifully balanced: always when I saw her naked I wanted to caress her, as I would want to caress a piece of sculpture, hefting the curves in the hollow of my hand, running a thumb down the long smooth lines, feeling the coolness, the velvet texture of the stone. Clerk, strike that last sentence, it will seem to mean too much.

Those burning noons, in that room and countless others like it – my God, I tremble to think of them now. I could not resist her careless nudity, the weight and density of that glimmering flesh. She would lie beside me, an abstracted

8

maya, gazing past me at the shadowy ceiling, or at that chink of hot white light between the shutters, until at last I managed, I never understood exactly how, to press a secret nerve in her, and then she would turn to me heavily, quickly, with a groan, and cling to me as if she were falling, her mouth at my throat, her blind-man's fingertips on my back. She always kept her eyes open, their dim soft grey gaze straying helplessly, flinching under the tender damage I was inflicting on her. I cannot express how much it excited me, that pained, defenceless look, so unlike her at any other time. I used to try to have her wear her spectacles when we were in bed like this, so she would seem even more lost, more defenceless, but I never succeeded, no matter what sly means I might employ. And of course I could not ask. Afterwards it would be as though nothing at all had happened, she would get up and stroll to the bathroom, a hand in her hair, leaving me prostrate on the soaked sheet, convulsed, gasping, as if I had suffered a heart attack, which I suppose I had, in a way.

She never knew, I believe, how deeply she affected me. I was careful that she should not know it. Oh, don't mistake me, it was not that I was afraid I would give myself into her power, or anything like that. It was just that such knowledge would have been, well, inappropriate between us. There was a reticence, a tactfulness, which from the first we had silently agreed to preserve. We understood each other, yes, but that did not mean we knew each other, or wanted to. How would we have maintained that unselfconscious grace that was so important to us both, if we had not also maintained the essential secretness of our inner selves?

How good it was to get up then in the cool of afternoon and amble down to the harbour through the stark geometry of sun and shadow in the narrow streets. I liked to watch Daphne walking ahead of me, her strong shoulders and her hips moving in a muffled, complex rhythm under the light stuff of her dress. I liked to watch the island men, too, hunched over their pastis and their thimbles of turbid coffee, swivelling their lizard eyes as she went past. That's right, you bastards, yearn, yearn.

On the harbour there was always a bar, always the same one whatever the island, with a few tables and plastic chairs outside, and crooked sun-umbrellas advertising Stella or Pernod, and a swarthy, fat proprietor leaning in the doorway picking his teeth. It was always the same people, too: a few lean, tough types in bleached denim, hard-eyed women gone leathery from the sun, a fat old guy with a yachting cap and grizzled sideburns, and of course a queer or two, with bracelets and fancy sandals. They were our crowd, our set, our friends. We rarely knew their names, or they ours, we called each other pal, chum, captain, darling. We drank our brandies or our ouzos, whatever was the cheapest local poison, and talked loudly of other friends, characters every one, in other bars, on other islands, all the while eyeing each other narrowly, even as we smiled, watching for we knew not what, an opening, perhaps, a soft flank left momentarily unguarded into which we might sink our fangs. Ladies and gentlemen of the jury, you have seen us, we were part of the local colour on your package holiday, you passed us by with wistful glances, and we ignored you.

We presided among this rabble, Daphne and I, with a kind of grand detachment, like an exiled king and queen waiting daily for word of the counter-rebellion and the summons from the palace to return. People in general, I noticed it, were a little afraid of us, now and again I detected it in their eyes, a worried, placatory, doggie sort of look, or else a resentful glare, furtive and sullen. I have pondered this phenomenon, it strikes me as significant. What was it in us – or rather, what was it *about* us – that impressed them? Oh, we are large, well-made, I am handsome, Daphne is beautiful, but that cannot have been the whole of it. No, after much thought the conclusion I have come to is this, that they imagined they recognised in us a coherence and wholeness, an essential authenticity, which they lacked, and of which they felt they were not entirely worthy. We were – well, yes, we were heroes.

I thought all this ridiculous, of course. No, wait, I am under oath here, I must tell the truth. I enjoyed it. I enjoyed sitting at ease in the sun, with my resplendent, disreputable consort at my side, quietly receiving the tribute of our motley court. There was a special, faint little smile I had, calm, tolerant, with just the tiniest touch of contempt, I bestowed it in particular on the sillier ones, the poor fools who prattled, cavorting before us in cap and bells, doing their pathetic tricks and madly laughing. I looked in their eyes and saw myself ennobled there, and so could forget for a moment what I was, a paltry, shivering thing, just like them, full of longing and loathing, solitary, afraid, racked by doubts, and dying.

That was how I got into the hands of crooks: I allowed myself to be lulled into believing I was inviolable. I do not seek, my lord, to excuse my actions, only to explain them. That life, drifting from island to island, encouraged illusions. The sun, the salt air, leached the significance out of things, so that they lost their true weight. My instincts, the instincts of our tribe, those coiled springs tempered in the dark forests of the north, went slack down there, your honour, really, they did. How could anything be dangerous, be wicked, in such tender, blue, watercolour weather? And then, bad things are always things that take place elsewhere, and bad people are never the people that one knows. The American, for instance, seemed no worse than any of the others among that year's crowd. In fact, he seemed to me no worse than I was myself – I mean, than I imagined myself to be, for this, of course, was before I discovered what things I was capable of.

I refer to him as the American because I did not know, or cannot remember, his name, but I am not sure that he was American at all. He spoke with a twang that might have been learned from the pictures, and he had a way of looking about him with narrowed eyes while he talked which reminded me of some film star or other. I could not take him seriously. I did a splendid impression of him – I have always been a good mimic – which made people laugh out loud in surprise and recognition. At first I thought he was quite a young man, but Daphne smiled and asked had I looked at his hands. (She noticed such things.) He was lean and muscular, with a hatchet face and boyish, close-cropped hair. He went in for tight jeans and high-heeled boots and leather belts with huge buckles. There was a definite touch of the cowpoke about him. I shall call him, let me see, I shall call him – Randolph. It was Daphne he was after. I watched him sidle up, hands stuck in his tight pockets, and start to sniff around her, at once cocksure and edgy, like so many others before him, his longing, like theirs, evident in a certain strained whiteness between the eyes. Me he treated with watchful affability, addressing me as friend, and even – do I imagine it? – as *pardner*. I remember the first time he sat himself down at our table, twining his spidery legs around the chair and leaning forward on an elbow. I expected him to fetch out a tobacco pouch and roll himself a smoke with one hand.

The waiter, Paco, or Pablo, a young man with hot eyes and aristocratic pretensions, made a mistake and brought us the wrong drinks, and Randolph seized the opportunity to savage him. The poor boy stood there, his shoulders bowed under the lashes of invective, and was what he had always been, a peasant's son. When he had stumbled away, Randolph looked at Daphne and grinned, showing a side row of long, fulvous teeth, and I thought of a hound sitting back proud as punch after delivering a dead rat at its mistress's feet. Goddamned spics, he said carelessly, and made a spitting noise out of the side of his mouth. I jumped up and seized the edge of the table and overturned it, pitching the drinks into his lap, and shouted at him to get up and reach for it, you sonofabitch! No, no, of course I didn't. Much as I might have liked to dump a table full of broken glass into his ludicrously overstuffed crotch, that was not the way I did things, not in those days. Besides, I had enjoyed as much as anyone seeing Pablo or Paco get his comeuppance, the twerp, with his soulful glances and his delicate hands and that horrible, pubic moustache.

Randolph liked to give the impression that he was a very dangerous character. He spoke of dark deeds perpetrated in a far-off country which he called Stateside. I encouraged these tales of derring-do, secretly delighting in the aw-shucks, 'tweren't-nuthin' way he told them. There was something wonderfully ridiculous about it all, the braggart's sly glance and slyly modest inflexion, his air of euphoric self-regard, the way he opened like a flower under the warmth of my silently nodding, awed response. I have always derived satisfaction from the little wickednesses of human beings. To treat a fool and a liar as if I esteemed him the soul of probity, to string him along in his poses and his fibs, that is a peculiar pleasure. He claimed he was a painter, until I put a few innocent questions to him on the subject, then he suddenly became a writer instead. In fact, as he confided to me one night in his cups, he made his money by dealing in dope among the island's transient rich. I was shocked, of course, but I recognised a valuable piece of information, and later, when –

But I am tired of this, let me get it out of the way. I asked him to lend me some money. He refused. I reminded him of that drunken night, and said I was sure the *guardia* would be interested to hear what he had told me. He was shocked. He thought about it. He didn't have the kind of dough I was asking for, he said, he would have to get it for me somewhere, maybe from some people that he knew. And he chewed his lip. I said that would be all right, I didn't mind where it came from. I was amused, and rather pleased with myself, playing at being a blackmailer. I had not really expected him to take me seriously, but it seemed I had underestimated his cravenness. He produced the cash, and for a few weeks Daphne and I had a high old time, and everything was grand except for Randolph dogging my steps wherever I went. He was distressingly literal-minded in his interpretation of words such as *lend* and *repay*. Hadn't I kept his grubby little secret, I said, was that not a fair return? These people, he said, with an awful, twitching attempt at a grin, these people didn't fool around. I said I was glad to hear it, one wouldn't want to think one had been dealing, even at second-hand, with the merely frivolous. Then he threatened to give them my name. I laughed in his face and walked away. I still could not take any of it seriously. A few days later a small package wrapped in brown paper arrived, addressed to me in a semi-literate hand. Daphne made the mistake of opening it. Inside was a tobacco tin – Balkan Sobranie, lending an oddly cosmopolitan touch – lined with cotton wool, in which nestled a curiously whorled, pale, gristly piece of meat crusted with dried blood. It took me a moment to identify it as a human ear. Whoever had cut it off had done a messy job, with something like a breadknife, to judge by the ragged serration. Painful. I suppose that was the intention. I remember thinking: How appropriate, an ear, in this land of the toreador! Quite droll, really.

I went in search of Randolph. He wore a large lint pad pressed to the left side of his head, held in place by a rakishly angled and none-too-clean bandage. He no longer made me think of the Wild West. Now, as if fate had decided to support his claim of being an artist, he bore a striking resemblance to poor, mad Vincent in that self-portrait made after he had disfigured himself for love. When he saw me I thought he was going to weep, he looked so sorry for himself, and so indignant. You deal with them yourself now, he said, you owe them, not me, I've paid, and he touched a hand grimly to his bandaged head. Then he called me a vile name and skulked off down an alleyway. Despite the noonday sun a shiver passed across my back, like a grey wind swarming over water. I tarried there for a moment, on that white corner, musing. An old man on a burro saluted me. Nearby a tinny churchbell was clanging rapidly. Why, I asked myself, why am I living like this?

That is a question which no doubt the court also would like answered. With my background, my education, my – yes – my culture, how could I live such a life, associate with such people, get myself into such scrapes? The answer is – I don't know the answer. Or I do, and it is too large, too tangled, for me to attempt here. I used to believe, like everyone else, that I was determining the course of my own life, according to my own decisions, but gradually, as I accumulated more and more past to look back on, I realised that I had done the things I did because I could do no other. Please, do not imagine, my lord, I hasten to say it, do not imagine that you detect here the insinuation of an apologia, or even of a defence. I wish to claim full responsibility for my actions – after all, they are the only things I can call my own – and I declare in advance that I shall accept without demur the verdict of the court. I am merely asking, with all respect, whether it is feasible to hold on to the principle of moral culpability once the notion of free will has been abandoned. It is, I grant you, a tricky one, the sort of thing we love to discuss in here of an evening, over our cocoa and our fags, when time hangs heavy.

As I've said, I did not always think of my life as a prison in which all actions are determined according to a random pattern thrown down by an unknown and insensate authority. Indeed, when I was young I saw myself as a masterbuilder who would one day assemble a marvellous edifice around myself, a kind of grand pavilion, airy and light, which would contain me utterly and yet wherein I would be free. Look, they would say, distinguishing this eminence from afar, look how sound it is, how solid: it's him all right, yes, no doubt about it, the man himself. Meantime, however, unhoused, I felt at once exposed and invisible. How shall I describe it, this sense of myself as something without weight, without moorings, a floating phantom? Other people seemed to have a density, a thereness, which I lacked. Among them, these big, carefree creatures, I was like a child among adults. I watched them, wide-eyed, wondering at their calm assurance in the face of a baffling and preposterous world. Don't mistake me, I was no wilting lily, I laughed and whooped and boasted with the best of them – only inside, in that grim, shadowed gallery I call my heart, I stood uneasily, with a hand to my mouth, silent, envious, uncertain. They understood matters, or accepted them, at least. They knew what they thought about things, they had opinions. They took the broad view, as if they did not realise that everything is infinitely divisible. They talked of cause and effect, as if they believed it possible to isolate an event and hold it up to scrutiny in a pure, timeless space, outside the mad swirl of things. They would speak of whole peoples as if they were speaking of a single individual, while to speak even of an individual with any show of certainty seemed to me foolhardy. Oh, they knew no bounds.

And as if people in the outside world were not enough, I had inside me too an exemplar of my own, a kind of invigilator, from whom I must hide my lack of conviction. For instance, if I was reading something, an argument in some book or other, and agreeing with it enthusiastically, and then I discovered at the end that I had misunderstood entirely what the writer was saying, had in fact got the whole thing arse-ways, I would be compelled at once to execute a somersault, quick as a flash, and tell myself, I mean my other self, that stern interior sergeant, that what was being said was true, that I had never really thought otherwise, and, even if I had, that it showed an open mind that I should be able to switch back and forth between opinions without even noticing it. Then I would mop my brow, clear my throat, straighten my shoulders and pass on delicately, in stifled dismay. But why the past tense? Has anything changed? Only that the watcher from inside has stepped forth and taken over, while the puzzled outsider cowers within.

Does the court realise, I wonder, what this confession is costing me?

I took up the study of science in order to find certainty. No, that's not it. Better say, I took up science in order to make the lack of certainty more manageable. Here was a way, I thought, of erecting a solid structure on the very sands that were everywhere, always, shifting under me. And I was good at it, I had a flair. It helped, to be without convictions as to the nature of reality, truth, ethics, all those big things – indeed, I discovered in science a vision of an unpredictable, seething world that was eerily familiar to me, to whom matter had always seemed a swirl of chance collisions. Statistics, probability theory, that was my field. Esoteric stuff, I won't go into it here. I had a certain cold gift that was not negligible, even by the awesome standards of the discipline. My student papers were models of clarity and concision. My professors loved me, dowdy old boys reeking of cigarette smoke and bad teeth, who recognised in me that rare, merciless streak the lack of which had condemned them to a life of drudgery at the lectern. And then the Americans spotted me.

How I loved America, the life there on that pastel, sun-drenched western coast, it spoiled me forever. I see it still in dreams, all there, inviolate, the ochre hills, the bay, the great delicate red bridge wreathed in fog. I felt as if I had ascended to some high, fabled plateau, a kind of Arcady. Such wealth, such ease, such innocence. From all the memories I have of the place I select one at random. A spring day, the university cafeteria. It is lunchtime. Outside, on the plaza, by the fountain, the marvellous girls disport themselves in the sun. We have listened that morning to a lecture by a visiting wizard, one of the grandmasters of the arcanum, who sits with us now at our table, drinking coffee from a paper cup and cracking pistachio nuts in his teeth. He is a lean, gangling person with a wild mop of frizzed hair going grey. His glance is humorous, with a spark of malice, it darts restlessly here and there as if searching for something that will make him laugh. The fact is, friends, he is saying, the whole damn thing is chance, pure chance. And he flashes suddenly a shark's grin, and winks at me, a fellow outsider. The faculty staff sitting around the table nod and say nothing, big, tanned, serious men in short-sleeved shirts and shoes with broad soles. One scratches his jaw, another consults idly a chunky wristwatch. A boy wearing shorts and no shirt passes by outside, playing a flute. The girls rise slowly, two by two, and slowly walk away, over the grass, arms folded, their books pressed to their chests like breastplates. My God, can I have been there, really? It seems to me now, in this place, more dream than memory, the music, the mild maenads, and us at our table, faint, still figures, the wise ones, presiding behind leaf-reflecting glass.

They were captivated by me over there, my accent, my bow-ties, my slightly sinister, old-world charm. I was twenty-four, among them I felt middle-aged. They threw themselves at me with solemn fervour, as if engaging in a form of self-improvement. One of their little foreign wars was in full swing just then, everyone was a protester, it seemed, except me – I would have no truck with their marches, their sit-downs, the ear-splitting echolalia that passed with them for argument – but even my politics, or lack of them, were no deterrent, and flower children of all shapes and colours fell into my bed, their petals trembling. I remember few of them with any precision, when I think of them I see a sort of hybrid, with this one's hands, and that one's eyes, and yet another's sobs. From those days, those nights, only a faint, bittersweet savour remains, and a trace, the barest afterglow, of that state of floating ease, of, how shall I say, of balanic, ataraxic bliss – yes, yes, I have got hold of a dictionary – in which they left me, my muscles aching from their strenuous ministrations, my flesh bathed in the balm of their sweat.

It was in America that I met Daphne. At a party in some professor's house one afternoon I was standing on the porch with a treble gin in my hand when I heard below me on the lawn the voice of home: soft yet clear, like the sound of water falling on glass, and with that touch of lethargy which is the unmistakable note of our set. I looked, and there she was, in a flowered dress and unfashionable shoes, her hair done up in the golliwog style of the day, frowning past the shoulder of a man in a loud jacket who was replying with airy gestures to something she had asked, while she nodded seriously, not listening to a word he said. I had just that glimpse of her and then I turned away, I don't quite know why. I was in one of my bad moods, and halfway drunk. I see that moment as an emblem of our life together. I would spend the next fifteen years turning away from her, in one way or another, until that morning when I stood at the rail of the island steamer, snuffling the slimed air of the harbour and waving half-heartedly to her and the child, the two of them tiny below me on the dockside. That day it was she who turned away from me, with what seems to me now a slow and infinitely sad finality.

I felt as much foolishness as fear. I felt ridiculous. It was unreal, the fix I had got myself into: one of those mad dreams that some ineffectual fat little man might turn into a third-rate film. I would dismiss it for long periods, as one dismisses a dream, no matter how awful, but presently it would come slithering back, the hideous, tentacled thing, and there would well up in me a hot flush of terror and shame – shame, that is, for my own stupidity, my wanton lack of prescience, that had landed me in such a deal of soup.

Since I had seemed, with Randolph, to have stumbled into a supporting feature, I had expected it would be played by a comic cast of ruffians, scarified fellows with low foreheads and little thin moustaches who would stand about me in a circle with their hands in their pockets, smiling horribly and chewing toothpicks. Instead I was summoned to an audience with a silver-haired hidalgo in a white suit, who greeted me with a firm, lingering handshake and told me his name was Aguirre. His manner was courteous and faintly sad. He fitted ill with his surroundings. I had climbed a narrow stairs to a dirty, low room above a bar. There was a table covered with oilcloth, and a couple of cane chairs. On the floor under the table a filthy infant was sitting, sucking a wooden spoon. An outsize television set squatted in a corner, on the blank, baleful screen of which I saw myself reflected, immensely tall and thin, and curved like a bow. There was a smell of fried food. Señor Aguirre, with a little moue of distaste, examined the seat of one of the chairs and sat down. He poured out wine for us, and tipped his glass in a friendly toast. He was a businessman, he said, a simple businessman, not a great professor – and smiled at me and gently bowed – but all the same he knew there were certain rules, certain moral imperatives. One of these in particular he was thinking of: perhaps I could guess which one? Mutely I shook my head. I felt like a mouse being toyed with by a sleek bored old cat. His sadness deepened. Loans, he said softly, loans must be repaid. That was the law on which commerce was founded. He hoped I would understand his position. There was a silence. A kind of horrified amazement had taken hold of me: this was the real world, the world of fear and pain and retribution, a serious place, not that sunny playground in which I had frittered away fistfuls of someone else's money. I would have to go home, I said at last, in a voice that did not seem to be mine, there were people who would help me, friends, family, I could borrow from them. He considered. Would I go alone? he wondered. For a second I did not see what he was getting at. Then I looked away from him and said slowly yes, yes, my wife and son would probably stay here. And as I said it I seemed to hear a horrible cackling, a jungle hoot of derision, just behind my shoulder. He smiled, and poured out carefully another inch of wine. The child, who had been playing with my shoelaces, began to howl. I was agitated, I had not meant to kick the creature. Señor Aguirre frowned, and shouted something over his shoulder. A door behind him opened and an enormously fat, angry-looking young woman put in her head and grunted at him. She wore a black, sleeveless dress with a crooked hem, and a glossy black wig as high as a beehive, with false eyelashes to match. She waddled forward, and with an effort bent and picked up the infant and smacked it hard across the face. It started in surprise, and, swallowing a mighty sob, fixed its round eyes solemnly on me. The woman glared at me too, and took the wooden spoon and threw it on the table in front of me with a clatter. Then, planting the child firmly on one tremendous hip, she stumped out of the room and slammed the door behind her. Señor Aguirre gave a slight, apologetic shrug. He smiled again, twinkling. What was my opinion of the island women? I hesitated. Come come, he said gaily, surely I had an opinion on such an important matter. I said they were lovely, quite lovely, quite the loveliest of their species I had ever encountered. He nodded happily, it was what he had expected me to say. No, he said, no, too dark, too dark all over, even in those places never exposed to the sun. And he leaned forward with his crinkled, silvery smile and tapped a finger lightly on my wrist. Northern women, now, ah, those pale northern women. Such white skin! So delicate! So fragile! Your wife, for instance, he said. There was another, breathless silence. I could hear faintly the brazen strains of music from a radio in the bar downstairs. Bullfight music. My chair made a crackling noise under me, like a muttered warning. Señor Aguirre joined his El Greco hands and looked at me over the spire of his fingertips. Your whife, he said, breathing on the word, your beautiful whife, you will come back quickly to her? It was not really a question. What could I say to him, what could I do? These are not really questions either.

I told Daphne as little as possible. She seemed to understand. She made no difficulties. That has always been the great thing about Daphne: she makes no difficulties.

It was a long trip home. The steamer landed in Valencia harbour at dusk. I hate Spain, a brutish, boring country. The city smelled of sex and chlorine. I took the night train, jammed in a third-class compartment with half a dozen reeking peasants in cheap suits. I could not sleep. I was hot, my head ached. I could feel the engine labouring up the long slope to the plateau, the wheels drumming their one phrase over and over. A washed-blue dawn was breaking in Madrid. I stopped outside the station and watched a flock of birds wheeling and tumbling at an immense height, and, the strangest thing, a gust of euphoria, or something like euphoria, swept through me, making me tremble, and bringing tears to my eyes. It was from lack of sleep, I suppose, and the effect of the high, thin air. Why, I wonder, do I remember so clearly standing there, the colour of the sky, those birds, that shiver of fevered optimism? I was at a turning point, you will tell me, just there the future forked for me, and I took the wrong path without noticing – that's what you'll tell me, isn't it, you, who must have meaning in everything, who lust after meaning, your palms sticky and your faces on fire! But calm, Frederick, calm. Forgive me this outburst, your honour. It is just that I do not believe such moments mean anything – or any other moments, for that matter. They have significance, apparently. They may even have value of some sort. But they do not mean anything.

There now, I have declared my faith.

Where was I? In Madrid. On my way out of Madrid. I took another train, travelling north. We stopped at every station on the way, I thought I would never get out of that terrible country. Once we halted for an hour in the middle of nowhere. I sat in the ticking silence and stared dully through the window. Beyond the littered tracks of the up-line there was an enormous, high, yellow field, and in the distance a range of blue mountains that at first I took for clouds. The sun shone. A tired crow flapped past. Someone coughed. I thought how odd it was to be there, I mean just there and not somewhere else. Not that being somewhere else would have seemed any less odd. I mean – oh, I don't know what I mean. The air in the compartment was thick. The seats gave off their dusty, sat-upon smell. A small, swarthy, low-browed man opposite me caught my eye and did not look away. At that instant it came to me that I was on my way to do something very bad, something really appalling, something for which there would be no forgiveness. It was not a premonition, that is too tentative a word. I knew. I cannot explain how, but I knew. I was shocked at myself, my breathing quickened, my face pounded as if from embarrassment, but as well as shock there was a sort of antic glee, it surged in my throat and made me choke. That peasant was still watching me. He sat canted forward a little, hands resting calmly on his knees, his brow lowered, at once intent and remote. They stare like that, these people, they have so little sense of themselves they seem to imagine their actions will not register on others. They might be looking in from a different world.

I knew very well, of course, that I was running away.

I HAD expected to arrive in rain, and at Holyhead, indeed, a fine, warm drizzle was falling, but when we got out on the channel the sun broke through again. It was evening. The sea was calm, an oiled, taut meniscus, mauve-tinted and curiously high and curved. From the forward lounge where I sat the prow seemed to rise and rise, as if the whole ship were straining to take to the air. The sky before us was a smear of crimson on the palest of pale blue and silvery green. I held my face up to the calm sea-light, entranced, expectant, grinning like a loon. I confess I was not entirely sober, I had already broken into my allowance of duty-free booze, and the skin at my temples and around my eyes was tightening alarmingly. It was not just the drink, though, that was making me happy, but the tenderness of things, the simple goodness of the world. This sunset, for instance, how lavishly it was laid on, the clouds, the light on the sea, that heartbreaking, blue-green distance, laid on, all of it, as if to console some lost, suffering wayfarer. I have never really got used to being on this earth. Sometimes I think our presence here is due to a cosmic blunder, that we were meant for another planet altogether, with other arrangements, and other laws, and other, grimmer skies. I try to imagine it, our true place, off on the far side of the galaxy, whirling and whirling. And the ones who were meant for here, are they out there, baffled and homesick, like us? No, they would have become extinct long ago. How could they survive, these gentle earthlings, in a world that was made to contain *us*?

The voices, that was what startled me first of all. I thought they must be putting on this accent, it sounded so like a caricature. Two raw-faced dockers with fags in their mouths, a customs man in a cap: my fellow countrymen. I walked through a vast, corrugated-iron shed and out into the tired gold of the summer evening. A bus went past, and a workman on a bike. The clocktower, its addled clock still showing the wrong time. It was all so affecting, I was surprised. I liked it here when I was a child, the pier, the promenade, that green bandstand. There was always a sweet sense of melancholy, of mild regret, as if some quaint, gay music, the last of the season, had just faded on the air. My father never referred to the place as anything but Kingstown: he had no time for the native jabber. He used to bring me here on Sunday afternoons, sometimes on weekdays too in the school holidays. It was a long drive from Coolgrange. He would park on the road above the pier and give me a shilling and slope off, leaving me to what he called my own devices. I see myself, the frog prince, enthroned on the high back seat of the Morris Oxford, consuming a cornet of ice cream, licking the diminishing knob of goo round and round with scientific application, and staring back at the passing promenaders, who blanched at the sight of my baleful eye and flickering, creamy tongue. The breeze from the sea was a soft, salt wall of air in the open window of the car, with a hint of smoke in it from the mailboat berthed below me. The flags on the roof of the yacht club shuddered and snapped, and a thicket of masts in the harbour swayed and tinkled like an oriental orchestra.

My mother never accompanied us on these jaunts. They were, I know now, just an excuse for my father to visit a poppet he kept there. I do not recall him behaving furtively, or not any more so than usual. He was a slight, neatly-made man, with pale eyebrows and pale eyes, and a small, fair moustache that was faintly indecent, like a bit of body fur, soft and downy, that had found its way inadvertently on to his face from some other, secret part of his person. It made his mouth startlingly vivid, a hungry, violent, red-coloured thing, grinding and snarling. He was always more or less angry, seething with resentment and indignation. Behind the bluster, though, he was a coward, I think. He felt sorry for himself. He was convinced the world had used him badly. In recompense he pampered himself, gave himself treats. He wore handmade shoes and Charvet ties, drank good claret, smoked cigarettes specially imported in airtight tins from a shop in the Burlington Arcade. I still have, or had, his malacca walking-cane. He was enormously proud of it. He liked to demonstrate to me how it was made, from four or was it eight pieces of rattan prepared and fitted together by a master craftsman. I could hardly keep a straight face, he was so laughably earnest. He made the mistake of imagining that his possessions were a measure of his own worth, and strutted and crowed, parading his things like a schoolboy with a champion catapult. Indeed, there was something of the eternal boy about him, something tentative and pubertal. When I think of us together I see him as impossibly young and me already grown-up, weary, embittered. I suspect he was a little afraid of me. By the age of twelve or thirteen I was as big as he, or as heavy, anyway, for although I have his fawn colouring, in shape I took after my mother, and already at that age was inclined towards flab. (Yes, m'lud, you see before you a middling man inside whom there is a fattie trying not to come out. For he was let slip once, was Bunter, just once, and look what happened.)

I hope I do not give the impression that I disliked my father. We did not converse much, but we were perfectly companionable, in the way of fathers and sons. If he did fear me a little, I too was wise enough to be wary of *him*, a relation easily mistaken, even by us at times, for mutual esteem. We had a great distaste for the world generally, there was that much in common between us. I notice I have inherited his laugh, that soft, nasal snicker which was his only comment on the large events of his time. Schisms, wars, catastrophes, what did he care for such matters? — the world, the only worthwhile world, had ended with the last viceroy's departure from these shores, after that it was all just a wrangle among peasants. He really did try to believe in this fantasy of a great good place that had been taken away from us and our kind — our kind being Castle Catholics, as he liked to say, yes, sir, Castle Catholics, and proud of it! But I think there was less pride than chagrin. I think he was secretly ashamed not to be a Protestant: he would have had so much less explaining, so much less justifying, to do. He portrayed himself as a tragic figure, a gentleman of the old school displaced in time. I picture him on those Sunday afternoons with his mistress, an ample young lady, I surmise, with hair unwisely curled and a generous décolletage, before whom he kneels, poised trembling on one knee, gazing rapt into her face, his moustache twitching, his moist red mouth open in supplication. Oh but I must not mock him like this. Really, really, I did not think unkindly of him — apart, that is, from wanting deep down to kill him, so that I might marry my mother, a novel and compelling notion which my counsel urges on me frequently, with a meaning look in his eye.

But I digress.

The charm I had felt in Kingstown, I mean Dun Laoghaire, did not endure into the city. My seat at the front on the top deck of the bus – my old seat, my favourite! – showed me scenes I hardly recognised. In the ten years since I had last been here something had happened, something had befallen the place. Whole streets were gone, the houses torn out and replaced by frightening blocks of steel and black glass. An old square where Daphne and I lived for a while had been razed and made into a vast, cindered car-park. I saw a church for sale – a church, for sale! Oh, something dreadful had happened. The very air itself seemed damaged. Despite the late hour a faint glow of daylight lingered, dense, dust-laden, like the haze after an explosion, or a great conflagration. People in the streets had the shocked look of survivors, they seemed not to walk but reel. I got down from the bus and picked my way among them with lowered gaze, afraid I might see horrors. Barefoot urchins ran along beside me, whining for pennies. There were drunks everywhere, staggering and swearing, lost in joyless befuddlement. An amazing couple reared up out of a pulsating cellar, a minatory, pockmarked young man with a crest of orange hair, and a stark-faced girl in gladiator boots and ragged, soot-black clothes. They were draped about with ropes and chains and what looked like cartridge belts, and sported gold studs in their nostrils. I had never seen such creatures, I thought they must be members of some fantastic sect. I fled before them, and dived into Wally's pub. Dived is the word.

I had expected it to be changed, like everything else. I

was fond of Wally's. I used to drink there when I was a student, and later on, too, when I worked for the government. There was a touch of sleaze to the place which I found congenial. I know much has been made of the fact that it was frequented by homosexuals, but I trust the court will dismiss the implications which have been tacitly drawn from this, especially in the gutter press. I am not queer. I have nothing against those who are, except that I despise them, of course, and find disgusting the thought of the things they get up to, whatever those things may be. But their presence lent a blowsy gaiety to the atmosphere in Wally's and a slight edge of threat. I liked that shiver of embarrassment and gleeful dread that ran like a bead of mercury up my spine when a bevy of them suddenly exploded in parrot shrieks of laughter, or when they got drunk and started howling abuse and breaking things. Tonight, when I hurried in to shelter from the stricken city, the first thing I saw was a half dozen of them at a table by the door with their heads together, whispering and giggling and pawing each other happily. Wally himself was behind the bar. He had grown fatter, which I would not have thought possible, but apart from that he had not changed in ten years. I greeted him warmly. I suspect he remembered me, though of course he would not acknowledge it: Wally prided himself on the sourness of his manner. I ordered a large, a gargantuan gin and tonic, and he sighed grudgingly and heaved himself off the high stool on which he had been propped. He moved very slowly, as if through water, billowing in his fat, like a jellyfish. I was feeling better already. I told him about the church I had seen for sale. He shrugged, he was not surprised, such things were commonplace nowadays. As he was setting my drink before me the huddled circle of queers by the door flew apart suddenly in a loud splash of laughter, and he frowned at them, pursing his little mouth so that it almost disappeared in the folds of his fat chin. He affected contempt for his clientele, though it was said he kept a bevy of boys himself, over whom he ruled with great severity, jealous and terrible as a Beardsleyan queen.

I drank my drink. There is something about gin, the tang in it of the deep wildwood, perhaps, that always makes me think of twilight and mists and dead maidens. Tonight it tinkled in my mouth like secret laughter. I looked about me. No, Wally's was not changed, not changed at all. This was my place: the murmurous gloom, the mirrors, the bottles ranged behind the bar, each one with its bead of ruby light. Yes, yes, the witch's kitchen, with a horrid fat queen, and a tittering band of fairy-folk. Why, there was even an ogre – Gilles the Terrible, *c'est moi*. I was happy. I enjoy the inappropriate, the disreputable, I admit it. In low dives such as this the burden of birth and education falls from me and I feel, I feel – I don't know what I feel. I don't know. The tense is wrong anyway. I turned to Wally and held out my glass, and watched in a kind of numbed euphoria as he measured out another philtre for me in a little silver chalice. That flash of blue when he added the ice, what am I thinking of? Blue eyes. Yes, of course.

I did say dead maidens, didn't I. Dear me.

So I sat in Wally's pub and drank, and talked to Wally of this and that – his side of the conversation confined to shrugs and dull grunts and the odd malevolent snigger – and gradually the buzz that travel always sets going in my head was stilled. I felt as if, instead of journeying by ship and rail, I had been dropped somehow through the air to land up in this spot at last, feeling groggy and happy, and pleasantly, almost voluptuously vulnerable. Those ten years I had passed in restless wandering were as nothing, a dream voyage, insubstantial. How distant all that seemed, those islands in a blue sea, those burning noons, and Randolph and Señor Aguirre, even my wife and child, how distant. Thus it was that when Charlie French came in I greeted him as if I had seen him only yesterday.

I know Charlie insists that he did not meet me in Wally's pub, that he never went near the place, but all I am prepared to admit is the possibility that it was not on that particular night that I saw him there. I remember the moment with perfect clarity, the queers whispering, and Wally polishing a glass with a practised and inimitably contemptuous wrist-action, and I sitting at the bar with a bumper of gin in my fist and my old pigskin suitcase at my feet, and Charlie pausing there in his chalkstripes and his scuffed shoes, a forgetful Eumaeus, smiling uneasily and eyeing me with vague surmise. All the same, it is possible that my memory has conflated two separate occasions. It is possible. What more can I say? I hope, Charles, this concession will soothe, even if only a little, your sense of injury.

People think me heartless, but I am not. I have much sympathy for Charlie French. I caused him great distress, no doubt of that. I humiliated him before the world. What pain that must have been, for a man such as Charlie. He behaved very well about it. He behaved beautifully, in fact. On that last, appalling, and appallingly comic occasion, when I was being led out in handcuffs, he looked at me not accusingly, but with a sort of sadness. He almost smiled. And I was grateful. He is a source of guilt and annoyance to me now, but he was my friend, and –

He was my friend. Such a simple phrase, and yet how affecting. I don't think I have ever used it before. When I wrote it down I had to pause, startled. Something welled up in my throat, as if I might be about to, yes, to weep. What is happening to me? Is this what they mean by rehabilitation? Perhaps I shall leave here a reformed character, after all.

Poor Charlie did not recognise me at first, and was distinctly uneasy, I could see, at being addressed in this place, in this familiar fashion, by a person who seemed to him a stranger. I was enjoying myself, it was like being in disguise. I offered to buy him a drink, but he declined, with elaborate politeness. He had aged. He was in his early sixties, but he looked older. He was stooped, and had a little egg-shaped paunch, and his ashen cheeks were inlaid with a filigree of broken veins. Yet he gave an impression of, what shall I call it, of equilibrium, which seemed new to him. It was as if he were at last filling out exactly his allotted space. When I knew him he had been a small-time dealer in pictures and antiques. Now he had presence, it was almost an air of imperium, all the more marked amid the gaudy trappings of Wally's bar. It's true, there was still that familiar expression in his eye, at once mischievous and sheepish, but I had to look hard to find it. He began to edge away from me, still queasily smiling, but then he in turn must have caught something familiar in my eye, and he knew me at last. Relieved, he gave a breathy laugh and glanced around the bar. That I did remember, that glance, as if he had just discovered his flies were open and was looking to see if anyone had noticed. Freddie! he said. Well well! He lit a cigarette with a not altogether steady hand, and released a great whoosh of smoke towards the ceiling. I was trying to recall when it was I had first met him. He used to come down to Coolgrange when my father was alive and hang about the house looking furtive and apologetic. They had been young together, he and my parents, in their cups they would reminisce about hunt balls before the war, and dashing up to Dublin for the Show, and all the rest of it. I listened to this stuff with boundless contempt, curling an adolescent's villous lip. They sounded like actors flogging away at some tired old drawing-room comedy, projecting wildly, my mother especially, with her scarlet fingernails and metallic perm and that cracked, gin-and-smoke voice of hers. But to be fair to Charles, I do not think he really subscribed to this fantasy of the dear dead days. He could not ignore the tiny trill of hysteria that made my mother's goitrous throat vibrate, nor the way my father looked at her sometimes, poised on the edge of his chair, tense as a whippet, pop-eyed and pale, with an expression of incredulous loathing. When they got going like this, the two of them, they forgot everything else, their son, their friend, everything, locked together in a kind of macabre trance. This meant that Charlie and I were often thrown into each other's company. He treated me tentatively, as if I were something that might blow up in his face at any moment. I was very fierce in those days, brimming with impatience and scorn. We must have been a peculiar pair, yet we got on, at some deep level. Perhaps I seemed to him the son he would never have, perhaps he seemed to me the father I had never had. (This is another idea put forward by my counsel. I don't know how you think of them, Maolseachlainn.) What was I saying? Charlie. He took me to the races one day, when I was a boy. He was all kitted out for the occasion, in tweeds and brown brogues and a little trilby hat tipped at a raffish angle over one eye. He even had a pair of binoculars, though he did not seem to be able to get them properly in focus. He looked the part, except for a certain stifled something in his manner that made it seem all the time as if he were about to break down in helpless giggles at himself and his pretensions. I was fifteen or sixteen. In the drinks marquee he turned to me blandly and asked what I would have, Irish or Scotch — and brought me home in the evening loudly and truculently drunk. My father was furious, my mother laughed. Charlie maintained an unruffled silence, pretending nothing was amiss, and slipped me a fiver as I was stumbling off to bed.

Ah Charles, I am sorry, truly I am.

Now, as if he too were remembering that other time, he insisted on buying a drink, and pursed his lips disapprovingly when I asked for gin. He was a whiskey man, himself. It was part of his disguise, like the striped suit and the worn-down, handmade shoes, and that wonderful, winged helmet of hair, now silvered all over, which, so my mother liked to say, had destined him for greatness. He had always managed to avoid his destiny, however. I asked him what he was doing these days. Oh, he said, I'm running a gallery. And he glanced about him with an abstracted, wondering smile, as if he were himself surprised at such a notion. I nodded. So that was what had bucked him up, what had given him that self-sufficient air. I saw him in some dusty room, a forgotten backwater, with a few murky pictures on the wall, and a frosty spinster for a secretary who bickered with him over tea money and gave him a tie wrapped in tissue-paper every Christmas. Poor Charlie, forced to take himself seriously at last, with a business to take care of, and painters after him for their money. Here, I said, let me, and peeled a note from my rapidly dwindling wad and slapped it on the bar.

To be candid, however, I was thinking of asking him for a loan. What prevented me was — well, there will be laughter in court, I know, but the fact is I felt it would be in bad taste. It is not that I am squeamish about these matters, in my time I have touched sadder cases than

Charlie for a float, but there was something in the present circumstances that held me back. We might indeed have been a father and son — not *my* father, of course, and certainly not *this* son — meeting by chance in a brothel. Constrained, sad, obscurely ashamed, we blustered and bluffed, knocking our glasses together and toasting the good old days. But it was no use, in a little while we faltered, and fell gloomily silent. Then suddenly Charlie looked at me, with what was almost a flash of pain, and in a low, impassioned voice said, Freddie, what have you done to yourself? At once abashed, he leaned away from me in a panic, desperately grinning, and puffed a covering cloud of smoke. First I was furious, and then depressed. Really, I was not in the mood for this kind of thing. I glanced at the clock behind the bar and, purposely misunderstanding him, said yes, it was true, it had been a long day, I was overdoing it, and I finished my drink and shook his hand and took up my bag and left.

There it was again, in another form, the same question: why, Freddie, why are you living like this? I brooded on it next morning on the way to Coolgrange. The day looked as I felt, grey and flat and heavy. The bus plunged laboriously down the narrow country roads, pitching and wallowing, with a dull zip and roar that seemed the sound of my own blood beating in my brain. The myriad possibilities of the past lay behind me, a strew of wreckage. Was there, in all that, one particular shard — a decision reached, a road taken, a signpost followed — that would show me just how I had come to my present state? No, of course not. My journey, like everyone else's, even yours, your honour, had not been a thing of signposts and decisive marching, but drift only, a kind of slow

37

subsidence, my shoulders bowing down under the gradual accumulation of all the things I had not done. Yet I can see that to someone like Charlie, watching from the ground, I must have seemed a creature of fable scaling the far peaks, rising higher and ever higher, leaping at last from the pinnacle into marvellous, fiery flight, my head wreathed in flames. But I am not Euphorion. I am not even his father.

The question is wrong, that's the trouble. It assumes that actions are determined by volition, deliberate thought, a careful weighing-up of facts, all that puppet-show twitching which passes for consciousness. I was living like that because I was living like that, there is no other answer. When I look back, no matter how hard I try I can see no clear break between one phase and another. It is a seamless flow – although flow is too strong a word. More a sort of busy stasis, a sort of running on the spot. Even that was too fast for me, however, I was always a little way behind, trotting in the rear of my own life. In Dublin I was still the boy growing up at Coolgrange, in America I was the callow young man of Dublin days, on the islands I became a kind of American. And nothing was enough. Everything was coming, was on the way, was about to be. Stuck in the past, I was always peering beyond the present towards a limitless future. Now, I suppose, the future may be said to have arrived.

None of this means anything. Anything of significance, that is. I am just amusing myself, musing, losing myself in a welter of words. For words in here are a form of luxury, of sensuousness, they are all we have been allowed to keep of the rich, wasteful world from which we are shut away.

O God, O Christ, release me from this place.

O Someone.

I must stop, I am getting one of my headaches. They come with increasing frequency. Don't worry, your lordship, no need to summon the tipstaff or the sergeant-at-arms or whatever he's called — they are just headaches. I shall not suddenly go berserk, clutching my temples and bawling for my — but speak of the devil, here she is, Ma Jarrett herself. Come, step into the witness box, mother.

It was early afternoon when I reached Coolgrange. I got down at the cross and watched the bus lumber away, its fat back-end looking somehow derisive. The noise of the engine faded, and the throbbing silence of summer settled again on the fields. The sky was still overcast, but the sun was asserting itself somewhere, and the light that had been dull and flat was now a tender, pearl-grey glow. I stood and looked about me. What a surprise the familiar always is. It was all there, the broken gate, the drive, the long meadow, the oak wood – home! – all perfectly in place, waiting for me, a little smaller than I remembered, like a scale-model of itself. I laughed. It was not really a laugh, more an exclamation of startlement and recognition. Before such scenes as this – trees, the shimmering fields, that mild soft light – I always feel like a traveller on the point of departure. Even arriving I seemed to be turning away, with a lingering glance at the lost land. I set off up the drive with my raincoat over my shoulder and my battered bag in my hand, a walking cliché, though it's true I was a bit long in the tooth, and a bit on the beefy side, for the part of the prodigal son. A dog slid out of the hedge at me with a guttural snarl, teeth bared to the gums.

I halted. I do not like dogs. This was a black-and-white thing with shifty eyes, it moved back and forth in a half-circle in front of me, still growling, keeping its belly close to the ground. I held the suitcase against my knees for a shield, and spoke sharply, as to an unruly child, but my voice came out a broken falsetto, and for a moment there was a sense of general merriment, as if there were faces hidden among the leaves, laughing. Then a whistle sounded, and the brute whined and turned guiltily toward the house. My mother was standing on the front steps. She laughed. Suddenly the sun came out, with a kind of soundless report. Good God, she said, it is you, I thought I was seeing things.

I hesitate. It is not that I am lost for words, but the opposite. There is so much to be said I do not know where to begin. I feel myself staggering backwards slowly, clutching in my outstretched arms a huge, unwieldy and yet weightless burden. She is so much, and, at the same time, nothing. I must go carefully, this is perilous ground. Of course, I know that whatever I say will be smirked at knowingly by the amateur psychologists packing the court. When it comes to the subject of mothers, simplicity is not permitted. All the same, I shall try to be honest and clear. Her name is Dorothy, though everyone has always called her Dolly, I do not know why, for there is nothing doll-like about her. She is a large, vigorous woman with the broad face and heavy hair of a tinker's wife. In describing her thus I do not mean to be disrespectful. She is impressive, in her way, at once majestic and slovenly. I recall her from my childhood as a constant but remote presence, statuesque, blank-eyed, impossibly handsome in an Ancient Roman sort of way, like a marble figure at the far side of a lawn. Later on, though, she grew to be top-heavy, with a big backside and slim legs, a contrast which, when I was an adolescent and morbidly interested in such things, led me to speculate on the complicated architecture that must be necessary to bridge the gap under her skirt between those shapely knees and that thick waist. Hello, mother, I said, and looked away from her, casting about me crossly for something neutral on which to concentrate. I was annoyed already. She has that effect on me, I have only to stand before her and instantly the irritation and resentment begin to seethe in my breast. I was surprised. I had thought that after ten years there would be at least a moment of grace between our meeting and the first attack of filial heartburn, but not a bit of it, here I was, jaw clenched, glaring venomously at a tuft of weed sprouting from a crack in the stone steps where she stood. She was not much changed. Her bosom, which cries out to be called ample, had descended to just above her midriff. Also she had grown a little moustache. She wore baggy corduroy trousers and a cardigan with sagging pockets. She came down the steps to me and laughed again. You have put on weight, Freddie, she said, you've got fat. Then she reached out and — this is true, I swear it — and took hold of a piece of my stomach and rolled it playfully between a finger and thumb. This woman, this woman — what can I say? I was thirty-eight, a man of parts, with a wife and a son and an impressive Mediterranean tan, I carried myself with gravitas and a certain faint air of menace, and she, what did she do? — she pinched my belly and laughed her phlegmy laugh. Is it any wonder I have ended up in jail? Is it? The dog, seeing that I was to be accepted, sidled up to me and tried to lick my hand, which gave me an opportunity to deliver it a good hard kick in the ribs. That made me feel better, but not much, and not for long.

Is there anything as powerfully, as piercingly evocative, as the smell of the house in which one's childhood was spent? I try to avoid generalisations, as no doubt the court has noticed, but surely this is a universal, this involuntary spasm of recognition which comes with the first whiff of that humble, drab, brownish smell, which is hardly a smell at all, more an emanation, a sort of sigh exhaled by the thousands of known but unacknowledged tiny things that collectively constitute what is called home. I stepped into the hall and for an instant it was as if I had stepped soundlessly through the membrane of time itself. I faltered, tottering inwardly. Hatstand with broken umbrella, that floor tile, still loose. Get out, Patch, damn you! my mother said behind me, and the dog yelped. The taste of apples unaccountably flooded my mouth. I felt vaguely as if something momentous had happened, as if in the blink of an eye everything around me had been whipped away and replaced instantly with an exact replica, perfect in every detail, down to the last dust-mote. I walked on, into this substitute world, tactfully keeping a blank expression, and seemed to hear a disembodied held breath being let go in relief that the difficult trick had worked yet again.

We went into the kitchen. It looked like the lair of some large, scavenging creature. Lord, mother, I said, are you *living* in here? Items of clothing, an old woman's nameless rags, were stuffed between the dishes on the dresser. The toes of three or four pairs of shoes peeped out from under a cupboard, an unnerving sight, as if the wearers might be huddled together in there, stubby arms clasped around each other's hunched shoulders, listening. Pieces of furniture had migrated here from all over the house, the narrow little bureau from my father's study, the walnut cocktail cabinet from the drawing-room, the velvet-covered recliner with balding armrests in which my Great-

Aunt Alice, a tiny, terrible woman, had died without a murmur one Sunday afternoon in summer. The huge old wireless that used to lord it over the lounge stood now at a drunken tilt on the draining-board, crooning softly to itself, its single green eye pulsing. The place was far from clean. A ledger was open on the table, and bills and things were strewn amid the smeared plates and the unwashed teacups. She had been doing the accounts. Briefly I considered bringing up the main matter straight away – money, that is – but thought better of it. As if she had an inkling of what was in my mind she glanced from me to the papers and back again with amusement. I turned away from her, to the window. Out on the lawn a stocky girl in jodhpurs was leading a string of Connemara ponies in a circle. I recalled dimly my mother telling me, in one of her infrequent and barely literate letters, about some hare-brained venture involving these animals. She came and stood beside me. We watched in silence the ponies plodding round and round. Ugly brutes, aren't they, she said cheerfully. The simmering annoyance I had felt since arriving was added to now by a sense of general futility. I have always been prone to accidie. It is a state, or, I might even say, a force, the significance of which in human affairs historians and suchlike seem not to appreciate. I think I would do anything to avoid it – anything. My mother was talking about her customers, mostly Japs and Germans, it seemed – They're taking over the bloody country, Freddie, I'm telling you. They bought the ponies as pets for their spoilt offspring, at what she happily admitted were outrageous prices. Cracked, the lot of them, she said. We laughed, and then fell vacantly silent again. The sun was on the lawn, and a vast white cloud was slowly unfurling above the sweltering beeches. I was thinking how strange it was to stand here glooming out at the day like this, bored and irritable, my hands in my pockets, while all the time, deep inside me somewhere, hardly acknowledged, grief dripped and dripped, a kind of silvery ichor, pure, and strangely precious. Home, yes, home is always a surprise.

She insisted that I come and look the place over, as she put it. After all, my boy, she said, someday all this will be yours. And she did her throaty cackle. I did not remember her being so easily amused in the past. There was something almost unruly in her laughter, a sort of abandon. I was a little put out by it, I thought it was not seemly. She lit up a cigarette and set off around the house, with the cigarette box and matches clutched in her left claw, and me trailing grimly in her smoking wake. The house was rotting, in places so badly, and so rapidly, that even she was startled. She talked and talked. I nodded dully, gazing at damp walls and sagging floors and mouldering window-frames. In my old room the bed was broken, and there was something growing in the middle of the mattress. The view from the window — trees, a bit of sloping field, the red roof of a barn — was exact and familiar as an hallucination. Here was the cupboard I had built, and at once I had a vision of myself, a small boy with a fierce frown, blunt saw in hand, hacking at a sheet of plywood, and my grieving heart wobbled, as if it were not myself I was remembering, but something like a son, dear and vulnerable, lost to me forever in the depths of my own past. When I turned around my mother was not there. I found her on the stairs, looking a little odd around the eyes. She set off again. I must see the grounds, she cried, the stables, the oak wood. She was determined I would see everything, everything.

Out of doors my spirits rose somewhat. How soft the air of summer here. I had been too long under harsh southern skies. And the trees, the great trees! those patient, quietly suffering creatures, standing stock-still as if in embarrassment, their tragic gazes somehow turned away from us. Patch the dog – I can see I am going to be stuck with this brute – Patch the dog appeared, rolling its mad eyes and squirming. It followed silently behind us across the lawn. The stable-girl, watching sidelong as we approached, seemed on the point of taking to her heels in fright. Her name was Joan, or Jean, something like that. Big bum, big chest – obviously mother had felt an affinity. When I spoke to her the poor girl turned crimson, and wincingly extended a calloused little paw as if she were afraid I might be going to keep it. I gave her one of my special, slow smiles, and saw myself through her eyes, a tall, tanned hunk in a linen suit, leaning over her on a summer lawn and murmuring dark words. Tinker! she yelped, get off! The lead pony, a stunted beast with a truculent eye, was edging sideways in that dully determined way that they have, nudging heavily against me. I put my hand on its flank to push it away, and was startled by the solidity, the actuality of the animal, the coarse dry coat, the dense unyielding flesh beneath, the blood warmth. Shocked, I took my hand away quickly and stepped back. Suddenly I had a vivid, queasy sense of myself, not the tanned pin-up now, but something else, something pallid and slack and soft. I was aware of my toenails, my anus, my damp, constricted crotch. And I was ashamed. I can't explain it. That is, I could, but won't. Then the dog began to bark, rushing at the pony's hoofs, and the pony snorted, peeling back its muzzle and snapping its alarming teeth. My mother kicked the dog, and the girl hauled the pony's head sideways. The dog howled, the line of ponies plunged and whinnied. What a racket! Everything, always, turns to farce. I remembered my hangover. I needed a drink.

★

Gin first, then some sort of awful sherry, then successive jorums of my late father's fine Bordeaux, the last, alas, of the bin. I was already half-soused when I went down to the cellar to fetch the claret. I sat on a crate amid the must and gloom, breathing gin fumes out of flared nostrils. A streaming lance of sunlight, seething with dust, pierced the low, cobwebbed window above my head. Things thronged around me in the shadows – a battered rocking-horse, an old high bicycle, a bundle of antique tennis racquets – their outlines blurred, greyish, fading, as if this place were a way-station where the past paused on its way down into oblivion. I laughed. Old bastard, I said aloud, and the silence rang like a rapped glass. He was always down here in those last months before he died. He had become a potterer, he who all his life had been driven by fierce, obsessive energies. My mother would send me down to look for him, in case something might have happened to him, as she delicately put it. I would find him poking about in corners, fiddling with things, or just standing, canted at an odd angle, staring at nothing. When I spoke he would give a great start and turn on me angrily, huffing, as if he had been caught at something shameful. But these spurts of animation did not last long, after a moment he would drift off again into vagueness. It was as if he were not dying of an illness, but of a sort of general distraction: as if one day in the midst of his vehement doings something had caught his attention, had beckoned to him out of the darkness, and, struck, he had turned aside and walked towards it, with a sleepwalker's pained, puzzled concentration. I was, what, twenty-two, twenty-three. The long process of his dying wearied and exasperated me in equal measure. Of course I pitied him, too, but I think pity is always, for me, only the permissible version of an urge to give weak things a good hard shake.

He began to shrink. Suddenly his shirt collars were too big for that wobbly tortoise-neck with its two slack harp-strings. Everything was too big for him, his clothes had more substance than he did, he seemed to rattle about inside them. His eyes were huge and haunted, already clouding. It was summer then, too. Light was not his medium any more, he preferred it down here, in the mossy half-dark, among the deepening shades.

I hauled myself to my feet and gathered an armful of dusty bottles and staggered with them up the damp stone steps.

Yet he died upstairs, in the big front bedroom, the airiest room in the house. It was so hot all that week. They opened wide the window, and he made them move his bed forward until the foot of it was right out on the balcony. He lay with the covers thrown back, his meagre chest bared, giving himself up to the sun, the vast sky, dying into the blue and gold glare of summer. His hands. The rapid beat of his breathing. His –

Enough. I was speaking of my mother.

I had set the bottles on the table, and was clawing the dust and cobwebs off them, when she informed me that she did not drink now. This was a surprise – in the old days she could knock it back with the best of them. I stared at her, and she shrugged and looked away. Doctor's orders, she said. I examined her with renewed attention. There was something wrong with her left eye, and her mouth drooped a little on that side. I recalled the odd way she had clutched the cigarette box and matches in her left hand when she was conducting me around the house. She shrugged again. A slight stroke, she said, last year. I thought what an odd term that is: a slight stroke. As if a benevolent but clumsy power had dealt her a fond, playful blow and accidentally damaged her. She glanced at me sidelong now with a tentative, almost girlish, melancholy little smile. She might have been confessing to something, some peccadillo, trivial but embarrassing. Sorry to hear it, old thing, I said, and urged her to go on, take a drop of wine, the doctors be damned. She seemed not to hear me. And then a really surprising thing happened. The girl, Joan or Jean – I'll compromise, and call her Jane – got up suddenly from her place, with a gulp of distress, and put her arm awkwardly around my mother's head, clutching her in a sort of wrestling hold, and laying a hand along her brow. I expected my mother to give her a good push and tell her to get off, but no, she sat there, suffering calmly the girl's embrace and looking at me still with that small smile. I stared back at her in startlement, holding the wine bottle suspended above my glass. It was the strangest thing. The girl's great hip was beside my mother's shoulder, and I thought irresistibly of the pony pressing against me on the lawn with that stubborn, brute regard. There was a silence. Then the girl, I mean Jane, caught my eye, and blenched, and withdrew her arm and sat down again hurriedly. Here is a question: if man is a sick animal, an insane animal, as I have reason to believe, then how account for these small, unbidden gestures of kindness and of care? Does it occur to you, my lord, that people of our kind – if I may be permitted to scramble up and join you on the bench for a moment – that we have missed out on something, I mean something in general, a universal principle, which is so simple, so obvious, that no one has ever thought to tell us about it? They all know what it is, my learned friend, this knowledge is the badge of their fellowship. And they are everywhere, the vast, sad, initiated crowd. They look up at us from the well of the court and say nothing, only smile a little, with that mixture of compassion and sympathetic irony, as my mother was smiling at me now. She reached

49

across and patted the girl's hand and told her not to mind me. I stared. What had I done? The child sat with eyes fixed on her plate, groping blindly for her knife and fork. Her cheeks were aflame, I could almost hear them hum. Had a look from me done all that? I sighed, poor ogre, and ate a potato. It was raw and waxen at the heart. More drink.

You're not getting into one of your moods, are you, Freddie? my mother said.

Have I mentioned my bad moods, I wonder. Very black, very black. As if the world had grown suddenly dim, as if something had dirtied the air. Even when I was a child my depressions frightened people. In them again, is he? they would say, and they would chuckle, but uneasily, and edge away from me. In school I was a terror — but no, no, I'll spare you the schooldays. I noticed my mother was no longer much impressed by my gloom. Her smile, with that slight droop at the side, was turning positively sardonic. I said I had seen Charlie French in town. Oh, Charlie, she said, and shook her head and laughed. I nodded. Poor Charlie, he is the kind of person about whom people say, Oh, like that, and laugh. Another, listless silence. Why on earth had I come back here. I picked up the bottle, and was surprised to find it empty. I opened another, clamping it between my knees and swaying and grunting as I yanked at the cork. Ah! and out it came with a jolly pop. Outside on the lawn the last of the day's sunlight thickened briefly, then faded. My mother was asking after Daphne and the child. At the thought of them something like a great sob, lugubrious, faintly comical, ballooned under my breastbone. Jane — no, I can't call her that, it doesn't fit — Joan cleared the table, and my mother produced, of all things, a decanter of port and pushed it across the table to me. You won't want us to withdraw, will you? she said, with that grin. You can think of me as a man, anyway, I'm ancient enough. I began earnestly to tell her about my financial troubles, but got into a muddle and had to stop. Besides, I suspected she was not really listening. She sat with her face half-turned to the nickel light of evening from the window, rheum-eyed and old, showing the broad brow and high cheekbones of her Dutch forebears, King Billy's henchmen. You should have a ruff, ma, I said, and a lace cap. I laughed loudly, then frowned. My face was going numb. Jean carefully offered me a cup of coffee. No, thank you, my dear, I said gravely, in my grandee's voice, indicating my port-glass, which, I noticed, was unaccountably empty. I refilled it, admiring the steadiness of the hand that held the decanter. Time passed. Birds were calling through the blue-grey dusk. I sat bemused, bolt-upright, in happy misery, listening to them. Then with a snort and a heave I roused myself and looked about me, smacking my lips and blinking. My mother and the girl were gone.

He died at evening. The room was still heavy with the long day's heat. I sat on a chair beside his bed in the open window and held his hand. His hand. The waxen feel of. How bright the air above the trees, bright and blue, like the limitless skies of childhood. I put my arm around him, laid a hand on his forehead. He said to me: don't mind her. He said to me —

Stop this, stop it. I was not there. I have not been present at anyone's death. He died alone, slipped away while no one was looking, leaving us to our own devices. By the time I arrived from the city they had trussed him up, ready for the coffin. He lay on the bed with his hands folded on his breast and his eyes shut tight, like a child being good. His hair was brushed in a neat lick across his forehead. His ears, I remember, were very white.

Extraordinary: all that anger and resentment, that furious, unfocused energy: gone.

I took what remained of the port and staggered away upstairs. My knees quaked, I felt as if I were lugging a body on my back. The light-switches seemed to have been moved, in the half-darkness I kept banging into things, swearing and laughing. Then I found my way by mistake into Joanne's room. (Joanne: that's it!) She must have been awake, listening to me barging about, I hardly got the door open before she switched on her lamp. I stood teetering on the threshold, goggling at her. She lay in a vast, sagging bed with the sheet pulled to her chin, and for some reason I was convinced that she was still wearing her jodhpurs and her baggy pullover, and even her riding boots. She said nothing, only smiled at me in fright, and for a wild moment I considered climbing in beside her, shoes and all, so that now she might cradle *my* poor whirling head in her plump young accommodating arm. I had not really noticed before her extraordinary flame-red hair, the sight of it spread out on the pillow in the lamplight almost made me cry. Then the moment was gone, and with a grave nod I withdrew silently, like an old sad grey fading ghost, and marched at a careful, dignified pace across the landing to the room where a bed had been made up for me. There I discovered that somewhere along the way I had mislaid the port.

I sat on the side of the bed, arms dangling between my knees, and was suddenly exhausted. My head fizzed, my eyes burned, but yet I could not make myself lie down to sleep. I might have been a child come home after a day of wild excursions. I had travelled far. Slowly, with underwater movements, I untied my shoelaces. One shoe dropped, and then –

I WOKE WITH A DREADFUL START, my ears ringing, as if there had been an explosion in my head. A dream: something about meat. It was light, but whether it was dawn or still dusk I was not sure. Grey. Nor did I know where I was. Even when I realised it was Coolgrange I did not recognise the room at first. Very high and long, with lofty windows that came down to the floor. Shabby, too, in a peculiar, offended way, as if it were conscious of once having been an important place. I got up carefully from the bed and went and looked down at the lawn. The grass was grey, and there were pigeon-coloured shadows under the trees. My brain thudded. It must be dawn: in the oak wood, under an iron sky, a solitary bird was testing out the lightening air with a single repeated flute-note. I pressed my forehead against the window-pane, and shivered at the clammy, cold touch of the glass. I had been travelling for the best part of a week, with scant food and too much alcohol, and now it was all catching up with me. I felt sick, sodden, reamed. My eyelids were scalding, my spit tasted of ash. It seemed to me the garden was watching me, in its stealthy, tightlipped way, or that it was at least somehow aware of me, framed here in the window, wringing my hands, a stricken starer-out – how many other such there must have been, down the years! – with the room's weightless dark pressing at my back. I had slept in my clothes.

The dream. (The court will need to hear about my dreams.) It came back to me suddenly. Nothing very much happened in it. My dreams are not the riotous tumble of events that others claim to enjoy, but states of feeling, rather, moods, particular humours, gusts of emotion, accompanied often by extreme physical effects: I weep, or thrash my limbs, grind my teeth, laugh, cry out. On this occasion it had been a dry retching, the ache in my throat when I woke was what brought it back to me. I had dreamed I was gnawing the ripped-out sternum of some creature, possibly human. It seemed to have been parboiled, for the meat on it was soft and white. Barely warm now, it crumbled in my mouth like suet, making me gag. Believe me, your lordship, I do not enjoy relating these things any more than the court enjoys hearing them. And there is worse to come, as you know. Anyway, there I was, mumbling these frightful gobs of flesh, my stomach heaving even as I slept. That is all there was, really, except for an underlying sensation of enforced yet horribly pleasurable transgression. Wait a moment. I want to get this right, it is important, I'm not sure why. Some nameless authority was making me do this terrible thing, was standing over me implacably with folded arms as I sucked and slobbered, yet despite this – or perhaps, even, because of it – despite the horror, too, and the nausea – deep inside me something exulted.

By the way, leafing through my dictionary I am struck by the poverty of the language when it comes to naming or describing badness. Evil, wickedness, mischief, these words imply an agency, the conscious or at least active doing of wrong. They do not signify the bad in its inert, neutral, self-sustaining state. Then there are the adjectives: dreadful, heinous, execrable, vile, and so on. They are not so much descriptive as judgmental. They carry a weight of censure mingled with fear. Is this not a queer state of affairs? It makes me wonder. I ask myself if perhaps the thing itself – *badness* – does not exist at all, if these strangely vague and imprecise words are only a kind of ruse, a kind of elaborate cover for the fact that nothing is there. Or perhaps the words are an attempt to make it be there? Or, again, perhaps there *is* something, but the words invented it. Such considerations make me feel dizzy, as if a hole had opened briefly in the world. What was I talking about? My dreams, yes. There was the recurring one, the one in which – but no, no, leave that to another time.

I am standing by the window, in my parents' bedroom. Yes, I had realised that it was, used to be, theirs. The grey of dawn was giving way to a pale wash of sunlight. My lips were tacky from last night's port. The room, the house, the garden and the fields, all was strange to me, I did not recognise it today – strange, and yet known, too, like a place in – yes – in a dream. I stood there in my wrinkled suit, with my aching head and soiled mouth, wide-eyed but not quite awake, staring fixedly into that patch of sunlit garden with an amnesiac's numbed amazement. But then, am I not always like that, more or less? When I think about it, I seem to have lived most of my life that way, stalled between sleep and waking, unable to distinguish between dream and the daylight world. In my mind there are places, moments, events, which are so still, so isolated, that I am not sure they can be real, but which if I had recalled them that morning would have struck me with more vividness and force than the real things surrounding me. For instance, there is the hallway of a farmhouse where I went once as a child to buy apples. I see the polished stone floor, cardinal red. I can smell the polish. There is a gnarled geranium in a pot, and a big pendulum clock with the minute-hand missing. I can hear the farmer's wife speaking in the dim depths of the house, asking something of someone. I can sense the fields all around, the light above the fields, the vast, slow, late-summer day. I am there. In such remembered moments I am there as I never was at Coolgrange, as I seem never to have been, or to be, anywhere, at any time, as I, or some essential part of me, was not there even on that day I am remembering, the day I went to buy apples from the farmer's wife, at that farm in the midst of the fields. Never wholly anywhere, never with anyone, either, that was me, always. Even as a child I seemed to myself a traveller who had been delayed in the middle of an urgent journey. Life was an unconscionable wait, walking up and down the platform, watching for the train. People got in the way and blocked my view, I had to crane to see past them. Yes, that was me, all right.

I picked my way down through the silent house to the kitchen. In the morning light the room had a scrubbed, eager aspect. I moved about warily, unwilling to disturb the atmosphere of hushed expectancy, feeling like an uninitiate at some grand, rapt ceremony of light and weather. The dog lay on a dirty old rug beside the stove, its muzzle between its paws, watching me, a crescent of white showing in each eye. I made a pot of tea, and was sitting at the table, waiting for it to draw, when Joanne came in. She was wearing a mouse-grey dressing-gown belted tightly about her midriff. Her hair was tied up at the back in a thick, appropriately equine plume. It really was remarkable in colour, a vernal russet blaze. Immediately, and not for the first time, I found myself picturing how she must be flossed elsewhere, and then was ashamed, as if I had misused the poor child. Seeing me, she halted, of course, ready to bolt. I lifted the teapot in a friendly gesture, and invited her to join me. She shut the door and edged around me with a panic-stricken smile, keeping the table between us, and took down a cup and saucer from the dresser. She had red heels and very white, thick calves. I thought she must be about seventeen. Through the fog of my hangover it occurred to me that she would be bound to know something about the state of my mother's finances – whether, for instance, those ponies were making money. I gave her what was intended to be a boyish, encouraging smile, though I suspect it came out a broken leer, and told her to sit down, that we must have a chat. The tea, however, was not for her, but for my mother – for Dolly, she said. Well! I thought, Dolly, no less! She made off at once, with the saucer grasped in both hands and her agitated smile fixed on the trembling liquid in the cup.

When she was gone I poked about morosely for a while, looking for the papers that had been on the table yesterday, the bills and ledgers and chequebook stubs, but found nothing. A drawer of the little bureau from my father's study was locked. I considered forcing it open, but restrained myself: in my hungover mood I might have smashed the whole thing to bits.

I wandered off through the house, carrying my teacup with me. In the drawing-room the carpet had been taken up, and a pane of glass in one of the windows was broken, and there was glass on the floor. I noticed I had no shoes on. I opened the garden door and stepped outside in my socks. There was a smell of sun-warmed grass and a faint tang of dung in the rinsed, silky air. The black shadow of the house lay across the lawn like a fallen stage-flat. I ventured a step or two on the yielding turf, the dew seeping up between my toes. I felt like an old man, going along shakily with my cup and saucer rattling and my trouser-cuffs wet and crumpled around my ankles. The rosebeds under the window had not been tended for years, and a tangle of briars rioted at the sills. The faded roses hung in clusters, heavy as cloth. Their particular wan shade of pink, and the chiaroscuro of the scene in general, put me in mind of something. I halted, frowning. The pictures — of course. I went back into the drawing-room. Yes, the walls were empty, with here and there a square patch where the wallpaper was not as faded as elsewhere. Surely she hadn't — ? I put my cup down carefully on the mantelpiece, taking slow, deep breaths. The bitch! I said aloud, I bet she has! My feet had left wet, webbed prints behind me on the floorboards.

I went through room after room, scanning the walls. Then I tackled the upstairs. But I knew there would be nothing. I stood on the first-floor landing, cursing under my breath. There were voices nearby. I flung open a bedroom door. My mother and Joanne were sitting up side by side in the girl's big bed. They looked at me in mild astonishment, and for a moment I faltered as something brushed past my consciousness, a wingbeat of incredulous speculation. My mother wore a knitted yellow bed-jacket with bobbles and tiny satin bows, which made her look like a monstrously overgrown Easter chick. Where, I said, with a calm that surprised me, where are the pictures, pray? There followed a bit of comic patter, with my mother saying *What? What?* and I shouting *The pictures! The pictures, damn it!* In the end we both had to shut up. The girl had been watching us, turning her eyes slowly from one to the other of us, like a spectator at a tennis match. Now she put a hand over her mouth and laughed. I

58

stared at her, and she blushed. There was a brief silence. I will see you downstairs, mother, I said, in a voice so stiff with ice it fairly creaked.

As I was going away from the door I thought I heard them both sniggering.

My mother arrived in the kitchen barefoot. The sight of her bunions and her big yellow toenails annoyed me. She had wrapped herself in an impossible, shot-silk tea-gown. She had the florid look of one of Lautrec's ruined doxies. I tried not to show too much of the disgust I felt. She pottered about with a show of unconcern, ignoring me. Well? I said, but she only raised her eyebrows blandly and said, Well what? She was almost smirking. That did it. I shouted, I waved my fists, I stamped about stiff-legged, beside myself. Where were they, the pictures, I cried, what had she done with them? I *demanded* to know. They were mine, my inheritance, my future and my son's future. And so on. My anger, my sense of outrage, impressed me. I was moved. I might almost have shed tears, I felt so sorry for myself. She let me go on like this for a while, standing with a hand on her hip and her head thrown back, contemplating me with sardonic calm. Then, when I paused to take a breath, she started. Demand, did I? – I, who had gone off and abandoned my widowed mother, who had skipped off to America and married without even informing her, who had never once brought my child, her grandson, to see her – I, who for ten years had stravaiged the world like a tinker, never doing a hand's turn of work, living off my dead father's few pounds and bleeding the estate dry – what right, she shrilled, what right had I to demand anything here? She stopped, and waited, as if really expecting an answer. I fell back a pace. I had forgotten what she is like when she gets going. Then I gathered myself and launched at her again. She rose magnificently to meet me. It was just like the old days. Hammer and tongs, oh, hammer and tongs! So stirring was it that even the dog joined in, barking and whining and dancing up and down on its front paws, until my mother gave it a clout and roared at it to lie down. I called her a bitch and she called me a bastard. I said if I was a bastard what did that make her, and quick as a flash she said, If I'm a bitch what does that make *you*, you cur! Oh, it was grand, a grand match. We were like furious children – no, not children, but big, maddened, primitive creatures – mastodons, something like that – tearing and thrashing in a jungle clearing amidst a storm of whipping lianas and uprooted vegetation. The air throbbed between us, blood-dimmed and thick. There was a sense of things ranged around us, small creatures cowering in the undergrowth, watching us in a trance of terror and awe. At last, sated, we disengaged tusks and turned aside. I nursed my pounding head in my hands. She stood at the sink, holding on to one of the taps and looking out the window at the garden, her chest heaving. We could hear ourselves breathe. The upstairs lavatory flushed, a muted, tentative noise, as if the girl were tactfully reminding us of her presence in the house. My mother sighed. She had sold the pictures to Binkie Behrens. I nodded to myself. Behrens: of course. All of them? I said. She did not answer. Time passed. She sighed again. You got the money, she said, what there was of it – he left me only debts. Suddenly she laughed. I should have known better, she said, than to marry a mick. She looked at me over her shoulder and shrugged. Now it was my turn to sigh. Dear me, I said. Oh, dear me.

Coincidences come out strangely flattened in court

testimony – I'm sure you have noticed this, your honour, over the years – rather like jokes that should be really funny but fail to raise a single laugh. Accounts of the most bizarre doings of the accused are listened to with perfect equanimity, yet the moment some trivial simultaneity of events is mentioned feet begin to shuffle in the gallery, and counsel clear their throats, and reporters take to gazing dreamily at the mouldings on the ceiling. These are not so much signs of incredulity, I think, as of embarrassment. It is as if someone, the hidden arranger of all this intricate, amazing affair, who up to now never put a foot wrong, has suddenly gone that bit too far, has tried to be just a little too clever, and we are all disappointed, and somewhat sad.

I am struck, for instance, by the frequent appearance which paintings make in this case. It was through art that my parents knew Helmut Behrens – well, not art, exactly, but the collecting of it. My father fancied himself a collector, did I mention that? Of course, he cared nothing for the works themselves, only for their cash value. He used his reputation as a horseman and erstwhile gay blade to insinuate himself into the houses of doddering acquaintances, on whose walls thirty or forty years before he had spotted a landscape, or a still-life, or a kippered portrait of a cross-eyed ancestor, which by now might be worth a bob or two. He had an uncanny sense of timing, often getting in only a step ahead of the heirs. I imagine him, at the side of a four-poster, in candlelight, still breathless from the stairs, leaning down and pressing a fiver urgently into a palsied, papery hand. He accumulated a lot of trash, but there were a few pieces which I thought were not altogether bad, and probably worth something. Most of these he had wheedled out of a distrait old lady whom his own father had courted briefly when she was a girl. He was hugely proud of this piece of chicanery, imagining, I suppose, that it put him on a par with the great robber barons of the past whom he so much admired, the Guggenheims and Pierpont Morgans and, indeed, the Behrenses. Perhaps these were the very pictures that led to his meeting Helmut Behrens. Perhaps they tussled for them over the old lady's death-bed, narrowing their eyes at each other, mouths pursed in furious determination.

It was through painting also that I met Anna Behrens – or met her again, I should say. We knew each other a little when we were young. I seem to remember once at Whitewater being sent outside to play with her in the grounds. Play! That's a good one. Even in those days she had that air of detachment, of faint, remote amusement, which I have always found unnerving. Later on, in Dublin, she would appear now and then, and glide through our student roisterings, poised, silent, palely handsome. She was nicknamed the Ice Queen, of course. I lost sight of her, forgot about her, until one day in Berkeley – this is where the coincidences begin – I spotted her in a gallery on Shattuck Avenue. I had not known she was in America, yet there was no sense of surprise. This is one of the things about Anna, she belongs exactly wherever she happens to be. I stood in the street for a moment watching her – admiring her, I suppose. The gallery was a large high white room with a glass front. She was leaning against a desk with a sheaf of papers in her hand, reading. She wore a white dress. Her hair, bleached silver by the sun, was done in a complicated fashion, with a single heavy braid hanging down at her shoulder. She might have been a piece on show, standing there so still in that tall, shadowless light behind sun-reflecting glass. I went in and spoke to her, admiring again that long, slightly off-centre, melancholy face with its close-set grey eyes and florentine mouth. I remembered the two tiny white spots on the bridge of her nose where the skin was stretched tight over the bone. She was friendly, in her distant way. She watched my lips as I talked. On the walls there were two or three vast canvases, done in the joky, minimalist style of the time, hardly distinguishable in their pastel bareness from the blank spaces surrounding them. I asked her if she was thinking of buying something. This amused her. I work here, she said, pushing back the blonde braid from her shoulder. I invited her to lunch, but she shook her head. She gave me her telephone number. When I stepped out into the sunlit street a jet plane was passing low overhead, its engines making the air rattle, and there was a smell of cypresses and car exhaust, and a faint whiff of tear-gas from the direction of the campus. All this was fifteen years ago. I crumpled the file card on which she had written her phone number, and started to throw it away. But I kept it.

She lived in the hills, in a mock-Tyrolean, shingled wooden house which she rented from a mad widow. More than once on the way there I stood up to get off the bus and go home, bored and half-annoyed already at the thought of Anna's amused, appraising glance, that impenetrable smile. When I called her she had spoken hardly a dozen words, and twice she put a hand over the phone and talked to someone with her in the room. Yet that morning I had shaved with particular care, and put on a new shirt, and selected an impressive volume of mathematical theory to carry with me. Now, as the bus threaded its way up these narrow roads, I was assailed by a sense of revulsion, I seemed to myself an obscurely shameful, lewd object, exposed and cringing, with my palped and powdered flesh, my baby-blue shirt, the floppy book clutched in my hand like a parcel of meat. The day was overcast, and there was mist in the pines. I climbed a zigzag of damp steps to the door, looking about me with an expression of bland interest, trying to appear blameless, as I always seem to do when I am on unfamiliar territory. Anna wore shorts, and her hair was loose. The sight of her there suddenly in the doorway, ash-blonde, at ease, her long legs bare, caused an ache at the root of my tongue. The house was dim inside. A few books, prints on the wall, a straw hat on a hook. The widow's cats had left a trace of themselves on the carpets and the chairs, a sharp, citrus stink, not wholly unpleasant.

Daphne was sitting cross-legged in a canvas chair, shelling peas into a nickel bowl. She wore a bathrobe, and her hair was wrapped in a towel. Another coincidence, you see.

What did we talk about that day, the three of us? What did I do? Sat down, I suppose, drank a beer, stretched out my legs and leaned back, playing at being relaxed. I cannot see myself. I am a sort of floating eye, watching, noting, scheming. Anna came and went between the living-room and the kitchen, bringing cheese and oranges and sliced avocados. It was Sunday. The place was quiet. I watched through the window the mist moving among the trees. The telephone rang and Anna answered it, turning away and murmuring into the receiver. Daphne smiled at me. Her glance was unfocused, a kind of soft groping among the objects around her. She rose and handed me the bowl and the remaining unshelled peas, and went away upstairs. When she came back in a while she was dressed, her hair was dried and she was wearing her spectacles, and at first I did not recognise her, and thought she was yet another tenant of the house. It was only then that I realised it was she I had seen on the lawn that day at Professor

Something's party. I started to tell her about it, about having seen her, but I changed my mind, for the same, unknown reason that I had turned away that first time without speaking to her. She took the bowl of peas from me and sat down again. Anna answered another phonecall, murmuring, quietly laughing. It occurred to me that my presence was hardly impinging on their day, that they would have done just these same things if I were not there. It was a soothing thought. I had not been invited to dinner, but it seemed accepted that I would stay. After we had eaten we sat on at the table for a long time. The fog thickened, pressing against the windows. I see the two of them opposite me there in that milky twilight, the dark one and the fair: they have an air of complicity, of secret amusement, as if they are sharing a mild, not very unkind joke at my expense. How distant it all seems, an age away, when we were still innocent, if that is the word, which I doubt.

I was, I confess it, captivated by them, their looks, their composure, their casual selfishness. They embodied an ideal that I had not known I harboured until now. I was still working at my science in those days, I was going to be one of those great, cold technicians, the secret masters of the world. Now suddenly another future had opened up, as if these two had caused a whole rockface before me to fall away and reveal beyond the swirling dust a vast, radiant distance. They were splendid, at once languorous and dashing. They reminded me of a pair of adventuresses out of the last century. They had arrived in New York the previous winter, and drifted by stages across the country to this tawny, sunlit shore, where they were poised now, as if on tiptoe, hands joined and arms extended, with the Pacific all before them. Though they had been in this house nearly half a year their impress was so light, so fleeting, that the rooms had barely registered their presence. They seemed to have no belongings – even the straw hat hanging on the door had been left behind by a previous tenant. There must have been friends, or acquaintances at least – I'm thinking of those phonecalls – but I never met them. Once in a while their landlady would descend on them, a darkly dramatic person with soulful eyes and very black hair twisted tight into a bun and skewered with a carved wooden pin. She dressed like an Indian squaw, festooning herself with beads and brightly coloured scarves. She would surge about the house distractedly, talking over her shoulder and trailing a dense, musky perfume, then fling herself with a balletic leap on to the couch in the living-room and sit for an hour telling of her woes – the result mostly of what with a throb in her voice she referred to as *man trouble* – meanwhile getting steadily, tearfully drunk on calvados, a supply of which she kept in a locked cupboard in the kitchen. A ghastly woman, I could not abide her, that leathery skin and daubed mouth, all that hysteria, that messy loneliness. The girls, however, found her greatly entertaining. They liked to do imitations of her, and made catchphrases of things she said. Sometimes, listening to them mimicking her, I wondered if perhaps, when I was not there, they treated *me* like this, lobbing remarks at each other in a comically solemn version of my voice and laughing softly, in that jaded way they had, as if the joke were not really funny, just ridiculous.

They thought the country, too, was a scream, especially California. We had a lot of fun together laughing at the Americans, who just then were entering that stage of doomed hedonistic gaiety through which we, the gilded children of poor old raddled Europe, had already passed, or so we believed. How innocent they seemed to us, with their flowers and their joss-sticks and their muddled religiosity. Of course, I felt a secret twinge of guilt, sneering at them like this. I had been captivated by the country when I first came there, now it was as if I had joined in mocking some happy, good-hearted creature, the fat girl at the party against whom only a moment ago I had been pressing myself, under cover of the general romp, in wordless, swollen ecstasy.

Perhaps contempt was for us a form of nostalgia, of homesickness, even? Living there, amid those gentle, paintbox colours, under that dome of flawless blue, was like living in another world, a place out of a story-book. (I used to dream of rain — real, daylong, Irish rain — as if it were something I had been told about but had never seen.) Or perhaps laughing at America was a means of defence? It's true, at times it crossed our minds, or it crossed *my* mind, at least, that we might be just the teeniest bit laughable ourselves. Was there not a touch of the preposterous about us, with our tweeds and our sensible shoes, our extravagant accents, our insolently polite manners? More than once I thought I detected a suppressed smile twitching the lips of some person who was supposed to be the unknowing butt of our ridicule. Even among ourselves there were moments of silence, of awkwardness, when a half-formed admission hovered between us, like a bad, embarrassing smell. A trio of expatriates meeting in this mellow playground — what could be more novelettish? We were a triangle, for God's sake!

We were a triangle. It happened, the inevitable, one afternoon a month or so after we met. We had been sitting on the porch at the back of the house drinking gin and smoking something with a horrid taste and the oddest effects. The day was hot and hazy. Above us a coin-coloured sun was stuck in the middle of a white sky. I was watching a cloud of hummingbirds sipping at a honeysuckle bush beside the porch steps. Daphne, in shorts and halter and high-heeled sandals, stood up, a little unsteadily, blinking, and wandered into the house. I followed her. I was not thinking of anything – I was fetching more ice, something like that. After the glare outside I could hardly see indoors, everywhere I turned the air had a huge dark hole in it. Idly I looked about for Daphne, following the sound of the ice tinkling in her glass, from the kitchen through the living-room to the bedroom. The blind was drawn. She was sitting on the side of the bed, gazing before her in the amber half-light. My head suddenly began to ache. She drained her drink in one long gulp, and was still holding the glass when we lay down together, and a bead of ice slid out of it and dropped into the hollow of my shoulder. Her lips were chill and wet. She began to say something, and laughed softly into my mouth. Our clothes seemed tight as bandages, I clawed at them, snorting. Then abruptly we were naked. There was a startled pause. Somewhere nearby children were playing. Daphne laid her hand on my hip. Her eyes were closed, and she was smiling with her eyebrows raised, as if she were listening to a distant, dreamy, and slightly funny melody. I heard a sound, and looked over my shoulder. Anna was standing in the doorway. I had a glimpse of myself as she would see me, my glimmering flanks and pale backside, my fish-mouth agape. She hesitated a moment, and then walked to the bed with her eyes on the ground, as if deep in thought, and sat down beside us and began to undress. Daphne and I lay quietly in each other's arms and watched her. She pulled her blouse over her head, and surfaced like a swimmer, tossing her hair. A metal clasp left its mauve imprint in the centre of her back. Why did she seem to me so much older now than us, world-weary, a little used, an adult joining tolerantly in a children's not quite permissible game? Daphne hardly breathed, her fingers steadily tightening on my hip. Her lips were parted, and she frowned a little, gazing at Anna's bared flesh, lost in a sort of vague amazement. I could feel her heartbeat, and my own. We might have been attending at a ritual disrobing.

A ritual, yes, that's how it was. We strove together slowly on the bed, the three of us, as if engaged in an archaic ceremonial of toil and worship, miming the fashioning and raising of something, a shrine, say, or a domed temple. How grave we were, how pensive, with what attentiveness we handled each other's flesh. No one spoke a word. The women had begun by exchanging a chaste kiss. They smiled, a little bashfully. My hands were trembling. I had felt this choking sense of transgression once before, long ago, when as a child I tussled with two girl cousins in the dark on the stairs one winter evening at Coolgrange – the same dread and incredulity, the same voluptuous, aching, infantile glee. Dreamily we delved and nuzzled, shivering, sighing. Now and then one of us would clutch at the other two with a child's impatient, greedy fervour and cry out softly, tinily, as if in pain or helpless sorrow. It seemed to me at times that there were not two women but one, a strange, remote creature, many-armed, absorbed behind an enamelled mask in something I could not begin to know. At the end, the final spasm gathering itself inside me, I raised myself up on trembling arms, with Daphne's heels pressed in the small of my back, and looked down at the two of them gnawing at each other with tender avidity, mouth on open mouth, and for a second, as the blood welled up in my eyes, I saw their heads merge, the fair one and the dark, the tawny and the panther-sleek. At once the shudder started in my groin, and I fell upon them, exultant and afraid.

But afterwards it was Daphne alone who lay in my arms, still holding me inside her, while Anna got up and walked to the window, and lifted the canvas blind at the side with one finger and stood gazing out into the hazy glare of afternoon. The children were still at play. There's a school, Anna murmured, up the hill. She laughed quietly and said, *But what do I know, I ask you?* It was one of the mad widow's catchphrases. Suddenly everything was sad and grey and waste. Daphne put her face against my shoulder and began to weep silently. I will always remember those children's voices.

It was a strange encounter, never to be repeated. I brood on it now, not for the obvious reasons, but because it puzzles me. The act itself, the troilism, was not so remarkable: in those days everyone was doing that sort of thing. No, what struck me then, and strikes me still, is the curious passiveness of my role in that afternoon's doings. I was the man among the three of us, yet I felt that it was I who was being softly, irresistibly penetrated. The wise will say that I was only the link along which the two of them had negotiated their way, hand over hand, into each other's arms. It may be true, but it is not of much significance, and certainly not the central thing. I could not rid myself of the feeling that a rite was being performed, in which Anna Behrens was the priestess and Daphne the sacrificial offering, while I was a mere prop. They wielded me like a stone phallus, bowing and writhing about me, with incantatory sighs. They were –

They were saying goodbye. Of course. It's just occurred to me. They were not finding each other, but parting. Hence the sadness and the sense of waste, hence Daphne's bitter tears. It was nothing to do with me, at all.

Well well. That's the advantage of jail, one has the time and leisure really to get to the heart of things.

The illusion of their melting into each other which I had experienced at the end of our bout on the bed that day was to last for a long time. Even yet when I think of them together it is a kind of double-headed coin that I see, on which are stamped their twin profiles, serene, emblematic, looking away, a stylised representation of paired virtues – Calm and Fortitude, let's say, or, better still, Silence and Sacrifice. I am remembering a certain moment, when Anna lifted her bruised, glistening mouth from between Daphne's legs and, glancing back at me with a complicitous, wry little smile, leaned aside so that I might see the sprawled girl's lap lying open there, intricate and innocent as a halved fruit. Everything was present, I see now, in that brief passage of renunciation and discovery. A whole future began just there.

I do not recall proposing to Daphne. Her hand, so to speak, had already been granted me. We were married one misty, hot afternoon in August. The ceremony was quick and squalid. I had a headache all through it. Anna and a colleague of mine from the university acted as witnesses. Afterwards the four of us went back to the house in the hills and drank cheap champagne. The occasion was not a success. My colleague made a limp excuse and departed after half an hour, leaving the three of us together in a restless, swirling silence. All sorts of unspoken things swam in the air between us like slithery, dangerous fish. Then Anna, with that smile, said she supposed we young things would want to be alone, and left. Suddenly I was prey to an absurd embarrassment. I jumped up and began collecting the empty bottles and the glasses, avoiding Daphne's eye. There was sun and mist in the kitchen window. I stood at the sink looking out at the blue-black

71

ghosts of trees on the hillside, and two great, fat, inexplicable tears gathered on the rims of my eyelids, but would not fall.

I do not know that I loved Daphne in the manner that the world understands by that word, but I do know that I loved her ways. Will it seem strange, cold, perhaps even inhuman, if I say that I was only interested really in what she was on the surface? Pah, what do I care how it seems. This is the only way another creature can be known: on the surface, that's where there is depth. Daphne walking through a room searching for her spectacles, touching things gently, quickly, reading things with her fingertips. The way she had of turning aside and peering into her purse, frowning, lips compressed, like a maiden aunt fetching up a shilling for sweets. Her stinginess, her sudden rushes of greed, childish and endearing. That time, years ago, I can't remember where, when I came upon her at the end of a party, standing by a window in a white dress in the half-light of an April dawn, lost in a dream – a dream from which I, tipsy and in a temper, unceremoniously woke her, when I could – dear Christ! – when I could have hung back in the shadows and painted her, down to the tiniest, tenderest detail, on the blank inner wall of my heart, where she would be still, vivid as in that dawn, my dark, mysterious darling.

We quickly agreed – tacitly, as always – to leave America. I gave up my studies, the university, my academic career, everything, with hardly a second thought, and before the year was out we had sailed for Europe.

MAOLSEACHLAINN MAC GIOLLA GUNNA, my counsel and, he insists, my friend, has a trick of seizing on the apparently trivial in the elaboration of his cases. Anecdotes of his methods circulate in the corridors of chancery, and around the catwalks in here. Details, details are his obsession. He is a large, lumbering, unhandy man — yards, literally yards of pinstripe — with a big square head and raggedy hair and tiny, haunted eyes. I think a life spent poking in the crevices of other people's nasty little tragedies has damaged something in him. He exudes an air of injured longing. They say he is a terror in court, but when he sits at the scarred table in the counsel room here, with his half-glasses hooked on that big head, crouched over his papers and writing out notes in a laborious, minute hand, panting a little and muttering to himself, I am reminded irresistibly of a certain fat boy from my schooldays, who was disconsolately in love with me, and whom I used to get to do my homework for me.

At present Maolseachlainn is deeply interested in why I went to Whitewater in the first place. But why should I not have gone there? I knew the Behrenses — or God knows I knew Anna, anyway. I had been away for ten years, I was paying a social call, as a friend of the family. This, however, is not good enough, it seems. Maolseach-lainn frowns, slowly shaking his great head, and without realising it goes into his court routine. Is it not true that I left my mother's house in anger only a day after my arrival there? Is it not the case that I was in a state of high indignation because I had heard my father's collection of pictures had been sold to Helmut Behrens for what I considered a paltry sum? And is it not further the case that I had reason already to feel resentment against the man Behrens, who had attempted to cuckold my father in – But hold on there, old man, I said: that last bit only came to light later on. He always looks so crestfallen when I stop him in his tracks like this. All the same, facts are facts.

It is true, I did fight with my mother again, I did storm out of the house (with the dog after me, of course, trying to bite my heels). However, Binkie Behrens was not the cause of the row, or not directly, anyway. As far as I remember it was the same old squabble: money, betrayal, my going to the States, my leaving the States, my marriage, my abandoned career, all that, the usual – and, yes, the fact that she had flogged my birthright for the price of a string of plug-ugly ponies out of which she had imagined she would make a fortune to provide for herself in the decrepitude of her old age, the deluded bloody bitch. There was as well the business of the girl Joanne. As I was leaving I paused and said, measuring my words, that I thought it hardly appropriate for a woman of my mother's position in society – her position! – in society! – to be so chummy with a stable-girl. I confess I had intended to cause outrage, but I am afraid I was the one who ended up goggle-eyed. My mother, after a moment's silence, stared me straight in the face, with brazen insouciance, and said that Joanne was not a child, that she was in fact twenty-seven years of age. She is – with a pause here for effect – she is like a son to me, the son I never had. Well, I said, swallowing hard, I'm happy for you both, I'm sure! and flounced out of the house. On the drive, though, I had to stop and wait for my indignation and resentment to subside a little before I could get my breath back. Sometimes I think I am an utter sentimentalist.

I got to Whitewater that evening. The last leg of the journey I made by taxi from the village. The driver was an immensely tall, emaciated man in a flat cap and an antique, blue-flannel suit. He studied me with interest in the driving-mirror, hardly bothering to watch the road ahead of us. I tried staring back at him balefully, but he was unabashed, and only grinned a little on one side of his thin face with a peculiarly friendly air of knowing. Why do I remember people like this so vividly? They clutter my mind, when I look up from the page they are thronged around me in the shadows, silent, mildly curious – even, it might be, solicitous. They are witnesses, I suppose, the innocent bystanders who have come, without malice, to testify against me.

I can never approach Whitewater without a small, involuntary gasp of admiration. The drive leads up from the road in a long, deep, treeless curve, so that the house seems to turn, slowly, dreamily, opening wide its Palladian colonnades. The taxi drew to a stop on the gravel below the great front steps, and with the sudden silence came the realisation – yes, Maolseachlainn, I admit it – that I had no reasonable cause to be there. I sat for a moment looking about me in groggy consternation, like a wakened sleepwalker, but the driver was watching me in the mirror now

75

with rapt expectancy, and I had to pretend to know what I was about. I got out of the car and stood patting my pockets and frowning importantly, but I could not fool him, his lopsided grin grew slyer still, for a second I thought he was going to wink at me. I told him brusquely to wait, and mounted the steps pursued by an unshakeable sensation of general mockery.

After a long time the door was opened by a wizened little angry man in what appeared at first to be a bus conductor's uniform. A few long strands of very black hair were plastered across his skull like streaks of boot polish. He looked at me with deep disgust. Not open today, he said, and was starting to shut the door in my face when I stepped smartly past him into the hall. I gazed about me, rubbing my hands slowly and smiling, playing the returned expatriate. Ah, I said, the old place! The great Tintoretto on the stairs, swarming with angels and mad-eyed martyrs, blared at me its vast chromatic chord. The doorman or whatever he was danced about anxiously behind me. I turned and loomed at him, still grinning, and said no, I wasn't a tripper, but a friend of the family – was Miss Behrens at home, by any chance? He dithered, distrustful still, then told me to wait, and scuttled off down the hall, splaying one flat foot as he went and carefully smoothing the oiled hairs on his pate.

I waited. All was silent save for the ticking of a tall, seventeenth-century German clock. On the wall beside me there was a set of six exquisite little Bonington water-colours, I could have put a couple of them under my arm there and then and walked out. The clock took a laboured breath and pinged the half-hour, and then, all about me, in farther and farther rooms, other clocks too let fall their single, silvery chimes, and it was as if a tiny tremor had passed through the house. I looked again at the

Tintoretto. There was a Fragonard, too, and a Watteau. And this was only the hallway. What was going on, what had happened, that it was all left unattended like this? I heard the taximan outside sounding his horn, a tentative, apologetic little toot. He must have thought I had forgotten about him. (I had.) Somewhere at the back of the house a door banged shut, and a second later a breath of cool air brushed past my face. I advanced creakingly along the hall, a hot, almost sensuous thrill of apprehensiveness pulsing behind my breastbone. I am at heart a timid man, large deserted places make me nervous. One of the figures in the Fragonard, a silken lady with blue eyes and a plump lower lip, was watching me sidelong with what seemed an expression of appalled but lively speculation. Cautiously I opened a door. The fat knob turned under my hand with a wonderful, confiding smoothness. I entered a long, high, narrow, many-windowed room. The wallpaper was the colour of tarnished gold. The air was golden too, suffused with the heavy soft light of evening. I felt as if I had stepped straight into the eighteenth century. The furnishings were sparse, there were no more than five or six pieces – some delicate, lyre-backed chairs, an ornate sideboard, a small ormolu table – placed just so, in such a way that not the things but the space around them, the light itself, seemed arranged. I stood quite still, listening, I did not know for what. On the low table there was a large and complicated jigsaw puzzle, half-assembled. Some of the pieces had fallen to the floor. I gazed at them, sprinkled on the parquet like puddles of something that had spilled, and once again a faint shiver seemed to pass through the house. At the far end of the room a french window stood wide-open, and a gauze curtain billowed in the breeze. Outside there was a long slope of lawn, whereon, in the middle distance, a lone, heraldic horse was prancing. Farther off was the river bend, the water whitening in the shallows, and beyond that there were trees, and then vague mountains, and then the limitless, gilded blue of summer. It struck me that the perspective of this scene was wrong somehow. Things seemed not to recede as they should, but to be arrayed before me – the furniture, the open window, the lawn and river and far-off mountains – as if they were not being looked at but were themselves looking, intent upon a vanishing-point here, inside the room. I turned then, and saw myself turning as I turned, as I seem to myself to be turning still, as I sometimes imagine I shall be turning always, as if this might be my punishment, my damnation, just this breathless, blurred, eternal turning towards her.

You have seen the picture in the papers, you know what she looks like. A youngish woman in a black dress with a broad white collar, standing with her hands folded in front of her, one gloved, the other hidden except for the fingers, which are flexed, ringless. She is wearing something on her head, a cap or clasp of some sort, which holds her hair drawn tightly back from her brow. Her prominent black eyes have a faintly oriental slant. The nose is large, the lips full. She is not beautiful. In her right hand she holds a folded fan, or it might be a book. She is standing in what I take to be the lighted doorway of a room. Part of a couch can be seen, or maybe a bed, with a brocade cover. The darkness behind her is dense and yet mysteriously weightless. Her gaze is calm, inexpectant, though there is a trace of challenge, of hostility, even, in the set of her mouth. She does not want to be here, and yet cannot be elsewhere. The gold brooch that secures the wings of her wide collar is expensive and ugly. All this you have seen, all this you know. Yet I put it to you, gentle connoisseurs of the jury, that even knowing all this you still know nothing, next to nothing. You do not know the fortitude and pathos of her presence. You have not come upon her suddenly in a golden room on a summer eve, as I have. You have not held her in your arms, you have not seen her asprawl in a ditch. You have not – ah no! – you have not killed for her.

I stood there, staring, for what seemed a long time, and gradually a kind of embarrassment took hold of me, a hot, shamefaced awareness of myself, as if somehow I, this soiled sack of flesh, were the one who was being scrutinised, with careful, cold attention. It was not just the woman's painted stare that watched me. Everything in the picture, that brooch, those gloves, the flocculent darkness at her back, every spot on the canvas was an eye fixed on me unblinkingly. I retreated a pace, faintly aghast. The silence was fraying at the edges. I heard cows lowing, a car starting up. I remembered the taxi, and turned to go. A maid was standing in the open french window. She must have come in just then and seen me there and started back in alarm. Her eyes were wide, and one knee was flexed and one hand lifted, as if to ward off a blow. For a moment neither of us stirred. Behind her a sudden breeze burnished the grassy slope. We did not speak. Then slowly, with her hand still raised, she stepped backwards carefully through the window, teetering a little as her heels blindly sought the level of the paved pathway outside. I felt an inexplicable, brief rush of annoyance – a presentiment, perhaps, a stray zephyr sent ahead of the storm that was to come. A telephone was ringing somewhere. I turned quickly and left the room.

There was no one in the hall. The telephone rang and rang, with peevish insistence. I could still hear it going as I descended the front steps. The taxi had left, of course. I swore, and set off down the drive, hobbling over the stony ground in my thin-soled Spanish shoes. The low sun glared in my face. When I looked back at the house the windows were ablaze, and seemed to be laughing fatly in derision. I began to perspire, and that brought on the midges. I asked myself again what had possessed me to come to Whitewater. I knew the answer, of course. It was the smell of money that had attracted me, as the smell of sweat was attracting these damned flies. I saw myself, as if from one of those sunstruck windows, skulking along here in the dust, hot, disgruntled, overweight, head bowed and fat back bent, my white suit rucked at the armpits and sagging in the arse, a figure of fun, the punchline of a bad joke, and at once I was awash with self-pity. Christ! was there no one who would help me? I halted, and cast a troubled glance around me, as if there might be a benefactor lurking among the trees. The silence had a sense of muffled gloating. I plunged on again, and heard the sound of engines, and presently an enormous black limousine came around the bend, followed by a sleek red sportscar. They were going at a stately pace, the limousine bouncing gently on its springs, and for a second I thought it was a funeral. I stepped on to the grass verge but kept on walking. The driver of the limousine, a large, crop-headed man, sat erect and vigilant, his hands lightly cupped on the rim of the steering-wheel, as if it were a projectile he might pluck from its moorings and throw with deadly aim. Beside him there was a stooped, shrunken figure, as the car swished past I glimpsed a dark eye and a liver-spotted skull, and huge hands resting one upon the other on the crook of a stick. A blonde woman wearing dark glasses was driving the sportscar. We gazed at each other with blank interest, like strangers, as she went by. I recognised her, of course.

Ten minutes later I was trudging along the road with

my thumb stuck out when I heard her pull up behind me. I knew it would be she. I stopped, turned. She remained in the car, her wrists folded before her on the steering-wheel. There was a brief, wordless tussle to see which one of us would make the first move. We compromised. I walked back to the car and she got out to meet me. I *thought* it was you, she said. We smiled, and were silent. She wore a cream suit and a white blouse. There was blood on her shoes. Her hair was yellower than I remembered, I wondered if she was dyeing it now. I told her she looked marvellous. I meant it, but the words sounded hollow, and I blushed. Anna, I said. I remembered, with a soft shock, how one day long ago I stole the envelope of one of her letters to Daphne, and took it into the lavatory and prised open the flap, my heart pounding, so that I might lick the gum where she had licked. The thought came to me: I loved her! and I gave a sort of wild, astonished laugh. She took off her sunglasses and looked at me quizzically. My hands were trembling. Come and see father, she said, he needs cheering up.

She drove very fast, working the controls probingly, as if she were trying to locate a pattern, a secret formula, hidden in this mesh of small, deft actions. I was impressed, even a little cowed. She was full of the impatient assurance of the rich. We did not speak. In a moment we were at the house, and pulled up in a spray of gravel. She opened her door, then paused and looked at me for a moment in silence and shook her head. Freddie Montgomery, she said. Well!

As we went up the steps to the front door she linked her arm lightly in mine. I was surprised. When I knew her, all those years ago, she was not one for easy intimacies – intimacies, yes, but not easy ones. She laughed and said, God, I'm a little drunk, I think. She had been to the hospital in the city – Behrens had suffered some sort of mild attack. The hospital was in an uproar. A bomb had gone off in a car in a crowded shopping street, quite a small device, apparently, but remarkably effective. She had wandered unchallenged into the casualty ward. There were bodies lying everywhere. She walked among the dead and dying, feeling like a survivor herself. Good God, Anna, I said. She gave a tense little laugh. What an experience, she said – luckily Flynn keeps a flask of something in the glove compartment. She had taken a few good swigs, and was beginning to regret it now.

We went into the house. The uniformed doorman was nowhere to be seen. I told Anna how he had gone off and left me to wander at will about the place. She shrugged. She supposed everyone had been downstairs watching the news of the bombing on television. All the same, I said, anyone could have got in. Why, she asked, do you think someone might come and plant a bomb here? And she looked at me with a peculiar, bitter smile.

She led the way into the gold salon. The french window was still open. There was no sign of the maid. A sort of shyness made me keep my eyes averted from the other end of the room, where the picture leaned out a little from the wall, as if listening intently. I sat down gingerly on one of the Louis Quinze chairs while Anna opened the carved and curlicued sideboard and poured out two whopping measures of gin. There was no ice, and the tonic was flat, but I didn't care, I needed a drink. I was still breathless with the notion of having been in love with her. I felt excited and bemused, and ridiculously pleased, like a child who has been given something precious to play with. I said it to myself again – *I loved her!* – trying it out for the sound of it. The thought, lofty, grand, and slightly mad, fitted well with the surroundings. She was pacing between me and the window, clutching her glass tightly in both hands. The gauze curtain bellied lazily at the edge of my vision. Something in the air itself seemed to be shaking. Suddenly the telephone on the low table beside me sprang to life with a crashing noise. Anna snatched it up and cried yes, yes, what? She laughed. It's some taximan, she said to me, looking for his fare. I took the phone and spoke harshly to the fellow. She watched me intently, with a kind of avid amusement. When I put down the receiver she said gaily, Oh, Freddie, you've got so pompous! I frowned. I was not sure how to respond. Her laughter, her glazed stare, were tinged with hysteria. But then, I too was less than calm. Look at that, she said. She was peering in annoyance at her bloodstained shoes. She clicked her tongue, and putting down her glass she quickly left the room. I waited. All this had happened before. I went and stood in the open window, a hand in my pocket, swigging my gin. Pompous, indeed — what did she mean? The sun was almost down, the light was gathering in bundles above the river. I stepped out on to the terrace. A balm of soft air breathed on my face. I thought how strange it was to be here like this, glass in hand, in the silence and calm of a summer evening, while there was so much darkness in my heart. I turned and looked up at the house. It seemed to be flying swiftly against the sky. I wanted my share of this richness, this gilded ease. From the depths of the room a pair of eyes looked out, dark, calm, unseeing.

Flynn, the crop-headed chauffeur, approached me from the side of the house with an air of tight-lipped politeness which was somehow menacing, rolling on the balls of his disproportionately dainty feet. He sported a bandit's drooping blue-black moustache, trimmed close and squared off at the ends, so that it looked as if it had been painted on to his large, pasty face. I do not like moustaches, have I mentioned that? There is something lewd about them which repels me. I have no doubt the prison shrink could explain what such an aversion signifies – and I've no doubt, too, that in my case he would be wrong. Flynn's was a particularly offensive specimen. The sight of it gave me heart suddenly, cheered me up, I don't know why. I followed him eagerly into the house. The dining-room was a great dim cavern full of the glint and gleam of precious things. Behrens came in leaning on Anna's arm, a tall, delicate figure in rich tweeds and a bow-tie. He moved slowly, measuring his steps. His head, trembling a little, was smooth and steeply domed, like a marvellous, desiccated egg. It must have been twenty years since I had seen him last. I confess I was greatly taken with him now. He had the fine high patina of something lovingly crafted, like one of those exquisite and temptingly pocket-sized jade figurines which I had been eyeing only a moment ago on the mantelpiece. He took my hand and squeezed it slowly in his strangler's grip, looking deep into my eyes as if he were trying to catch a glimpse of someone else in there. Frederick, he said, in his breathy voice. So like your mother.

We dined at a rickety table in the bay of a tall window overlooking the garden. The cutlery was cheap, the plates mismatched. It was something I remembered about Whitewater, the makeshift way that life was lived in odd corners, at the edge of things. The house was not meant for people, all that magnificence would not tolerate their shoddy doings in its midst. I watched Behrens cutting up a piece of bleeding meat. Those enormous hands fascinated me. I was always convinced that at some time in the past he had killed someone. I tried to imagine him young, in flannels and a blazer, carrying a tennis racquet – *Oh look, here's Binkie!* – but it was impossible. He talked about the bombing. Five dead – or was it six by now? – from a mere two pounds of explosive! He sighed and shook his head. He seemed more impressed than shocked. Anna hardly spoke. She was pale, and looked tired and distracted. I noticed for the first time how she had aged. The woman I knew fifteen years ago was still there, but fixed inside a coarser outline, like one of Klimt's gem-encrusted lovers. I looked out into the luminous grey twilight, aghast and in an obscure way proud at the thought of what I had lost, of what might have been. Piled clouds, a last, bright strip of sky. A blackbird whistled suddenly. Someday I would lose all this too, I would die, and it would all be gone, this moment at this window, in summer, on the tender brink of night. It was amazing, and yet it was true, it would happen. Anna struck a match and lighted a candle on the table between us, and for a moment there was a sense of hovering, of swaying, in the soft, dark air.

My mother, I said to Behrens, and had to stop and clear my throat – my mother gave you some pictures, I believe. He turned his raptor's gaze on me. *Sold*, he said, and it was almost a whisper, sold, not gave. He smiled. There was a brief silence. He was quite at ease. He was sorry, he said, if I had come in the hope of seeing the pictures again. He could understand that I might be attached to them. But he had got rid of them almost at once. He smiled again, gently. There were one or two quite nice things, he said, but they would not have been comfortable, here, at White-water.

There you are, father, I thought, so much for your connoisseur's eye.

I wanted to do something for your mother, you see, Behrens was saying. She had been ill, you know. I gave her much more than the market value – you mustn't tell her that, of course. She wanted to set up in business of some kind, I think. He laughed. Such a spirited woman! he said. There was another silence. He fiddled with his knife, amused, waiting. I realised, with some astonishment, that he must have thought I had come to demand the return of the collection. Then, of course, I began to wonder if despite his protestations he had cheated on the price. The notion bucked me up immensely. Why, you old scoundrel, I thought, laughing to myself, you're just like all the rest of us. I looked at Anna's profile faintly reflected in the window before me. What was she, too, but an ageing spinster, with her wrinkles and her dyed hair – probably Flynn serviced her once a month or so, between hosing down the car and taking his moustache to the barber's for a trim. Damn you all! I poured myself a brimming glass of wine, and spilled some on the tablecloth, and was glad. Oh dark, dark.

I expected to be asked to stay the night, but when we had drunk our coffee Anna excused herself, and came back in a minute and said she had phoned for a taxi. I was offended. I had come all this way to see them and they would not even offer me a bed. An ugly silence fell. Behrens at my prompting had been talking about Dutch painters. Did I imagine it, or did he glance at me with a sly smile when he asked if I had been into the garden room? Before I realised it was the gilded salon that he meant he had passed on. Now he sat, head trembling, his mouth open a little, staring dully at the candle-flame. He lifted a hand, as if he were about to speak again, but let it fall slowly. The lights of a car swept the window and a horn tooted. Behrens did not get up. So good to see you, he murmured, giving me his left hand. So good.

Anna walked with me to the front door. I felt I had somehow made a fool of myself, but could not think how, exactly. In the hall our footsteps sounded very loud, a confused and faintly absurd racket. It's Flynn's night off, Anna said, or I would have had him drive you. I said stiffly that was quite all right. I was asking myself if we could be the same two people who had rolled with Daphne naked on a bed one hot Sunday afternoon on the other side of the world, on the other side of time. How could I have imagined I had ever loved her. Your father seems well, I said. She shrugged. Oh, she said, he's dying. At the door, I don't know what I was thinking of, I fumbled for her hand and tried to kiss her. She stepped back quickly, and I almost fell over. The taxi tooted again. Anna! I said, and then could think of nothing to add. She laughed bleakly. Go home, Freddie, she said, with a wan smile, and shut the door slowly in my face.

I knew who would be driving the taxi, of course. Don't say anything, I said to him sternly, not a word! He looked at me in the mirror with a mournful, accusing eye, and we lumbered off down the drive. I realised I had nowhere to go.

IT IS SEPTEMBER. I have been here now for two months. It seems longer than that. The tree that I can glimpse from the window of my cell has a drab, dusty look, it will soon begin to turn. It trembles, as if in anticipation, at night I fancy I can hear it, rustling excitedly out there in the dark. The skies in the morning are splendid, immensely high and clear. I like to watch the clouds building and dispersing. Such huge, delicate labour. Today there was a rainbow, when I saw it I laughed out loud, as at a wonderful, absurd joke. Now and then people pass by, under the tree. It must be a shortcut, that way. At nine come the office girls with cigarettes and fancy hairdos, and, a little later, the dreamy housewives lugging shopping bags and babies. At four every afternoon a schoolboy straggles by, bearing an enormous satchel on his back like a hump. Dogs come too, walking very fast with an air of determination, stop, give the tree a quick squirt, pass on. Other lives, other lives. Lately, since the season began to change, they all seem to move, even the boy, with a lighter tread, borne up, as if they are flying, somehow, through the glassy blue autumnal air.

At this time of year I often dream about my father. It is

88

always the same dream, though the circumstances vary. The person in it is indeed my father, but not as I ever knew him. He is younger, sturdier, he is cheerful, he has a droll sense of humour. I arrive at a hospital, or some such large institution, and, after much searching and confusion, find him sitting up in bed with a steaming mug of tea in his hand. His hair is boyishly rumpled, he is wearing someone else's pyjamas. He greets me with a sheepish smile. On impulse, because I am flustered and have been so worried, I embrace him fervently. He suffers this unaccustomed display of emotion with equanimity, patting my shoulder and laughing a little. Then I sit down on a chair beside the bed and we are silent for a moment, not quite knowing what to do, or where to look. I understand that he has survived something, an accident, or a shipwreck, or a hectic illness. Somehow it is his own foolhardiness, his recklessness (my father, reckless!), that has got him into danger, and now he is feeling silly, and comically ashamed of himself. In the dream it is always I who have been responsible for his lucky escape, by raising the alarm, calling for an ambulance, getting the lifeboat out, something like that. My deed sits between us, enormous, unmanageable, like love itself, proof at last of a son's true regard. I wake up smiling, my heart swollen with tenderness. I used to believe that in the dream it was death I was rescuing him from, but lately I have begun to think that it is, instead, the long calamity of his life I am undoing at a stroke. Now perhaps I'll have another, similar task to perform. For they told me today my mother has died.

By the time the taxi got me to the village the last bus to the city had left, as my driver, with melancholy enjoyment, had assured me would be the case. We sat in the darkened main street, beside a hardware shop, the engine purring. The driver turned around in his seat, lifting his cap for a rapid, one-finger scratch, and settled down to see what I would do next. Once again I was struck by the way these people stare, the dull, brute candour of their interest. I had better give him a name – it is Reck, I'm afraid – for I shall be stuck with him for a while yet. He would be happy, he said, to drive me into the city himself. I shook my head: it was a good thirty miles, and I already owed him money. Otherwise, he said, with an awful, ingratiating smile, his mother might put me up – Mrs Reck, it seemed, ran a public house with a room upstairs. The idea did not appeal to me, but the street was dark and grimly silent, and there was something very depressing about those tools in that shop window, and yes, I said faintly, with a hand to my forehead, yes, take me to your mother.

But she was not there, or asleep or something, and he led me up the back stairs himself, going on tiptoe like a large, shaky spider. The room had a little low window, one chair, and a bed with a hollow in the middle, as if a cadaver had lately been removed from it. There was a smell of piss and porter. Reck stood smiling at me shyly, kneading his cap in his hands. I bade him a firm goodnight, and he withdrew, lingeringly. The last I saw of him was a bony hand slowly pulling the door closed behind him. I walked back and forth once or twice gingerly, the floorboards creaking. Did I wring my hands, I wonder? The low window and the sagging bed gave me a vertiginous sense of disproportion, I seemed too tall, my feet too big. I sat on the side of the bed. A faint radiance lingered in the window. If I leaned down sideways I could see a crooked chimney pot and a silhouette of trees. I felt like the gloomy hero in a Russian novel, brooding in my bolthole above the dramshop in the village of Dash, in the year Dot, with my story all before me, waiting to be told.

I did not sleep. The sheets were clammy and somehow slippery, and I was convinced I was not the first to have tossed and turned between them since their last laundering. I tried to lie, tensed like a spring, in such a way that as little of me as possible came in contact with them. The hours were marked by a distant churchbell with a peculiarly dull note. There was the usual barking of dogs and bellowing of cattle. The sound of my own fretful sighs infuriated me. Now and then a car or a lorry passed by, and a box of lighted geometry slid rapidly over the ceiling and down the walls and poured away in a corner. I had a raging thirst. Waking dreams assailed me with grotesque and bawdy visions. Once, on the point of sleep, I had a sudden, dreadful sense of falling, and I sprang awake with a jerk. Though I tried to put her out of my mind I kept returning to the thought of Anna Behrens. What had happened to her, that she should lock herself away in that drear museum, with only a dying old man for company? But perhaps nothing had happened, perhaps that was it. Perhaps the days just went by, one by one, without a sound, until at last it was too late, and she woke up one morning and found herself stuck fast in the middle of her life. I imagined her there, sad and solitary, bewitched in her magic castle, year after year, and — oh, all sorts of mad notions came into my head, I am too embarrassed to speak of them. And as I was thinking these things, another thought, on another, murkier level, was winding and winding its dark skein. So it was out of a muddled conflation of ideas of knight errantry and rescue and reward that my plan originated. I assure you, your honour, this is no sly attempt at exoneration: I only wish to explain my motives, I mean the deepest ones, if such a thing is possible. As the hours went on, and stars flared in the little window and then slowly faded again, Anna Behrens merged in my mind with the other women who were in some way in my care – Daphne, of course, and even my mother, even the stable-girl, too – but in the end, when the dawn came, it was that Dutch figure in the picture in the garden room who hovered over the bed and gazed at me, sceptical, inquisitive and calm. I got up and dressed, and sat on the chair by the window and watched the ashen light of day descend upon the rooftops and seep into the trees. My mind was racing, my blood fizzled in my veins. I knew now what I would do. I was excited, and at the same time I had a deep sense of dread. There were stirrings downstairs. I wanted to be out, out, being and doing. I started to leave the room, but paused and lay on the bed for a moment to calm myself, and fell at once into a profound and terrible sleep. It was as if I had been struck down. I cannot describe it. It lasted no more than a minute or two. I woke up shaking. It was as if the very heart of things had skipped a beat. So it was that the day began, as it would continue, in the horrors.

Mrs Reck was tall and thin. No, she was short and fat. I do not remember her clearly. I do not wish to remember her clearly. For God's sake, how many of these grotesques am I expected to invent? I'll call her for a witness, and you can do the job yourselves. At first I thought she was in pain, but it was only a terrible, tongue-tied shyness that was making her duck and flinch. She fed me sausages and rashers and black pudding in the parlour behind the bar (it was the executioner who ate a hearty breakfast). An intricate silence filled the room, I could hear myself swallow. Shadows hung down the walls like fronds of cobweb. There was a picture of Jesus with his dripping heart on show, done in thick shades of crimson and cream, and a photograph of some pope or other blessing the multitudes from a Vatican balcony. A feeling of gloom settled like heartburn in my breast. Reck appeared, in his braces and shirt-sleeves, and asked coyly if everything was all right. Grand, I said stoutly, grand! He stood and gazed at me, smiling tenderly, with a sort of happy pride. I might have been something he had left to propagate overnight. Ah, these poor, simple lives, so many, across which I have dragged my trail of slime. He had not once mentioned the monies I owed him – even on the phone he had apologised for not waiting for me. I rose and edged past him in the doorway. Just popping out for a moment, I said, get a breath of air. I could feel my horrible smile, like something sticky that had dripped on to my face. He nodded, and a little flicker of sadness passed over his brow and down his sheep's muzzle. You knew I was going to do a flit, didn't you? Why did you not stop me? I don't understand these people. I have said it before. I don't understand them.

The sun was shining through a thinning haze. It was still impossibly early. I walked down one side of the main street and up the other, twitching with impatience. Few people were about. Where did the notion come from that country folk are early risers? A van passed by, towing a trailer with a pig in it. At the end of the street there was a bridge over a shallow brown stream. I sat on the parapet and watched the water for a while. I needed a shave. I thought of going back to Reck's and borrowing a razor from him, but even I was not ruffian enough for such effrontery. The day was growing hot already. I began to feel light-headed there in the sun, watching the water squiggle and gulp below me. Presently a large, ancient man came along and began to address me earnestly. He wore sandals, and a torn mackintosh slung like a kern's tartan over one shoulder, and carried a thick ash stave. His hair was long, his beard matted. For some reason I found myself picturing his head borne aloft on a platter. He spoke calmly, in a loud, strong voice. I could not understand a word he said – he seemed to have lost the power of articulation – yet I found something oddly affecting in the way he stood there, leaning on his ashplant, with one knee flexed, his eyes fixed on me, speaking out his testament. I watched his mouth working in the thicket of his beard, and nodded my head slowly, seriously. Madmen do not frighten me, or even make me uneasy. Indeed, I find that their ravings soothe me. I think it is because everything, from the explosion of a nova to the fall of dust in a deserted room, is to them of vast and equal significance, and therefore meaningless. He finished, and continued regarding me in silence for a moment. Then he nodded gravely, and, with a last, meaningful stare, turned and strode away, over the bridge.

Your honour, I know I have spoken of having a plan, but it was a plan only in the broadest sense. I have never been much good at details. In the night, when the egg hatched and the thing first flexed its sticky, brittle wings, I had told myself that when morning came and real life started up again I would laugh at such a preposterous notion. And I did laugh, even if it was in a thoughtful sort of way, and I believe, I really do, that if I had not been stranded in that hole, with nothing to pass the time except my own dark thoughts, none of this would have happened. I would have gone to Charlie French and borrowed some money from him, and returned to the island and paid my debt to Señor Aguirre, and then I would have taken my wife and child and come home, to Coolgrange, to make my peace with my mother, and settle down, and become a squireen like my father, and live, and be happy. Ah –

What was I saying? My plan, yes. Your lordship, I am no mastermind. The newspapers, which from the start have been quite beside themselves – it was the silly season, after all, and I gave them a glorious, running story – have portrayed me both as a reckless thug and a meticulous, ice-cool, iron-willed blond beast. But I swear, it was all just drift, like everything else. I suppose at first I played with the idea, telling it to myself as a sort of story, as I lay there, the sleepless prince, in Mother Reck's gingerbread house, while the innocent stars crowded silently in the window. In the morning I rose and held it up to the light, and already it had begun to harden, to set. Strangely, it was like the work of someone else, which had been given to me to measure and to test. This process of distancing seems to have been an essential preliminary to action. Perhaps this accounts for the peculiar sensation which came over me there on the bridge above that gurgling river. It's hard to describe. I felt that I was utterly unlike myself. That is to say, I was perfectly familiar with this large, somewhat overweight, fair-haired man in a wrinkled suit sitting here fretfully twiddling his thumbs, yet at the same time it was as if I – the real, thinking, sentient I – had somehow got myself trapped inside a body not my own. But no, that's not it, exactly. For the person that was inside was also strange to me, stranger by far, indeed, than the familiar, physical creature. This is not clear, I know. I say the one within was strange to *me*, but which version of *me* do I mean? No, not clear at all. But it was not a new sensation. I have always felt – what is the word – bifurcate, that's it. Today, however, this feeling was stronger, more pronounced than usual. Bunter was restive, aching to get out. He had been shut up for so long, burbling and grumbling and taunting in there, and I knew that when he burst out at last he would talk and talk and talk. I felt dizzy. Grey nausea made my insides cringe. I wonder if the court appreciates what a state my nerves were in, not just that day, but throughout that period? My wife and child were being held hostage by wicked people, I was practically broke, my quarterly allowance from the pittance left me by my father was not due for another two months, and here I was, after a ghastly night, red-eyed, unshaven, stranded in the middle of nowhere and contemplating desperate actions. How would I not have been dizzy, how would I not have felt sick to my guts?

Eventually I sensed the village behind me coming sluggishly to life, and I walked back along the main street, keeping an eye out in case I should encounter an importunate Reck or, worse, Reck's mother. The morning was sunny and still, dew-laden, and a little dazed, as if drunk on its own newness. There were patches of damp on the pavements. It would be a glorious day. Oh yes, glorious.

I did not know until I found it that I was looking for the hardware shop where Reck had stopped the taxi the night before. My arm reached out and pushed open the door, a bell pinged, my legs walked me inside.

Gloom, a smell of paraffin and linseed oil, and clusters of things pendent overhead. A short, stout, elderly, balding man was sweeping the floor. He wore carpet slippers, and a cinnamon-coloured shopcoat such as I had not seen since I was a child. He smiled and nodded at me, and put aside his brush. He would not speak, however – professional etiquette, no doubt – until he had taken up position behind the counter, leaning forward on his arms with his head cocked to one side. Wire-rimmed glasses, I thought, would have completed the effect. I liked him straight away. Good day to you, sir, he said, in a cheery, hand-rubbing sort of voice. I felt better already. He was polite to just the correct degree, without undue subservience, or any hint of nosiness. I bought a ball of twine and a roll of brown wrapping-paper. Also a hank of rope – coiled, I recall, in a tight cylinder, very like a hangman's knot – good hard smooth hemp, not that modern plastic stuff. I had little notion of what I intended to do with these things. The rope, for instance, was pure indulgence. I didn't care. It was years – decades! – since I had experienced such simple, greedy pleasure. The shopman placed my purchases lovingly before me on the counter, crooning a little under his breath, smiling, pursing his lips approvingly. It was playtime. In this pretend-world I could have anything I wanted. A tenon-saw, for instance, with rosewood stock. A set of brass fire-irons, their handles made in the shape of crouching monkeys. That white enamelled bucket, with a delicate, flesh-blue shadow down one side. Oh, anything! Then I spotted the hammer. One moulded, polished piece of stainless steel, like a bone from the thigh of some swift animal, with a velvety, black rubber grip and a blued head and claw. I am utterly unhandy, I do not think I could drive a nail straight, but I confess I had always harboured a secret desire to have a hammer like that. More laughter in court, of course, more ribald guffaws from the wiseacres in the gallery. But I insist, your honour, gentle handymen of the jury, I insist it was an innocent desire, a wish, an ache, on the part of the deprived child inside me – not Bunter, not him, but the true, lost ghost of my boyhood – to possess this marvellous toy. For the first time my fairy-godfather hesitated. There are other models, he ventured, less – a hurried, breathy whisper – less expensive, sir. But no, no, I could not resist it. I must have it. That one. Yes, that one, there, with the tag on it. Exhibit A, in other words.

I stumbled out of the shop with my parcel under my arm, bleared and grinning, happy as a drunken schoolboy. The shopkeeper came to the door to watch me go. He had shaken hands with me in an odd, cryptic manner. Perhaps he was a mason, and was testing to see if I too might be a member of the brotherhood? – but no, I prefer to think he was merely a decent, kindly, well-meaning man. There are not many such, in this testimony.

I felt by now that I knew the village. I felt in fact that I had been here before, and even that I had done all these things before, walked about aimlessly in the early morning, and sat on the bridge, and gone into a shop and purchased things. I have no explanation: I only felt it. It was as if I had dreamed a prophetic dream and then forgotten it, and this was the prophecy coming true. But then, something of that sense of inevitability infected everything I did that day – inevitable, mind you, does not mean excusable, in my vocabulary. No indeed, a strong mixture of Catholic and Calvinist blood courses in my veins.

It came to me suddenly, with happy inconsequentiality, that it was midsummer day.

This is a wonderful country, a man with a decent accent can do almost anything. I thought I was heading for the bus-stop, to see if there was a bus to the city, but instead – more inevitability – I found myself outside a tumbledown garage in the village square. A boy in filthy overalls a number of sizes too small for him was heaving tyres and whistling tunelessly out of the side of his face. A rusty tin sign nailed to the wall above his head proclaimed: *Melmoth's ar Hire.* The boy paused and looked at me blankly. He had stopped whistling, but kept his lips puckered. Car? I said, pointing to the sign, for hire, yes? I jiggled an invisible steering wheel. He said nothing, only frowned in deep puzzlement, as if I had asked for something utterly outlandish. Then a stout, big-bosomed woman came out of the cash office and spoke to him sharply. She wore a crimson blouse and tight black trousers and high-heeled, toeless sandals. Her hair, black as a crow's wing, was piled up in a brioche shape, with ringlets trailing down at the sides. She reminded me of someone, I could not think who. She led me into the office, where with a lurch I spied, among a cluster of gaudy postcards tacked to the wall behind her desk, a view of the island, and the harbour, and the very bar where I had first encountered Randolph the American. It was unnerving, an omen, even a warning, perhaps. The woman was studying me up and down with a sort of smouldering surmise. With another shock I realised who it was she reminded me of: the mother of the squalling baby in Señor Aguirre's apartment.

The car was a Humber, a great, heavy, high model, not old enough to be what they call vintage, just hopelessly out of fashion. It seemed to have been built for a simpler, more innocent age than this, one peopled by a species of big children. The upholstery had a vaguely fecal smell. I drove sedately through the village in third gear, perched high above the road as if I were being borne along on a palanquin. The engine made a noise like muffled cheering. I had paid a deposit of five pounds, and signed a document in the name of Smyth (I thought the *y* a fiendishly clever touch). The woman had not even asked to see a driving licence. As I say, this is a wonderful country. I felt extraordinarily light-hearted.

Speaking of jaunts: I went to my mother's funeral today. Three plain-clothes men took me in a closed car, I was very impressed. We sped through the city with the siren hee-hawing, it was like my arrest all over again, but in reverse. A lovely, sunny, crisp morning, pale smoke in the air, a few leaves down already on the pavements. I felt such a strange mingling of emotions – a certain rawness, of course, a certain pain, but elation, too, and something like grief that yet was not without sweetness. I was grieving not for my mother only, perhaps not for her at all, but for things in general. Maybe it was just the usual September melancholy, made unfamiliar by the circumstances. We drove by the river under a sky piled high with bundles of luminous Dutch clouds, then south through leafy suburbs. The sea surprised me, as it always does, a bowl of blue, moving metal, light rising in flakes off the surface. All three detectives were chain-smokers, they worked at it grimly, as if it were a part of their duties. One of them offered me a cigarette. Not one of my vices, I said, and they laughed politely. They seemed embarrassed, and kept glancing warily out the windows, as if they had been forced to come on an outing with a famous and disreputable relative and were afraid of being spotted by someone they knew. Now we were in the country, and there was mist on the fields still, and the hedges were drenched. She was buried in the family plot in the old cemetery at Coolgrange. I was not allowed to leave the car, or even to open a window. I was secretly glad, for somehow I could not conceive of myself stepping out suddenly like this, into the world. The driver parked as near as possible to the graveside, and I sat in a fug of cigarette smoke and watched the brief, hackneyed little drama unfold beyond the fogged glass, among the leaning headstones. There were few mourners: an aunt or two, and an old man who had worked years ago for my father in the stables. The girl Joanne was there, of course, red-eyed, her poor face blotched and swollen, dressed in a lumpy pullover and a crooked skirt. Charlie French stood a little apart from the rest, with his hands awkwardly clasped. I was surprised to see him. Decent of him to come, courageous, too. Neither he nor the girl looked in my direction, though they must have felt the pressure of my humid gaze. The coffin seemed to me surprisingly small, they got it down into the hole with room to spare. Poor Ma. I can't believe that she's gone, I mean the fact of it has not sunk in yet. It is somehow as if she had been bundled away to make room for something more important. Of course, the irony of the situation does not escape me: if I had only waited a few months there would have been no need to – but no, enough of that. They'll read the will without me, which is only right. The last time I saw her I fought with her. That was the day I left for Whitewater. She did not visit me in jail. I don't blame her. I never even brought the child for her to see. She was not as tough as I imagined. Did I destroy her life, too? All these dead women.

When the ceremony was over Charlie walked past the car with his head down. He seemed to hesitate, but changed his mind and went on. I think he would have spoken to me, had it not been for the presence of the detectives, and my aunts agog behind him, and, oh, just the general awfulness of everything.

So I AM DRIVING away from the village, in the Humber Hawk, with a foolish grin on my face. I felt, for no good reason, that I was escaping all my problems, I pictured them dwindling in space and time like the village itself, a quaint jumble of things getting steadily smaller and smaller. If I had stopped for a moment to think, of course, I would have realised that what I was leaving behind me was not my tangled troubles, as I fondly imagined, but, on the contrary, a mass of evidence, obvious and unmistakable as a swatch of matted hair and blood. I had skipped Ma Reck's without paying for my lodgings, I had bought a burglar's kit in the village shop, and now I had as good as stolen a car – and all this not five miles from what would soon come to be known as the scene of the crime. The court will agree, these are hardly the marks of careful premeditation. (Why is it that every other thing I say sounds like the sly preamble to a plea of mitigation?) The fact is, I was not thinking at all, not what could really be called thinking. I was content to sail through sun and shade along these dappled back roads, one hand on the wheel and an elbow out the window, with the scents of the countryside in my nostrils and the breeze whipping my hair. Everything would be well, everything would work itself out. I do not know why I felt so elated, perhaps it was a form of delirium. Anyway, I told myself, it was only a madcap game I was playing, I could call it off whenever I wished.

Meanwhile here was Whitewater, rising above the trees.

An empty tour bus was parked at the gate. The driver's door was open, and the driver was lounging in the stepwell, sunning himself. He watched me as I swung past him into the drive. I waved to him. He wore tinted glasses. He did not smile. He would remember me.

Afterwards the police could not understand why I showed so little circumspection, driving up brazenly like that, in broad daylight, in that unmistakable motor car. But I believed, you see, that the matter would be entirely between Behrens and me, with Anna perhaps as go-between. I never imagined there would be anything so vulgar as a police investigation, and headlines in the papers, and all the rest of it. A simple business transaction between civilised people, that's what I intended. I would be polite but firm, no more than that. I was not thinking in terms of threats and ransom demands, certainly not. When later I read what those reporters wrote – the Midsummer Manhunt, they called it – I could not recognise myself in their depiction of me as a steely, ruthless character. Ruthless – me! No, as I drove up to Whitewater it was not police I was thinking of, but only the chauffeur Flynn, with his little pig eyes and his boxer's meaty paws. Yes, Flynn was a man to avoid.

Halfway up the drive there was

God, these tedious details.

Halfway up there was a fork in the drive. A wooden arrow with HOUSE written on it in white paint pointed to the right, while to the left a sign said STRICTLY

PRIVATE. I stopped the car. See me there, a big blurred face behind the windscreen peering first this way, then that. It is like an illustration from a cautionary tract: the sinner hesitates at the parting of the ways. I drove off to the left, and my heart gave an apprehensive wallop. Behold, the wretch forsakes the path of righteousness.

I rounded the south wing of the house, and parked on the grass and walked across the lawn to the garden room. The french window was open. Deep breath. It was not yet noon. Far off in the fields somewhere a tractor was working, it made a drowsy, buzzing sound that seemed the very voice of summer, I hear it still, that tiny, distant, prelapsarian song. I had left the rope and the hammer in the car, and brought with me the twine and the roll of wrapping paper. It struck me suddenly how absurd the whole thing was. I began to laugh, and laughing stepped into the room.

The painting is called, as everyone must know by now, *Portrait of a Woman with Gloves*. It measures eighty-two centimetres by sixty-five. From internal evidence − in particular the woman's attire − it has been dated between 1655 and 1660. The black dress and broad white collar and cuffs of the woman are lightened only by a brooch and gold ornamentation on the gloves. The face has a slightly Eastern cast. (I am quoting from the guidebook to Whitewater House.) The picture has been variously attributed to Rembrandt and Frans Hals, even to Vermeer. However, it is safest to regard it as the work of an anonymous master.

None of this means anything.

I have stood in front of other, perhaps greater paintings, and not been moved as I am moved by this one. I have a reproduction of it on the wall above my table here − sent to me by, of all people, Anna Behrens − when I look at it my heart contracts. There is something in the way the woman regards me, the querulous, mute insistence of her eyes, which I can neither escape nor assuage. I squirm in the grasp of her gaze. She requires of me some great effort, some tremendous feat of scrutiny and attention, of which I do not think I am capable. It is as if she were asking me to let her live.

She. There is no she, of course. There is only an organisation of shapes and colours. Yet I try to make up a life for her. She is, I will say, thirty-five, thirty-six, though people without thinking still speak of her as a girl. She lives with her father, the merchant (tobacco, spices, and, in secret, slaves). She keeps house for him since her mother's death. She did not like her mother. Her father dotes on her, his only child. She is, he proclaims, his treasure. She devises menus – father has a delicate stomach – inspects the kitchen, she even supervises his wine cellar. She keeps an inventory of the household linen in a little notebook attached to her belt by a fine gold chain, using a code of her own devising, for she has never learned to read or write. She is strict with the servants, and will permit no familiarities. Their dislike she takes for respect. The house is not enough to absorb her energies, she does good works besides: she visits the sick, and is on the board of visitors of the town's almshouse. She is brisk, sometimes impatient, and there are mutterings against her among the alms-folk, especially the old women. At times, usually in spring and at the beginning of winter, everything becomes too much for her. Notice the clammy pallor of her skin: she is prey to obscure ailments. She takes to her bed and lies for days without speaking, hardly breathing, while outside in the silvery northern light the world goes about its busy way. She tries to pray, but God is distant. Her father comes to visit her at evening, walking on tiptoe. These periods of prostration frighten him, he remembers his wife dying, her terrible silence in the last weeks. If he were to lose his daughter too – But she gets up, wills herself to it, and very soon the servants are feeling the edge of her tongue again, and he cannot contain his relief, it comes out in little laughs, roguish endearments, a kind of clumsy skittishness. She considers him wryly, then turns back to her tasks. She cannot understand this notion he has got into his head: he wants to have her portrait painted. I'm old, is all he will say to her, I am an old man, look at me! And he laughs, awkwardly, and avoids her eye. My portrait? she says, mine? – I am no fit subject for a painter. He shrugs, at which she is first startled, then grimly amused: he might at least have attempted to contradict her. He seems to realise what is going through her mind, and tries to mend matters, but he becomes flustered, and, watching him fuss and fret and pluck at his cuffs, she realises with a pang that it's true, he has aged. Her father, an old man. The thought has a touch of bleak comedy, which she cannot account for. You have fine hands, he says, growing testy, annoyed both at himself and her, your mother's hands – we'll tell him to make the hands prominent. And so, to humour him, but also because she is secretly curious, she goes along one morning to the studio. The squalor is what strikes her first of all. Dirt and daubs of paint everywhere, gnawed chicken bones on a smeared plate, a chamber-pot on the floor in the corner. The painter matches the place, with that filthy smock, and those fingernails. He has a drinker's squashed and pitted nose. She thinks the general smell is bad until she catches a whiff of his breath. She discovers that she is relieved: she had expected someone young, dissolute, threatening, not this pot-bellied old soak. But then he fixes his little wet eyes on her, briefly, with a kind of impersonal intensity, and she flinches, as if caught in a burst of strong light. No one has ever looked at her like this before. So this is what it is to be known! It is almost indecent. First he puts her standing by the window, but it does not suit, the light is wrong, he says. He shifts her about, grasping her by the upper arms and walking her backwards from one place to another. She feels she should be indignant, but the usual responses do not seem to function here. He is shorter than her by a head. He makes some sketches, scribbles a colour note or two, then tells her to come tomorrow at the same time. And wear a darker dress, he says. Well! She is about to give him a piece of her mind, but already he has turned aside to another task. Her maid, sitting by the door, is biting her lips and smirking. She lets the next day pass, and the next, just to show him. When she does return he says nothing about the broken appointment, only looks at her black dress – pure silk, with a broad collar of Spanish lace – and nods carelessly, and she is so vexed at him it surprises her, and she is shocked at herself. He has her stand before the couch. Remove your gloves, he says, I am to emphasise the hands. She hears the note of amused disdain in his voice. She refuses. (*Her* hands, indeed!) He insists. They engage in a brief, stiff little squabble, batting icy politenesses back and forth between them. In the end she consents to remove one glove, then promptly tries to hide the hand she has bared. He sighs, shrugs, but has to suppress a grin, as she notices. Rain streams down the windows, shreds of smoke fly over the rooftops. The sky has a huge silver hole in it. At first she is restless, standing there, then she seems to pass silently through some barrier, and a dreamy calm comes over her. It is the same, day after day, first there is agitation, then the breakthrough, then silence and a kind of softness, as if she were floating away, away, out of herself. He mutters under his breath as he works. He is choleric, he swears, and clicks his tongue, sending up sighs and groans. There are long, fevered passages when he works close up against the canvas, and she can only see his stumpy legs and his old, misshapen boots. Even his feet seem busy. She wants to laugh when he pops his head out at the side of the easel and peers at her sharply, his potato nose twitching. He will not let her see what he is doing, she is not allowed even a peek. Then one day she senses a kind of soundless, settling crash at his end of the room, and he steps back with an expression of weary disgust and waves a hand dismissively at the canvas, and turns aside to clean his brush. She comes forward and looks. For a second she sees nothing, so taken is she by the mere sensation of stopping like this and turning: it is as if – as if somehow she had walked out of herself. A long moment passes. The brooch, she says, is wonderfully done. The sound of her own voice startles her, it is a stranger speaking, and she is cowed. He laughs, not bitterly, but with real amusement and, so she feels, a curious sort of sympathy. It is an acknowledgement, of – she does not know what. She looks and looks. She had expected it would be like looking in a mirror, but this is someone she does not recognise, and yet knows. The words come unbidden into her head: Now I know how to die. She puts on her glove, and signals to her maid. The painter is speaking behind her, something about her father, and money, of course, but she is not listening. She is calm. She is happy. She feels numbed, hollowed, a walking shell. She goes down the stairs, along the dingy hall, and steps out into a commonplace world.

Do not be fooled: none of this means anything either.

I had placed the string and the wrapping-paper carefully on the floor, and now stepped forward with my arms outstretched. The door behind me opened and a large woman in a tweed skirt and a cardigan came into the room. She halted when she saw me there, with my arms flung wide before the picture and peering wildly at her over my shoulder, while I tried with one foot to conceal the paper and the ball of twine on the floor. She had blue-grey hair, and her spectacles were attached to a cord around her neck. She frowned. You must stay with the party, she said loudly, in a cross voice – really, I don't know how many times I have to say it. I stepped back. A dozen gaudily dressed people were crowding in the doorway behind her, craning to get a look at me. Sorry, I heard myself say meekly, I got lost. She gave an impatient toss of the head and strode to the middle of the room and began at once to speak in a shouted singsong about Carlin tables and Berthoud clocks, and weeks later, questioned by the police and shown my photograph, she would deny ever having seen me before in her life. Her charges shuffled in, jostling surreptitiously in an effort to stay out of her line of sight. They took up position, standing with their hands clasped before them, as if they were in church, and looked about them with expressions of respectful vacancy. One grizzled old party in a Hawaiian shirt grinned at me and winked. I confess I was rattled. There was a knot in the pit of my stomach and my palms were damp. All the elation I had felt on the way here had evaporated, leaving behind it a stark sense of foreboding. I was struck, for the first time, really, by the enormity of what I was embarked on. I felt like a child whose game has led him far into the forest, and now it is nightfall, and there are shadowy figures among the trees. The guide had finished her account of the treasures in the room – the picture, *my* picture, was given two sentences, and a misattribution – and walked out now with one arm raised stiffly above her head, still talking, shepherding the party behind her. When they had gone I waited, staring fixedly at the doorknob, expecting her to come back and haul me out briskly by the scruff of the neck. Somewhere inside me a voice was moaning softly in panic and fright. This is something that does not seem to be appreciated – I have remarked on it before – I mean how timorous I am, how easily daunted. But she did not return, and I heard them tramping away up the stairs. I set to work again feverishly. I see myself, like the villain in an old three-reeler, all twitches and scowls and wriggling eyebrows. I got the picture off the wall, not without difficulty, and laid it flat on the floor – shying away from that black stare – and began to tear off lengths of wrapping-paper. I would not have thought that paper would make so much noise, such scuffling and rattling and ripping, it must have sounded as if some large animal were being flayed alive in here. And it was no good, my hands shook, I was all thumbs, and the sheets of paper kept rolling back on themselves, and I had nothing to cut the twine with, and anyway the picture, with its thick, heavy frame, was much too big to be wrapped. I scampered about on my knees, talking to myself and uttering little squeaks of distress. Everything was going wrong. Give it up, I told myself, oh please, please, give it up now, while there's still time! but another part of me gritted its teeth and said, no you don't, you coward, get up, get on your feet, do it. So I struggled up, moaning and snivelling, and grasped the picture in my arms and staggered with it blindly, nose to nose, in the direction of the french window. Those eyes were staring into mine, I almost blushed. And then – how shall I express it – then somehow I sensed, behind that stare, another presence, watching me. I stopped, and lowered the picture, and there she was, standing in the open window, just as she had stood the day before, wide-eyed, with one hand raised. This, I remember thinking bitterly, this is the last straw. I was outraged.

How dare the world strew these obstacles in my path. It was not fair, it was just not fair! Right, I said to her, here, take this, and I thrust the painting into her arms and turned her about and marched her ahead of me across the lawn. She said nothing, or if she did I was not listening. She found it hard going on the grass, the picture was too heavy for her, and she could hardly see around it. When she faltered I prodded her between the shoulder-blades. I really was very cross. We reached the car. The cavernous boot smelled strongly of fish. There was the usual jumble of mysterious implements, a jack, and spanners and things – I am not mechanically minded, or handed, have I mentioned that? – and a filthy old pullover, which I hardly noticed at the time, thrown in a corner with deceptive casualness by the hidden arranger of all these things. I took out the tools and threw them behind me on to the grass, then lifted the painting from the maid's arms and placed it face-down on the worn felt matting. This was the first time I had seen the back of the canvas, and suddenly I was struck by the antiquity of the thing. Three hundred years ago it had been stretched and sized and left against a lime-washed wall to dry. I closed my eyes for a second, and at once I saw a workshop in a narrow street in Amsterdam or Antwerp, smoky sunlight in the window, and hawkers going by outside, and the bells of the cathedral ringing. The maid was watching me. She had the most extraordinary pale, violet eyes, they seemed transparent, when I looked into them I felt I was seeing clear through her head. Why did she not run away? Behind her, in one of the great upstairs windows, a dozen heads were crowded, goggling at us. I could make out the guide-woman's glasses and the American's appalling shirt. I think I must have cried aloud in rage, an old lion roaring at the whip and chair, for the maid flinched and stepped back a pace. I caught her wrist in an iron claw and, wrenching open the car door, fairly flung her into the back seat. Oh, why did she not run away! When I got behind the wheel, fumbling and snarling, I caught a whiff of something, a faint, sharp, metallic smell, like the smell of worn pennies. I could see her in the mirror, crouched behind me as in a deep glass box, braced between the door and the back of the seat, with her elbows stuck out and fingers splayed and her face thrust forward, like the cornered heroine in a melodrama. A fierce, choking gust of impatience surged up inside me. Impatience, yes, that was what I felt most strongly – that, and a grievous sense of embarrassment. I was mortified. I had never been so exposed in all my life. People were looking at me – she in the back seat, and the tourists up there jostling at the window, but also, it seemed, a host of others, of phantom spectators, who must have been, I suppose, an intimation of all that horde who would soon be crowding around me in fascination and horror. I started the engine. The gears shrieked. In my agitation I kept getting ahead of myself and having to go back and repeat the simplest actions. When I had got the car off the grass and on to the drive I let the clutch out too quickly, and the machine sprang forward in a series of bone-shaking lurches, the bonnet going up and down like the prow of a boat caught in a wash and the shock absorbers grunting. The watchers at the window must have been in fits by now. A bead of sweat ran down my cheek. The sun had made the steering-wheel almost too hot to hold, and there was a blinding glare on the windscreen. The maid was scrabbling at the door handle, I roared at her and she stopped at once, and looked at me wide-eyed, like a rebuked child. Outside the gate the bus driver was still sitting in the sun. When she saw him she tried to get the window open, but in vain, the mechanism must have been broken. She pounded on the glass with her fists. I spun the wheel and the car lumbered out into the road, the tyres squealing. We were shouting at each other now, like a married couple having a fight. She pummelled me on the shoulder, got a hand around in front of my face and tried to claw my eyes. Her thumb went up my nose, I thought she would tear off the nostril. The car was going all over the road. I trod with both feet on the brake pedal, and we sailed in a slow, dragging curve into the hedge. She fell back. I turned to her. I had the hammer in my hand. I looked at it, startled. The silence rose around us like water. Don't, she said. She was crouched as before, with her arms bent and her back pressed into the corner. I could not speak, I was filled with a kind of wonder. I had never felt another's presence so immediately and with such raw force. I saw her now, really saw her, for the first time, her mousy hair and bad skin, that bruised look around her eyes. She was quite ordinary, and yet, somehow, I don't know – somehow radiant. She cleared her throat and sat up, and detached a strand of hair that had caught at the corner of her mouth.

You must let me go, she said, or you will be in trouble.

It's not easy to wield a hammer in a motor car. When I struck her the first time I expected to feel the sharp, clean smack of steel on bone, but it was more like hitting clay, or hard putty. The word *fontanel* sprang into my mind. I thought one good bash would do it, but, as the autopsy would show, she had a remarkably strong skull – even in that, you see, she was unlucky. The first blow fell just at the hairline, above her left eye. There was not much blood, only a dark-red glistening dent with hair matted in it. She shuddered, but remained sitting upright, swaying a little, looking at me with eyes that would not focus properly. Perhaps I would have stopped then, if she had not suddenly launched herself at me across the back of the seat, flailing and screaming. I was dismayed. How could this be happening to me – it was all so *unfair*. Bitter tears of self-pity squeezed into my eyes. I pushed her away from me and swung the hammer in a wide, backhand sweep. The force of the blow flung her against the door, and her head struck the window, and a fine thread of blood ran out of her nostril and across her cheek. There was blood on the window, too, a fan-shaped spray of tiny drops. She closed her eyes and turned her face away from me, making a low, guttural noise at the back of her throat. She put a hand up to her head just as I was swinging at her again, and when the blow landed on her temple her fingers were in the way, and I heard one of them crack, and I winced, and almost apologised. Oh! she said, and suddenly, as if everything inside her had collapsed, she slithered down the seat on to the floor.

There was silence again, clear and startling. I got out of the car and stood a moment, breathing. I was dizzy. Something seemed to have happened to the sunlight, everywhere I looked there was an underwater gloom. I thought I had driven only a little way, and expected to see the gates of Whitewater, and the tour bus, and the driver running towards me, but to my astonishment the road in both directions was empty, and I had no idea where I was. On one side a hill rose steeply, and on the other I could see over the tops of pine trees to far-off, rolling downs. It all looked distinctly improbable. It was like a hastily painted backdrop, especially that smudged, shimmering distance, and the road winding innocently away. I found I was still clutching the hammer. With a grand sweep of my arm I flung it from me, and watched it as it flew, tumbling slowly end over end, in a long, thrilling arc, far, far out over the blue pine-tops. Then abruptly I bent forward and vomited up the glutinous remains of the breakfast I had consumed an age ago, in another life.

I crawled back into the car, keeping my eyes averted from that crumpled thing wedged behind the front seat. The light in the windscreen was a splintered glare, I thought for a second the glass was smashed, until I put a hand to my face and discovered I was crying. This I found encouraging. My tears seemed not just a fore-token of remorse, but the sign of some more common, simpler urge, an affect for which there was no name, but which might be my last link, the only one that would hold, with the world of ordinary things. For everything was changed, where I was now I had not been before. I trembled, and all around me trembled, and there was a sluggish, sticky feel to things, as if I and all of this – car, road, trees, those distant meadows – as if we had all a moment ago struggled mute and amazed out of a birthhole in the air. I turned the key in the ignition, bracing myself, convinced that instead of the engine starting something else would happen, that there would be a terrible, rending noise, or a flash of light, or that slime would gush out over my legs from under the dashboard. I drove in second gear along the middle of the road. Smells, smells. Blood has a hot, thick smell. I wanted to open the windows, but did not dare, I was afraid of what might come in – the light outside seemed moist and dense as glair, I imagined it in my mouth, my nostrils.

I drove and drove. Whitewater is only thirty miles or so from the city, but it seemed hours before I found myself in the suburbs. Of the journey I remember little. That is to say, I do not remember changing gears, accelerating and slowing down, working the pedals, all that. I see myself moving, all right, as if in a crystal bubble, flying sound- lessly through a strange, sunlit, glittering landscape. I think I went very fast, for I recall a sensation of pressure in my ears, a dull, rushing blare. So I must have driven in circles, round and round those narrow country roads. Then there were houses, and housing estates, and straggling factories, and supermarkets big as aircraft hangers. I stared through the windscreen in dreamy amazement. I might have been a visitor from another part of the world altogether, hardly able to believe how much like home everything looked and yet how different it was. I did not know where I was going, I mean I was not going anywhere, just driving. It was almost restful, sailing along like that, turning the wheel with one finger, shut off from everything. It was as if all my life I had been clambering up a steep and difficult slope, and now had reached the peak and leaped out blithely into the blue. I felt so free. At the first red traffic light the car drifted gently to a stop as if it were subsiding into air. I was at the junction of two suburban roads. On the left there was a little green rise with a chestnut tree and a neat row of new houses. Children were playing on the grassy bank. Dogs gambolled. The sun shone. I have always harboured a secret fondness for quiet places such as this, unremarked yet cherished domains of building and doing and tending. I leaned my head back on the seat and smiled, watching the youngsters at play. The lights changed to green, but I did not stir. I was not really there, but lost somewhere, in some sunlit corner of my past. There was a sudden rapping on the window beside my ear. I jumped. A woman with a large, broad, horsy face – she reminded me, dear God, of my mother! – was peering in at me and saying something. I rolled down the window. She had a loud voice, it sounded very loud to me, at any rate. I could not understand her, she was talking about an accident, and asking me if I was all right. Then she pressed her face forward and squinnied over my shoulder, and opened her

mouth and groaned. Oh, she said, the poor child! I turned
my head. There was blood all over the back seat now, far
too much, surely, for just one person to have shed. For a
mad instant, in which a crafty spark of hope flared and
died, I wondered if there *had* been a crash, which somehow
I had not noticed, or had forgotten, if some overloaded
vehicle had ploughed into the back of us, flinging bodies
and all this blood in through the rear window. I could not
speak. I had thought she was dead, but there she was,
kneeling between the seats and groping at the window
beside her, I could hear her fingers squeaking on the glass.
Her hair hung down in bloodied ropes, her face was a clay
mask streaked with copper and crimson. The woman
outside was gabbling into my ear about telephones and
ambulances and the police – the police! I turned to her
with a terrible glare. Madam! I said sternly (she would
later describe my voice as *cultured* and *authoritative*), will
you please get on about your business! She stepped back,
staring in shock. I confess I was myself impressed, I would
not have thought I could muster such a commanding tone.
I rolled up the window and jammed the car into gear and
shot away, noticing, too late, that the lights had turned to
red. A tradesman's van coming from the left braked
sharply and let out an indignant squawk. I drove on.
However, I had not gone more than a street or two when
suddenly an ambulance reared up in my wake, its siren
yowling and blue light flashing. I was astonished. How
could it have arrived so promptly? In fact, this was another
of those appalling coincidences in which this case abounds.
The ambulance, as I would later learn, was not looking for
me, but was returning from – yes – from the scene of a car
crash, with – I'm sorry, but, yes – with a dying woman in
the back. I kept going, haring along with my head down,
my nose almost touching the rim of the wheel. I do not

think I could have stopped, locked in fright as I was. The ambulance drew alongside, swaying dangerously and trumpeting like a frenzied big beast. The attendant in the passenger seat, a burly young fellow in shirt-sleeves, with a red face and narrow sideburns, looked at the blood-streaked window behind me with mild, professional interest. He conferred briefly with the driver, then signalled to me, with complicated gestures, nodding and mouthing, to follow them. They thought I was coming from the same crash, ferrying another victim to hospital. They surged ahead. I followed in their wake, befuddled with alarm and bafflement. I could see nothing but this big square clumsy thing scudding along, whooshing up dust and wallowing fatly on its springs. Then abruptly it braked and swung into a wide gateway, and an arm appeared out of the side window and beckoned me to follow. It was the sight of that thick arm that broke the spell. With a gulp of demented laughter I drove on, past the hospital gate, plunging the pedal to the floor, and the noise of the siren dwindled behind me, a startled plaint, and I was free.

I peered into the mirror. She was sitting slumped on the seat with her head hanging and her hands resting palm upwards on her thighs.

Suddenly the sea was on my left, far below, blue, unmoving. I drove down a steep hill, then along a straight cement road beside a railway track. A pink and white hotel, castellated, with pennants flying, rose up on my right, enormous and empty. The road straggled to an end in a marshy patch of scrub and thistles, and there I stopped, in the midst of a vast and final silence. I could hear her behind me, breathing. When I turned she lifted her sibyl's fearsome head and looked at me. *Help me*, she whispered. *Help me*. A bubble of blood came out of her mouth and burst. *Tommy!* she said, or a word like that, and then:

Love. What did I feel? Remorse, grief, a terrible – no no no, I won't lie. I can't remember feeling anything, except that sense of strangeness, of being in a place I knew but did not recognise. When I got out of the car I was giddy, and had to lean on the door for a moment with my eyes shut tight. My jacket was bloodstained, I wriggled out of it and flung it into the stunted bushes – they never found it, I can't think why. I remembered the pullover in the boot, and put it on. It smelled of fish and sweat and axle-grease. I picked up the hangman's hank of rope and threw that away too. Then I lifted out the picture and walked with it to where there was a sagging barbed-wire fence and a ditch with a trickle of water at the bottom, and there I dumped it. What was I thinking of, I don't know. Perhaps it was a gesture of renunciation or something. Renunciation! How do I dare use such words. The woman with the gloves gave me a last, dismissive stare. She had expected no better of me. I went back to the car, trying not to look at it, the smeared windows. Something was falling on me: a delicate, silent fall of rain. I looked upwards in the glistening sunlight and saw a cloud directly overhead, the merest smear of grey against the summer blue. I thought: I am not human. Then I turned and walked away.

II

ALL MY ADULT LIFE I have had a recurring dream (yes, yes, dreams again!), it comes once or twice a year and leaves me disturbed for days afterwards. As usual it is not a dream in the ordinary sense, for not much happens in it, really, and nothing is explicit. There is mainly an undefined but profound and mounting sensation of unease, which rises at the end to full-fledged panic. A long time ago, it seems, I have committed a crime. No, that is too strong. I have done something, it is never clear what, precisely. Perhaps I stumbled upon something, it may even have been a corpse, and covered it up, and almost forgot about it. Now, years later, the evidence has been found, and they have come to question me. As yet there is nothing to suggest that I was directly involved, not a hint of suspicion attaches to me. I am merely another name on a list. They are mild, soft-spoken, stolidly deferential, a little bored. The young one fidgets. I respond to their questions politely, with a certain irony, smiling, lifting an eyebrow. It is, I tell myself smugly, the performance of my life, a masterpiece of dissembling. Yet the older one, I notice, is regarding me with deepening interest, his shrewd eyes narrowing. I must have said something. What have I said? I begin to blush, I cannot help it. A horrible constriction takes hold of me. I babble, what is intended as a relaxed little laugh turns into a strangled gasp. At length I run down, like a clockwork toy, and sit and gape at them helplessly, panting. Even the younger one, the sergeant, is interested now. An appalling silence descends, it stretches on and on, until at last my sleeping self makes a bolt for it and I start awake, aghast and sweating. What is peculiarly awful in all this is not the prospect of being dragged before the courts and put in jail for a crime I am not even sure I have committed, but the simple, terrible fact of having been found out. This is what makes me sweat, what fills my mouth with ashes and my heart with shame.

And now, as I hurried along the cement road, with the railway track beside me and the sea beyond, I had that same feeling of ignominy. What a fool I had been. What trouble there would be in the days, the weeks, the years ahead. Yet also there was a sensation of lightness, of buoyancy, as if I had thrown off an awkward burden. Ever since I had reached what they call the use of reason I had been doing one thing and thinking another, because the weight of things seemed so much greater than that of thoughts. What I said was never exactly what I felt, what I felt was never what it seemed I should feel, though the feelings were what felt genuine, and right, and inescapable. Now I had struck a blow for the inner man, that guffawing, fat foulmouth who had been telling me all along I was living a lie. And he had burst out at last, it was he, the ogre, who was pounding along in this lemon-coloured light, with blood on his pelt, and me slung helpless over his back. Everything was gone, the past, Coolgrange, Daphne, all my previous life, gone, abandoned, drained of its essence, its significance. To do the worst thing, the very worst thing, that's the way to be free. I would never again need to pretend to myself to be what I was not. The thought made my head spin and my empty stomach heave.

I was prey to a host of niggling worries. This pullover was smelly, and too tight for me. The knee of my left trouser-leg had a small rip in it. People would notice that I had not shaved today. And I needed, I positively longed, to wash my hands, to plunge up to the elbows in scalding suds, to sluice myself, to drench, rinse, scour – to be clean. Opposite the deserted hotel there was a jumble of grey buildings that had once been a railway station. Weeds were growing on the platform, and all the windows in the signal box were smashed. A pockmarked enamel sign with a lovingly painted pointing hand indicated a cement blockhouse set at a discreet distance down the platform. A clump of purple buddleia was flourishing by the doorway of the gents. I went into the ladies – there were no more rules, after all. The air here was chill and dank. There was a quicklime smell, and something green and glistening was growing up the walls. The fittings had been ripped out long ago, even the stall doors were gone. It was apparent from the state of the floor, however, that the place was still in frequent use. In a corner there was a little heap of stuff – used condoms, I think, discoloured wads of cotton, even bits of clothing – from which I quickly averted my eyes. A single tap on a green copper pipe stuck out of the wall where the handbasins had been. When I turned the spigot there was a distant groaning and clanking, and presently a rusty dribble came out. I washed my hands as best I could and dried them on the tail of my shirt. Yet when I had finished, and was about to leave, I discovered a drop of blood between my fingers. I don't know where it came from. It may have been on the pullover, or even in my hair. The blood was thick by now, dark, and sticky.

Nothing, not the stains in the car, the smears on the windows, not her cries, not even the smells of her dying, none of it affected me as did this drop of brownish gum. I plunged my fists under the tap again, whining in dismay, and scrubbed and scrubbed, but I could not get rid of it. The blood went, but something remained, all that long day I could feel it there, clinging in the fork of tender flesh between my fingers, a moist, warm, secret stain.

I am afraid to think what I have done.

For a while I sat on a broken bench on the platform in the sun. How blue the sea was, how gay the little flags fluttering and snapping on the hotel battlements. All was quiet, save for the sea-breeze crooning in the telegraph wires, and something somewhere that creaked and knocked, creaked and knocked. I smiled. I might have been a child again, daydreaming here, in these toy surroundings. I could smell the sea, and the sea-wrack on the beach, and the cat-smell of the sand. A train was on the way, yes, a puff-puff, the rails were humming and shivering in anticipation. Not a soul to be seen, not a grown-up anywhere, except, away down the beach, a few felled sunbathers on their towels. I wonder why it was so deserted there? Perhaps it wasn't, perhaps there were seaside crowds all about, and I didn't notice, with my inveterate yearning towards backgrounds. I closed my eyes, and something swam up dreamily, a memory, an image, and sank again without breaking the surface. I tried to catch it before it was gone, but there was only that one glimpse: a doorway, I think, opening on to a darkened room, and a mysterious sense of expectancy, of something or someone about to appear. Then the train came through, a slow, rolling thunder that made my diaphragm shake. The passengers were propped up in the wide windows like manikins, they gazed at me blankly as they were borne slowly past. It occurred to me I should have turned my face away: everyone was a potential witness now. But I thought it did not matter. I thought I would be in jail within hours. I looked about me, taking great breaths, drinking my fill of the world that I would soon be losing. A gang of boys, three or four, had appeared in the grounds of the hotel. They straggled across the unkempt lawns, and stopped to throw stones at a for-sale sign. I rose, with a leaden sigh, and left the station and set off along the road again.

I took a bus into the city. It was a single-decker, on an infrequent route, coming from far out. The people on it all seemed to know each other. At each stop when someone got on there was much banter and friendly raillery. An old chap with a cap and a crutch was the self-appointed host of this little travelling club. He sat near the front, behind the driver, his stiff left leg stuck out into the aisle, and greeted each newcomer with a start of feigned surprise and a rattle of his crutch. Oh! watch out! here he comes! he would say, mugging at the rest of us over his shoulder, as if to alert us to the arrival of some terrible character, when what had appeared up the step was a ferret-faced young man with a greasy season-ticket protruding from his fist like a discoloured tongue. Girls provoked gallantries, which made them smirk, while for the housewives off to town to do their shopping there were winks and playful references to that stiff limb of his. Now and again he would let a glance slide over me, quick, tentative, a little queasy, like that of an old trouper spotting a creditor in the front row. It struck me, indeed, that there was something faintly theatrical about the whole thing. The rest of the passengers had the self-conscious nonchalance of a first-night audience.

They too had a part of sorts to play. Behind the chatter and the jokes and the easy familiarity they seemed worried, their eyes were full of uncertainty and tiredness, as if they had got the text by heart but still were not sure of their cues. I studied them with deep interest. I felt I had discovered something significant, though what it was, or what it signified, I was not sure. And I, what was I among them? A stage-hand, perhaps, standing in the wings envying the players.

When we reached town I could not decide where to get off, one place seemed as good as another. I must say something about the practicalities of my situation. I should have been shaking in fear. I had a five-pound note and some coins – mostly foreign – in my pocket, I looked, and smelled, like a tramp, and I had nowhere to go. I did not even have a credit card with which to bluff my way into a hotel. Yet I could not worry, could not make myself be concerned. I seemed to float, bemused, in a dreamy detachment, as if I had been given a great dose of local anaesthetic. Perhaps this is what it means to be in shock? No: I think it was just the certainty that at any moment a hand would grasp me by the shoulder while a terrible voice boomed out a caution. By now they would have my name, a description would be in circulation, hard-eyed men in bulging jackets would be cruising the streets on the look-out for me. That none of this was so is still a puzzle to me. The Behrenses must have known at once who it was that would take that particular picture, yet they said nothing. And what about the trail of evidence I left behind me? What about the people who saw me, the Recks, the señorita at the garage, the man in the hardware shop, that woman who looked like my mother who came upon me sitting like a loon at the traffic lights? Your lordship, I would not wish to encourage potential wrongdoers, but I must say, it is easier to get away with something, for a time at least, than is generally acknowledged. Vital days – how easily one slips into the lingo! – *vital days* were to pass before they even began to know who it was they were after. If I had not continued to be as rash as I was at the start, if I had stopped and taken stock, and considered carefully, I believe I might not be here now, but in some sunnier clime, nursing my guilt under an open sky. But I did not stop, did not consider. I got off the bus and set off at once in the direction in which I happened to be facing, since my fate, I was convinced, awaited me all around, in the open arms of the law. Capture! I nursed the word in my heart. It comforted me. It was the promise of rest. I dodged along through the crowds like a drunk, surprised that they did not part before me in horror. All round me was an inferno of haste and noise. A gang of men stripped to the waist was gouging a hole in the road with pneumatic drills. The traffic snarled and bellowed, sunlight flashing like knives off the windshields and the throbbing roofs of cars. The air was a poisonous hot blue haze. I had become unused to cities. Yet I was aware that even as I struggled here I was simultaneously travelling smoothly forward in time, it seemed a kind of swimming without effort. Time, I thought grimly, time will save me. Here is Trinity, the Bank. Fox's, where my father used to come on an annual pilgrimage, with great ceremony, to buy his Christmas cigars. My world, and I an outcast in it. I felt a deep, dispassionate pity for myself, as for some poor lost wandering creature. The sun shone mercilessly, a fat eye stuck in the haze above the streets. I bought a bar of chocolate and devoured it, walking along. I bought an early edition of an evening paper, too, but there was nothing in it. I dropped it on the ground and shambled on. An urchin picked it up – Eh, mister! – and ran after me with it. I thanked him, and he grinned, and I almost burst into tears. I stood there, stalled, and looked about me blearily, a baffled hulk. People crowded past me, all faces and elbows. That was my lowest point, I think, that moment of helplessness and dull panic. I decided to give myself up. Why had I not thought of it before? The prospect was wonderfully seductive. I imagined myself being lifted tenderly and carried through a succession of cool white rooms to a place of calm and silence, of luxurious surrender.

In the end, instead, I went to Wally's pub.

It was shut. I did not understand. At first I thought wildly that it must be something to do with me, that they had found out I had been there and had closed it down. I pushed and pushed at the door, and tried to see through the bottle-glass of the windows, but all was dark inside. I stepped back. Next door there was a tiny fashion boutique where a pair of pale girls, frail and blank as flowers, stood motionless, staring at nothing, as if they were themselves a part of the display. When I spoke they turned their soot-rimmed eyes on me without interest. Holy hour, one said, and the other giggled wanly. I retreated, simpering, and went to the pub and pounded on the door with renewed force. After some time there were dragging footsteps inside and the sound of locks being undone. What do you want, Wally said crossly, blinking in the harsh sunlight slanting down from the street. He was wearing a purple silk dressing-gown and shapeless slippers. He looked me up and down with distaste, noting the stubble and the filthy pullover. I told him my car had broken down, I needed to make a phonecall. He gave a sardonic snort and said, A phonecall! as if it were the richest thing he'd heard in ages. He shrugged. It was nearly opening time anyway. I followed him inside. His calves were plump and white and hairless, I wondered where I had seen others like them recently. He switched on a pink-shaded lamp behind the bar. There's the phone, he said with a wave, pursing his lips derisively. I asked if I could have a gin first. He sniffed, his sceptic's heart gratified, and permitted himself a thin little smile. Have a smash-up, did you? he said. For a second I did not know what he was talking about. Oh, the car, I said, no, no it just – stopped. And I thought, with bleak amusement: There's the first question answered and I haven't lied. He turned away to make my drink, priest-like in his purple robe, then set it before me and propped himself on the edge of his stool with his fat arms folded. He knew I had been up to something, I could see it from the look in his eye, at once eager and disdainful, but he could not bring himself to ask. I grinned at him and drank my drink, and gleaned a grain of enjoyment from his dilemma. I said it was a good idea, wasn't it, the siesta. He raised an eyebrow. I pointed a finger at his dressing-gown. A nap, I said, in the middle of the day: good idea. He did not think that was funny. From somewhere in the shadowy reaches behind me a tousle-haired young man appeared, clad only in a drooping pair of underpants. He gave me a bored glance and asked Wally if the paper was in yet. Here, I said, take mine, go ahead. I must have been twisting it in my hands, it was rolled into a tight baton. He prised it open and read the headlines, his lips moving. Fucking bombers, he said, fucking lunatics. Wally had fixed him with a terrible glare. He threw the paper aside and wandered off, scratching his rump. I held out my glass for a refill. We still charge for drinks, you know, Wally said. We'll accept money. I gave him my last fiver. A thin blade of light had got in through a chink in a shutter somewhere and stood at a slant beside me, embedded in the floor. I watched Wally's plump back as he refilled my glass. I wondered if I might tell him what I had done. It seemed perfectly possible. Nothing, I told myself, nothing shocks Wally, after all. I could almost believe it. I imagined him looking at me with a twist of the mouth and one eyebrow arched, trying not to leer as I recounted my horrid tale. The thought of confessing gave me a little lift, it was so splendidly irresponsible. It made the whole thing seem no more than a spot of high jinks, a jape that had gone wrong. I chuckled mournfully into my glass. You look like shit, Wally said complacently. I asked for another gin, a double this time.

Distinctly in my head her voice again said: Don't.

The boy with the curls came back, now wearing tight jeans and a shiny tight green shirt. He was called Sonny. Wally left him in charge of the bar and waddled off to his quarters, his dressing-gown billowing behind him. Sonny poured a generous measure of crème de menthe into a tumbler and filled it up with ice cubes, then perched himself on the stool, squirming his narrow little nates, and examined me without much enthusiasm. You're new, he said, making it sound like an accusation. No I'm not, I said, you are, and I smirked, pleased with myself. He made a wide-eyed face. Well excuse me, he said, I'm sure. Wally came back, dressed and coiffed and reeking of pomade. I had another double. My face was growing taut, it felt like a mud mask. I had reached that stage of inebriation where everything was settling into another version of reality. It seemed not drunkenness, but a form of enlightenment, almost a sobering-up. A crowd of theatre people came in, prancing and squawking. They looked at my appearance and then at each other, brimming with merriment. Talk about rough trade, one said, and Sonny tittered. And I thought, that's what I'll do, I'll get one of them to take me home and hide me, Lady Macbeth there with the mascara and the blood-red nails, or that laughing fellow in the harlequin shirt – why not? Yes, that's what I should do, I should live henceforth among actors, practise among them, study their craft, the grand gesture and the fine nuance. Perhaps in time I would learn to play my part sufficiently well, with enough conviction, to take my place among the others, the naturals, those people on the bus, and all the rest of them.

It was only when Charlie French came in that I realised it was for him I had been waiting. Good old Charlie. My heart flooded with fondness, I felt like embracing him. He was in his chalkstripes, carrying a battered, important-looking briefcase. Although he had seen me three days ago he tried at first not to know me. Or perhaps he really didn't recognise me, in my dishevelled, wild-eyed state. He said he had thought I was going down to Coolgrange. I said I had been there, and he asked after my mother. I told him about her stroke. I laid it on a bit, I think – I may even have shed a tear. He nodded, looking past my left ear and jingling the coins in his trouser pocket. There was a pause, during which I snuffled and sighed. So, he said brightly, you're off on your travels again, are you? I shrugged. His car's broke down, isn't it, Wally said, and expelled an unpleasant little chuckle. Charlie assumed a sympathetic frown. Is that right? he said slowly, with a dreamy lack of emphasis. The crowd of actors behind us suddenly shrieked, so piercingly that glasses chimed, but he might not have heard them, he did not even blink. He had perfected a pose for places and occasions such as this, by which he managed to be at once here and not here. He stood very straight, his black brogues planted firmly together and his briefcase leaning against his leg, with one fist on the bar — oh, I can see him! — and the other hand holding his whiskey glass suspended halfway to his lips, just as if he had stumbled in here by mistake and was too much the gentleman to cut and run before partaking of a snifter and exchanging a few civilities with the frantic denizens of the place. He could maintain this air of being just about to leave throughout a whole night's drinking. Oh yes, Charlie could act them all into a cocked hat.

The more I drank the fonder I became of him, especially as he kept paying for gins as fast as I could drink them. But it was not just that. I was — I am — genuinely fond of him, I think I have said so already. Did I mention that he got me my job at the Institute? We had kept in touch during my years in college — or at least *he* had kept in touch with *me*. He liked to think of himself as the wise old family friend watching over with an avuncular eye the brilliant only son of the house. He took me out for treats. There were teas at the Hibernian, the odd jaunt to the Curragh, the dinner at Jammet's every year on my birthday. They never quite worked, these occasions, they smacked too much of contrivance. I was always afraid that someone would see me with him, and while I squirmed and scowled he would sink into a state of restless melancholy. When we were ready to part there would be a sudden burst of hearty chatter which was nothing but relief badly disguised, then we would each turn and slink away guiltily. Yet he was not deterred, and the day after my return with Daphne from America he took me for a drink in the Shelbourne and suggested that, as he put it, I might like to give the chaps at the Institute a hand. I was still feeling groggy — we had made a hideous winter crossing, on what was hardly more than a tramp steamer — and he was so diffident, and employed such elaborate depreciations, that it was a while before I realised he was offering me a job. The work, he assured me hurriedly, would be right up my street – hardly work at all, and to such as I, he fancied, more a form of play – the money was decent, the prospects were limitless. I knew at once, of course, from his suppliant, doggy manner, that all this was at my mother's prompting. Well, he said, showing his big yellow teeth in a strained smile, what do you think? First I was annoyed, then amused. I thought: why not?

If the court pleases, I shall skim lightly over this period of my life. It is a time that is still a source of vague unease in my mind, I cannot say why, exactly. I have the feeling of having done something ridiculous by taking that job. It was unworthy of me, of course, of my talent, but that is not the whole source of my sense of humiliation. Perhaps that was the moment in my life at which – but what am I saying, there are no moments, I've said that already. There is just the ceaseless, slow, demented drift of things. If I had any lingering doubts of that the Institute extinguished them finally. It was housed in a great grey stone building from the last century which always reminded me, with its sheer flanks, its buttresses and curlicues and blackened smokestacks, of a grand, antiquated ocean liner. No one knew what exactly it was we were expected to achieve. We did statistical surveys, and produced thick reports bristling with graphs and flow-charts and complex appendices, which the government received with grave words of praise and then promptly forgot about. The director was a large, frantic man who sucked fiercely on an enormous black pipe and had a tic in one eye and tufts of hair sprouting from his ears. He plunged about the place, always on his way elsewhere. All queries and requests he greeted with a harsh, doomed laugh. Try that on the Minister! he would cry over his shoulder as he strode off, emitting thick gusts of smoke and sparks in his wake. Inevitably there was a high incidence of looniness among the staff. Finding themselves with no fixed duties, people embarked furtively on projects of their own. There was an economist, a tall, emaciated person with a greenish face and unruly hair, who was devising a foolproof system for betting on the horses. He offered one day to let me in on it, clutching my wrist in a trembling claw and hissing urgently into my ear, but then something happened, I don't know what, he grew suspicious, and in the end would not speak to me, and avoided me in the corridors. This was awkward, for he was one of a select band of savants with whom I had to treat in order to gain access to the computer. This machine was at the centre of all our activities. Time on it was strictly rationed, and to get an uninterrupted hour at it was a rare privilege. It ran all day and through the night, whirring and crunching in its vast white room in the basement. At night it was tended by a mysterious and sinister trio, a war criminal, I think, and two strange boys, one with a damaged face. Three years I spent there. I was not violently unhappy. I just felt, and feel, as I say, a little ridiculous, a little embarrassed. And I never quite forgave Charlie French.

It was late when we left the pub. The night was made of glass. I was very drunk. Charlie helped me along. He was worrying about his briefcase, and clutched it tightly under his arm. Every few yards I had to stop and tell him how good he was. No, I said, holding up a hand commandingly, no, I want to say it, you're a good man, Charles, a good man. I wept copiously, of course, and retched drily a few times. It was all a sort of glorious, grief-stricken, staggering rapture. I remembered that

Charlie lived with his mother, and wept for that, too. But how is she, I shouted sorrowfully, tell me, Charlie, how is she, that sainted woman? He would not answer, pretended not to hear, but I kept at it and at last he shook his head irritably and said, She's dead! I tried to embrace him, but he walked away from me. We came upon a hole in the street with a cordon of red and white plastic ribbon around it. The ribbon shivered and clicked in the breeze. It's where the bomb in the car went off yesterday, Charlie said. Yesterday! I laughed and laughed, and knelt on the road at the edge of the hole, laughing, with my face in my hands. Yesterday, the last day of the old world. Wait, Charlie said, I'll get a taxi. He went off, and I knelt there, rocking back and forth and crooning softly, as if I were a child I was holding in my arms. I was tired. It had been a long day. I had come far.

I WOKE IN SPLINTERED sunlight with a shriek fading in my ears. Big sagging bed, brown walls, a smell of damp. I thought I must be at Coolgrange, in my parents' room. For a moment I lay without moving, staring at sliding waterlights on the ceiling. Then I remembered, and I shut my eyes tight and hid my head in my arms. The darkness drummed. I got up and dragged myself to the window, and stood amazed at the blue innocence of sea and sky. Far out in the bay white sailboats were tacking into the wind. Below the window was a little stone harbour, and beyond that the curve of the coast road. An enormous seagull appeared and flung itself on flailing pinions at the glass, shrieking. They must think you are Mammy, Charlie said behind me. He was standing in the doorway. He wore a soiled apron, and held a frying-pan in his hand. The gulls, he said, she used to feed them. At his back a white, impenetrable glare. This was the world I must live in from now on, in this searing, inescapable light. I looked at myself and found I was naked.

I sat in the vast kitchen, under a vast, grimy window, and

watched Charlie making breakfast in a cloud of fat-smoke. He did not look too good in daylight, he was hollow and grey, with flakes of dried shaving soap on his jaw and bruised bags under his phlegm-coloured eyes. Besides the apron he wore a woollen cardigan over a soiled string vest, and sagging flannel trousers. Used to wait till I was gone, he said, then throw the food out the window. He shook his head and laughed. A terrible woman, he said, terrible. He brought a plate of rashers and fried bread and a swimming egg and set it down in front of me. There, he said, only thing for a sore head. I looked up at him quickly. *A sore head?* Had I blurted something out to him last night, some drunken confession? But no, Charlie would not make that kind of joke. He went back to the stove and lit a cigarette, fumbling with the matches.

Look, Charlie, I said, I may as well tell you, I've got into a bit of a scrape.

I thought at first he had not heard me. He went slack, and a dreamy vacancy came over him, his mouth open and drooping a little on one side and his eyebrows mildly lifted. Then I realised that he was being tactful. Well, if he didn't want to know, that was all right. But I wish to have it in the record, m'lud, that I would have told him, if he had been prepared to listen. As it was I merely let a silence pass, and then asked if I might borrow a razor, and perhaps a shirt and tie. Of course, he said, of course, but he would not look me in the eye. In fact, he had not looked at me at all since I got up, but edged around me with averted gaze, busying himself with the teapot and the pan, as if afraid that if he paused some awful awkward thing would arise which he would not know how to deal with. He suspected something, I suppose. He was no fool. (Or not a great fool, anyway.) But I think too it was simply that he did not quite know how to accommodate my presence. He fidgeted, moving things about, putting things away in drawers and cupboards and then taking them out again, murmuring to himself distractedly. People did not come often to this house. Some of the weepy regard I had felt for him last night returned. He seemed almost maternal, in his apron and his old felt slippers. He would take care of me. I gulped my tea and gloomed at my untouched fry congealing on its plate. A car-horn tooted outside, and Charlie with an exclamation whipped off his apron and hurried out of the kitchen. I listened to him blundering about the house. In a surprisingly short time he appeared again, in his suit, with his briefcase under his arm, and sporting a raffish little hat that made him look like a harassed bookie. Where are you based, he said, frowning at a spot beside my left shoulder, Coolgrange, or − ? I said nothing, only looked at him appealingly, and he said, Ah, and nodded slowly, and slowly withdrew. Suddenly, though, I did not want him to go − alone, I would be alone! − and I rushed after him and made him come back and tell me how the stove worked, and where to find a key, and what to say if the milkman called. He was puzzled by my vehemence, I could see, and faintly alarmed. I followed him into the hall, and was still talking to him as he backed out the front-door, nodding at me warily, with a fixed smile, as if I were − ha! I was going to say, a dangerous criminal. I scampered up the stairs to the bedroom, and watched as he came out on the footpath below, a clownishly foreshortened figure in his hat and his baggy suit. A large black car was waiting at the kerb, its twin exhaust pipes discreetly puffing a pale-blue mist. The driver, a burly, dark-suited fellow with no neck, hopped out smartly and held open the rear door. Charlie looked up at the window where I stood, and the driver followed his glance. I saw myself as they would see me, a blurred face floating behind the glass, blear-eyed, unshaven, the very picture of a fugitive. The car slid away smoothly and passed along the harbour road and turned a corner and was gone. I did not stir. I wanted to stay like this, with my forehead against the glass and the summer day all out there before me. How quaint it all seemed, the white-tipped sea, and the white and pink houses, and the blurred headland in the distance, quaint and happy, like a little toy world laid out in a shop window. I closed my eyes, and again that fragment of memory swam up out of the depths – the doorway, and the darkened room, and the sense of something imminent – but this time it seemed to be not my own past I was remembering.

The silence was swelling like a tumour at my back.

Hurriedly I fetched my plate with the fried egg and greying rashers from the kitchen, taking the stairs three at a time, and came back and opened the window and clambered on to the narrow, wrought-iron balcony outside. A strong, warm wind was blowing, it startled me, and left me breathless for a moment. I picked up the pieces of food and flung them into the air, and watched the gulls swooping after the rich tidbits, crying harshly in surprise and greed. From behind the headland a white ship glided soundlessly into view, shimmering in the haze. When the food was gone I threw the plate away too, I don't know why, skimmed it like a discus out over the road and the harbour wall. It slid into the water with hardly a splash. There were strings of lukewarm fat between my fingers and egg-yolk under my nails. I climbed back into the room and wiped my hands on the bedclothes, my heart pounding in excitement and disgust. I did not know what I was doing, or what I would do next. I did not know myself. I had become a stranger, unpredictable and dangerous.

I explored the house. I had never been here before. It was a great, gaunt, shadowy place with dark drapes and big brown furniture and bald spots in the carpets. It was not exactly dirty, but there was a sense of staleness, of things left standing for too long in the same spot, and the air had a grey, dull feel to it, as if a vital essence in it had been used up long ago. There was a smell of must and stewed tea and old newspapers, and, everywhere, a flattish, faintly sweet something which I took to be the afterglow of Mammy French. I suppose there will be guffaws if I say I am a fastidious man, but it's true. I was already in some distress before I started poking among Charlie's things, and I feared what I might find. His sad little secrets were no nastier than mine, or anyone else's, yet when here and there I turned over a stone and they came scuttling out, I shivered, and was ashamed for him and for myself. I steeled myself, though, and persevered, and was rewarded in the end. There was a rolltop desk in his bedroom, which took me ten minutes of hard work with a kitchen knife to unlock, squatting on my heels and sweating beads of pure alcohol. Inside I found some banknotes and a plastic wallet of credit cards. There were letters, too – from my mother, of all people, written thirty, forty years before. I did not read them, I don't know why, but put them back reverently, along with the credit cards, and even the cash, and locked the desk again. As I was going out I exchanged a shamefaced little grin with my reflection in the wardrobe mirror. That German, what's his name, was right: money is abstract happiness.

The bathroom was on the first-floor return, a sort of wooden lean-to with a gas geyser and a gigantic, claw-footed bath. I crouched over the hand-basin and scraped off two days' growth of stubble with Charlie's soap-encrusted razor. I had thought of growing a beard, for disguise, but I had lost enough of myself already, I did not want my face to disappear as well. The shaving-glass had a concave, silvery surface in which my magnified features – a broad, pitted jaw, one black nose-hole with hairs, a single, rolling eyeball – bobbed and swayed alarmingly, like things looming in the window of a bathysphere. When I had finished I got into the tub and lay with my eyes shut while the water cascaded down on me from the geyser. It was good, at once a solace and a scalding chastisement, if the gas had not eventually gone out I might have stayed there all day, lost to myself and everything else in that roaring, tombal darkness. When I opened my eyes tiny stars were whizzing and popping in front of me. I padded, dripping, into Charlie's room, and spent a long time deciding what to wear. In the end I chose a dark-blue silk shirt and a somewhat louche, flowered bow-tie to go with it. Black socks, of course – silk again: Charlie is not one to stint himself – and a pair of dark trousers, baggy but well cut, of a style which was antique enough to have come back into fashion. For the present I would do without underwear: even a killer on the run has his principles, and mine precluded getting into another man's drawers. My own clothes – how odd they looked, thrown on the bedroom floor, as if waiting to be outlined in chalk – I gathered in a bundle, and with my face averted carried them to the kitchen and stuffed them into a plastic garbage bag. Then I washed and dried the breakfast things, and was standing in the middle of the floor with a soiled tea-towel in my hand when the image of her bloodied face shot up in front of me like something in a fairground stall, and I had to sit down, winded and shaking. For I kept forgetting, you see, forgetting all about it, for quite long periods. I suppose my mind needed respite, in order to cope. Wearily I looked about the big dank kitchen. I wondered if Charlie would notice there was a plate missing. Why did I throw it into the sea, why did I do that? It was not yet noon. Time opened its black maw in my face. I went into one of the front rooms – net curtains, vast dining-table, a stuffed owl under glass – and stood at the window looking out at the sea. All that blue out there was daunting. I paced the floor, stopped, stood listening, my heart in my mouth. What did I expect to hear? There was nothing, only the distant noise of other lives, a tiny ticking and plinking, like the noise of an engine cooling down. I remembered days like this in my childhood, strange, empty days when I would wander softly about the silent house and seem to myself a kind of ghost, hardly there at all, a memory, a shadow of some more solid version of myself living, oh, living marvellously, elsewhere.

I must stop. I'm sick of myself, all this.

Time. The days.

Go on, go on.

Disgust, now, that is something I know about. Let me say a word or two about disgust. Here I sit, naked under my prison garb, wads of pallid flesh trussed and bagged like badly packaged meat. I get up and walk around on my hind legs, a belted animal, shedding an invisible snow of scurf everywhere I move. Mites live on me, they lap my sweat, stick their snouts into my pores and gobble up the glop they find there. Then the split skin, the cracks, the crevices. Hair: just think of hair. And this is only the surface. Imagine what is going on inside, the purple pump shuddering and squelching, lungs fluttering, and, down in the dark, the glue factory at its ceaseless work. Animate carrion, slick with gleet, not ripe enough yet for the worms. Ach, I should –

Calm, Frederick. Calm.

My wife came to see me today. This is not unusual, she comes every week. As a remand prisoner I have the right to unrestricted visiting, but I have not told her this, and if she knows it she has said nothing. We prefer it this way. Even at its most uneventful the Thursday visiting hour is a bizarre, not to say uncanny ritual. It is conducted in a large, square, lofty room with small windows set high up under the ceiling. A partition of plywood and glass, an ugly contraption, separates us from our loved ones, with whom we converse as best we can by way of a disinfected plastic grille. This state of virtual quarantine is a recent imposition. It is meant to keep out drugs, we're told, but I think it is really a way of keeping *in* those interesting viruses which lately we have begun to incubate in here. The room has a touch of the aquarium about it, with that wall of greenish glass, and the tall light drifting down from above, and the voices that come to us out of the plastic lattices as if bubbled through water. We inmates sit with shoulders hunched, leaning grimly on folded arms, wan, bloated, vague-eyed, like unhoused crustaceans crouching at the bottom of a tank. Our visitors exist in a different element from ours, they seem more sharply defined than we, more intensely present in their world. Sometimes we catch a look in their eyes, a mixture of curiosity and compassion, and faint repugnance, too, which strikes us to the heart. They must feel the force of our longing, must hear it, almost, the mermen's song, a high needle-note of pure woe buzzing in the glass that separates us from them. Their concern for our plight is not a comfort, but distresses

145

us, rather. This is the tenderest time of our week, we desire tranquillity, decorum, muted voices. We are constantly on edge, worried that someone's wife or girlfriend out there will make a scene, jump up and shout, pound her fists on the partition, weep. When such a thing does happen it is awful, just awful, and afterwards the one that it happened to is an object of sympathy and awe amongst us, as if he had suffered a bereavement.

No fear of Daphne making a scene. She maintains an admirable poise at all times. Today, for instance, when she told me about the child, she spoke quietly, looking away from me with her usual air of faint abstraction. I confess I was annoyed at her, I couldn't hide it. She should have told me she was having him tested, instead of just presenting me with the diagnosis out of the blue like this. She gave me a quizzical look, tilting her head to one side and almost smiling. Are you surprised? she said. I turned my face away crossly and did not answer. Of course I was not surprised. I knew there was something wrong with him, I always knew – I told her so, long before she was ready to admit it. From the start there was the way he moved, warily, quaking, on his scrawny little legs, as if trying not to drop some large, unmanageable thing that had been dumped into his arms, looking up at us in bewilderment and supplication, like a creature looking up out of a hole in the ground. Where did you take him, I said, what hospital, what did they say exactly? She shrugged. They were very nice, she said, very sympathetic. The doctor talked to her for a long time. It is a very rare condition, somebody's syndrome, I have forgotten the name already, some damn Swiss or Swede – what does it matter. He will never speak properly. He'll never do anything properly, it seems. There is something wrong with his brain, something is missing, some vital bit. She explained it all to me, repeating what the doctor told her, but I was only half-listening. A sort of weariness had come over me, a sort of lethargy. Van is his name, have I mentioned that? Van. He's seven. When I get out he will probably be, what, thirty-something? Jesus, almost as old as I am now. A big child, that's what the country people will call him, not without fondness, at Coolgrange. A big child.

I will not, I will not weep. If I start now I'll never stop.

In the afternoon I broke into Charlie's desk again, and took some cash and ventured out to the newsagent's on the harbour. What a strange, hot thrill of excitement I felt, stepping into the shop, my stomach wobbled, and I seemed to be treading slowly through some thick, resistant medium. I think a part of me hoped – no, expected – that somehow I would be saved, that as in a fairy-tale everything would be magically reversed, that the wicked witch would disappear, that the spell would be lifted, that the maid would wake from her enchanted sleep. And when I picked up the papers it seemed for a moment as if some magic had indeed been worked, for at first I could see nothing in them except more stuff about the bombing and its aftermath. I bought three mornings, and an early-evening edition, noting (is this only hindsight?) the hard look that the pimpled girl behind the counter gave me. Then I hurried back to the house, my heart going at a gallop, as if it were some choice erotica I was clutching under my arm. Indoors again, I left the papers on the kitchen-table and ran to the bathroom, where in my agitation I managed to pee on my foot. After a lengthy, feverish search I found a quarter-full bottle of gin and took a good slug from the neck. I tried to find something else to do, but it was no good, and with leaden steps I returned to the kitchen and sat down slowly at the table and spread out the papers in front of me. There it was, a few paragraphs in one of the mornings, squeezed under a photograph of a bandaged survivor of the bombing sitting up in a hospital bed. In the evening edition there was a bigger story, with a photograph of the boys I had seen playing in the hotel grounds. It was they who had found her. There was a photograph of her, too, gazing out solemn-eyed from a blurred background, it must have been lifted from a group shot of a wedding, or a dance, she was wearing a long, ugly dress with an elaborate collar, and was clutching something, flowers, perhaps, in her hands. Her name was Josephine Bell. There was more inside, a file picture of Behrens and a view of Whitewater House, and an article on the Behrens collection, littered with mis-spellings and garbled dates. A reporter had been sent down the country to talk to Mrs Brigid Bell, the mother. She was a widow. There was a photograph of her standing awkwardly in front of her cottage, a big, raw-faced woman in an apron and an old cardigan, peering at the camera in a kind of stolid dismay. Her Josie, she said, was a good girl, a decent girl, why would anyone want to kill her. And suddenly I was back there, I saw her sitting in the mess of her own blood, looking at me, a bleb of pink spittle bursting on her lips. *Mammy* was what she said, that was the word, not Tommy, I've just this moment realised it. *Mammy*, and then: *Love*.

I THINK THE TIME I spent in Charlie French's house was the strangest period of my life, stranger even and more disorienting than my first days here. I felt, in the brownish gloom of those rooms, with all that glistening marine light outside, as if I were suspended somehow in mid-air, in a sealed flask, cut off from everything. Time was split in two: there was clock time, which moved with giant slowness, and then there was that fevered rush inside my head, as if the mainspring had broken and all the works were spinning madly out of control. I did sentry-go up and down the kitchen for what seemed hours on end, shoulders hunched and hands stuck in my pockets, furiously plotting, unaware how the distance between turns was steadily decreasing, until in the end I would find myself at a shuddering stop, glaring about me in bafflement, like an animal that had blundered into a net. I would stand in the big bedroom upstairs, beside the window, with my back pressed to the wall, watching the road, for so long, sometimes, that I forgot what it was I was supposed to be watching for. There was little traffic in this backwater, and I soon got to recognise the regular passers-by, the girl with the orange hair from the flat in the house next door, the smooth, shady-looking fellow with the salesman's sample-case, the few old bodies who walked their pugs or shuffled to the shops at the same hour every day. Anyway, there would be no mistaking the others, the grim ones, when they came for me. Probably I would not even see them coming. They would surround the house, and kick in the door, and that would be the first I would know of it. But still I stood there, watching and watching, more like a pining lover than a man on the run.

Everything was changed, everything. I was estranged from myself and all that I had once supposed I was. My life up to now had only the weightless density of a dream. When I thought about my past it was like thinking of what someone else had been, someone I had never met but whose history I knew by heart. It all seemed no more than a vivid fiction. Nor was the present any more solid. I felt light-headed, volatile, poised at an angle to everything. The ground under me was stretched tight as a trampoline, I must keep still for fear of unexpected surges, dangerous leaps and bounces. And all around me was this blue and empty air.

I could not think directly about what I had done. It would have been like trying to stare steadily into a blinding light. It was too big, too bright, to contemplate. It was incomprehensible. Even still, when I say *I did it*, I am not sure I know what I mean. Oh, do not mistake me. I have no wish to vacillate, to hum and haw and kick dead leaves over the evidence. I killed her, I admit it freely. And I know that if I were back there today I would do it again, not because I would want to, but because I would have no choice. It would be just as it was then, this spider, and this moonlight between the trees, and all, all the rest of it. Nor can I say I did not mean to kill her – only, I am not clear as to when I began to mean it. I was flustered, impatient, angry, she attacked me, I swiped at her, the swipe became a blow, which became the prelude to a second blow – its apogee, so to speak, or perhaps I mean perigee – and so on. There is no moment in this process of which I can confidently say, there, that is when I decided she should die. Decided? – I do not think it was a matter of deciding. I do not think it was a matter of thinking, even. That fat monster inside me just saw his chance and leaped out, frothing and flailing. He had scores to settle with the world, and she, at that moment, was world enough for him. I could not stop him. Or could I? He is me, after all, and I am he. But no, things were too far gone for stopping. Perhaps that is the essence of my crime, of my culpability, that I let things get to that stage, that I had not been vigilant enough, had not been enough of a dissembler, that I left Bunter to his own devices, and thus allowed him, fatally, to understand that he was free, that the cage door was open, that nothing was forbidden, that everything was possible.

After my first appearance in court the newspapers said I showed no sign of remorse when the charges were read out. (What did they expect, that I would weep, rend my garments?) They were on to something, in their dim-witted way. Remorse implies the expectation of for-giveness, and I knew that what I had done was unforgivable. I could have feigned regret and sorrow, guilt, all that, but to what end? Even if I had felt such things, truly, in the deepest depths of my heart, would it have altered anything? The deed was done, and would not be cancelled by cries of anguish and repentance. Done, yes, finished, as nothing ever before in my life had been finished and done – and yet there would be no end to it, I saw that straight away. I was, I told myself, responsible, with all the weight that word implied. In killing Josie Bell

I had destroyed a part of the world. Those hammer-blows had shattered a complex of memories and sensations and possibilities – a life, in short – which was irreplaceable, but which, somehow, must be replaced. For the crime of murder I would be caught and put away, I knew this with the calmness and certainty which only an irrelevance could inspire, and then they would say I had paid my debt, in the belief that by walling me up alive they had struck a sort of balance. They would be right, according to the laws of retribution and revenge: such balance, however, would be at best a negative thing. No, no. What was required was not my symbolic death – I recognised this, though I did not understand what it meant – but for her to be brought back to life. That, and nothing less.

That evening when Charlie returned he put his head cautiously around the door as if he feared there might be a bucket of water balanced on it. I leered at him, swaying. I had finished the gin, and moved on, reluctantly, to whiskey. I was not drunk, exactly, but in a kind of numbed euphoria, as if I had just come back from a lengthy and exquisitely agonising visit to the dentist. Under the new buzz the old hangover lurked, biding its time. My skin was hot and dry all over, and my eyes felt scorched. Cheers! I cried, with a fatuous laugh, and the ice cubes chuckled in my glass. Charlie was darting sidelong looks at my outfit. Hope you don't mind, I said. Didn't think we'd be the same size. Ah, he said, yes, well, I've shrunk in my old age, you see. And he gave a graveyard laugh. I could see he had been hoping I would be gone when he came home. I followed him out to the hall, where he took off his bookie's titfer and put it with his briefcase on the bog-oak hallstand. He went into the dining-room and poured himself a modest whiskey, adding a go of flattish soda from a screw-top bottle. He took a sip, and stood for a little while as if stalled, with a hand in his pocket, frowning at his feet. My presence was interfering with his evening rituals. He put away the whiskey bottle without offering me a refill. We traipsed back to the kitchen, where Charles donned his apron and rooted about in cupboards and on murky shelves for the makings of a stew. While he worked he talked distractedly over his shoulder, with a cigarette hanging from a corner of his lopsided mouth and one eye screwed shut against the smoke. He was telling me about a sale he had made, or a picture he had bought, or something like that. I think he only spoke for fear of the prospect of silence. Anyway I was not really listening. I watched him glugging the better half of a fifty-pound bottle of Pommerol into the stew. An inch of cigarette ash went into the pot as well, he tried vainly to fish it out with a spoon, clucking in annoyance. You can imagine what it's like for me, he said, actually parting with pictures! I nodded solemnly. In fact, what I was imagining was Charlie in his poky gallery, bowing and scraping and wringing his hands in front of some fur-coated bitch reeking of face-powder and perspiration, whose hubby had given her the money to bag a bauble for her birthday. I was depressed suddenly, and suddenly tired.

He served up the stew, spilling some on the floor. He was not good with implements, they tended to turn treacherous in his hands, to wobble and veer and let things slither off. We carried our plates into the dining-room and sat down at the table under the stuffed owl's virulent, glassy stare. We drank the rest of the Pommerol, and Charles fetched another bottle. He continued to make an elaborate business of avoiding my eye, smiling about him at the floor, the furniture, the fire-irons in the grate, as if the commonplace had suddenly presented itself to his attention with a new and unexpected charm. The lowering sun was shining full upon me through the tall window at my back. The stew tasted of burnt fur. I pushed my plate aside and turned and looked out at the harbour. There was a shimmering flaw in the window-pane. Something made me think of California, something about the light, the little yachts, the gilded evening sea. I was so tired, so tired, I could have given up then and there, could have drifted out into that summer dusk as easily as a breeze, unknown, planless, free. Charlie squashed out a sodden fag-end on the rim of his plate. Did you see that thing about Binkie Behrens in the paper? he said. I poured myself another fill of wine. No, I said, what was that, Charles?

By the by, what would I have done in all this affair without the solace of drink and its deadening effect? I seem to have got over those days in a series of quaking lunges from one brief state of drunken equilibrium to another, like a fugitive fleeing across a zigzag of slimed stepping-stones. Even the colours, gin-blue and claret-red, are they not the very emblems of my case, the court-colours of my testimony? Now that I have sobered up forever I look back not only on that time but on all my life as a sort of tipsy but not particularly happy spree, from which I knew I would have to emerge sooner or later, with a bad headache. This, ah yes, this is hangover time with a vengeance.

The rest of that evening, as I recall it, was a succession of distinct, muffled shocks, like falling downstairs slowly in a dream. That was when I learned that my father had kept a mistress. I was first astonished, then indignant. I had been his alibi, his camouflage! While I sat for hours in the back of the car above the yacht club in Dun Laoghaire on

Sunday afternoons, he was off fucking his fancy-woman. Penelope was her name – Penelope, for God's sake! Where did they meet, I wanted to know, was there a secret love-nest where he kept her, a bijou little hideaway with roses round the door and a mirror on the bedroom ceiling? Charlie shrugged. Oh, he said, they used to come here. At first I could not take it in. Here? I cried. Here? But what about –? He shrugged again, and gave a sort of grin. Mammy French, it seems, did not mind. On occasion she even had the lovers join her for tea. She and Penelope exchanged knitting patterns. You see, she knew – Charlie said, but stopped, and a spot of colour appeared in the cracked skin over each cheekbone, and he ran a finger quickly around the inside of his shirt collar. I waited. She knew I was fond of your – of Dolly, he said at last. By now I was fairly reeling. Before I could speak he went on to tell me how Binkie Behrens too had been after my mother, how he would invite her and my father to Whitewater and ply my father with drink so he would not notice Binkie's gamy eye and wandering hands. And then my mother would come and tell Charlie all about it, and they would laugh together. Now he shook his head and sighed. Poor Binkie, he said. I sat aghast, lost in wonderment and trying to hold my wine-glass straight. I felt like a child hearing for the first time of the doings of the gods: they crowded in my buzzing head, these tremendous, archaic, flawed figures with their plots and rivalries and impossible loves. Charlie was so matter-of-fact about it all, half wistful and half amused. He spoke mostly as if I were not there, looking up now and then in mild surprise at my squeaks and snorts of astonishment. And you, I said, what about you and my –? I could not put it into words. He gave me a look at once arch and sly.

Here, he said, finish the bottle.

I think he told me something more about my mother, but I don't remember what it was. I do remember phoning her later that night, sitting cross-legged in the dark on the floor in the hall, with tears in my eyes and the telephone squatting in my lap like a frog. She seemed immensely far away, a miniature voice booming at me tinily out of a thrumming void. Freddie, she said, you're drunk. She asked why had I not come back, to collect my bag if for nothing else. I wanted to say to her, Mother, how could I go home, now? We were silent for a moment, then she said Daphne had called her, wondering where I was, what I was doing. Daphne! I had not thought of her for days. Through the doorway at the end of the hall I watched Charlie pottering about in the kitchen, rattling the pots and pans and pretending he was not trying to hear what I was saying. I sighed, and the sigh turned into a thin little moan. Ma, I said, I've got myself into such trouble. There was a noise on the line, or maybe it was in my head, like a great rushing of many wings. What? she said, I can't hear you — what? I laughed, and two big tears ran down the sides of my nose. Nothing, I shouted, nothing, forget it! Then I said, Listen, do you know who Penelope is — was — do you know about her? I was shocked at myself. Why did I say such a thing, why did I want to wound her? She was silent for a moment, and then she laughed. That bitch? she said, of course I knew about her. Charlie had come to the doorway, and stood, with a rag in one hand and a plate in the other, watching me. The light was behind him, I could not see his face. There was another pause. You're too hard on yourself, Freddie, my mother said at last, in that reverberant, faraway voice, you make things too hard on yourself. I did not know what she meant. I still don't. I waited a moment, but she said nothing more, and I could not speak. Those were the last words we would ever exchange. I put down the receiver gently, and got to my feet, not without difficulty. One of my knees was asleep. I limped into the kitchen. Charlie was bent over the sink doing the washing-up, with a cigarette dangling from his lip, sleeves rolled, his waistcoat unbuckled at the back. The sky in the window in front of him was a pale shade of indigo, I thought I had never seen anything so lovely in my life.

Charlie, I said, swaying, I need a loan.

I had always been a weeper, but now any hint of kindness could make me blub like a babe. When there and then he sat down at the kitchen table and wrote out a cheque – I have it still: spidery black scrawl, an illegible signature, a stewy thumb-print in one corner – I tried to seize his liver-spotted hand, I think I meant to kiss it. He made a little speech, I don't remember it well. My mother figured in it, Daphne too. I think even Penelope's name was mentioned. I wonder if he was drunk? He kept looming into focus and fading out again, yet I felt this was less an effect of my blurred vision than of a sort of tentativeness on his part. Oh, Charlie, you should have heeded that niggle of suspicion, you should have thrown me out that night, fuddled and defenceless though I was.

The next thing I recall is being on my knees in the lavatory, puking up a ferruginous torrent of wine mixed with fibrous strands of meat and bits of carrot. The look of this stuff gushing out filled me with wonder, as if it were not vomit, but something rich and strange, a dark stream of ore from the deep mine of my innards. Then there is an impression of everything swaying, of glistening darkness and things in it spinning past me, as though I were being whirled round and round slowly on a wobbly carousel made of glass. Next I was lying on my back on the big, disordered bed upstairs, shivering and sweating. There was a light on, and the window was a box of deep, glistening darkness. I fell asleep, and after what seemed a moment woke again with the sun shining in my face. The house was silent around me, but there was a thin, continuous ringing which I seemed to feel rather than hear. The sheets were a sodden tangle. I did not want to move, I felt as fragile as crystal. Even my hair felt breakable, a shock of erect, minute filaments bristling with static. I could hear the blood rushing along my veins, quick and heavy as mercury. My face was swollen and hot, and strangely smooth to the touch: a doll's face. When I closed my eyes a crimson shape pulsed and faded and pulsed again on the inside of my lids, like the repeated after-image of a shell bursting in blackness. When I swallowed, the ringing in my ears changed pitch. I dozed, and dreamed I was adrift in a hot lake. When I woke it was afternoon. The light in the window, dense, calm, unshadowed, was a light shining straight out of the past. My mouth was dry and swollen, my head seemed packed with air. Not since childhood had I known this particular state of voluptuous distress. It was not really illness, more a kind of respite. I lay for a long time, hardly stirring, watching the day change, listening to the little noises of the world. The brazen sunlight slowly faded, and the sky turned from lilac to mauve, and a single star appeared. Then suddenly it was late, and I lay in a sleepy daze in the soft summer darkness and would not have been surprised if my mother had appeared, young and smiling, in a rustle of silk, with a finger to her lips, to say goodnight to me on her way out for the evening. It was not Maman who came, however, but only Charlie, he opened the door cautiously on its wheezy hinges and peered in at me, craning his tortoise neck, and I shut my eyes and he withdrew softly and creaked away down the stairs. And I saw in my mind another doorway, and another darkness – that fragment of memory, not mine, yet again – and waited, hardly breathing, for something or someone to appear. But there was nothing.

I think of that brief bout of ague as marking the end of an initial, distinct phase of my life as a murderer. By the morning of the second day the fever had abated. I lay in a clammy tangle of sheets with my arms flung wide, just breathing. I felt as if I had been wading frantically through waist-high water, and now at last I had gained the beach, exhausted, trembling in every limb, and yet almost at peace. I had survived. I had come back to myself. Outside the window the seagulls were crying, looking for Mammy French, they rose and fell with stiff wings spread wide, as if suspended on elastic cords. I rose shakily and crossed the room. There was wind and sun, and the sea glared, a rich, hazardous blue. Below in the little stone harbour the yachts bobbed and slewed, yanking at their mooring-ropes. I turned away. There was something in the gay, bright scene that seemed to rebuke me. I put on Charlie's dressing-gown and went down to the kitchen. Silence everywhere. In the calm matutinal light everything stood motionless as if under a spell. I could not bear the thought of food. I found an open bottle of Apollinaris in the refrigerator and drank it off. It was flat, and tasted faintly of metal. I sat down at the table and rested my forehead in my hands. My skin felt grainy, as if the surface layer had crumpled to a sort of clinging dust. Charlie's breakfast things were still on the table, and there was spilled cigarette ash and a saucer of crushed butts. The newspapers I had bought on Thursday were stuffed in the rubbish bin. This was Saturday. I had missed, what, nearly two days, two days of accumulating evidence. I looked for the plastic bag in which I had put my clothes, but it was gone. Charlie must have put it out for the binmen, it would be on some dump by now. Perhaps at this very moment a rag-picker was rummaging in it. A spasm of horror swarmed over me. I jumped up and paced the floor, my hands clasped together to keep them from shaking. I must do something, anything. I ran upstairs and swept from room to room like a mad king, the tail of the dressing-gown flying out behind me. I shaved, glaring at myself in the fish-eye mirror, then I put on Charlie's clothes again, and broke into his desk and took his cash and his wallet of credit cards, and went down the stairs three at a time and stormed out into the world.

And paused. Everything was in its place, the boats in the harbour, the road, the white houses along the coast, the far headland, those little clouds on the horizon, and yet − and yet it was all different somehow from what I had expected, from what something inside me had expected, some nice sense of how things should be ordered. Then I realised it was I, of course, who was out of place.

I went into the newsagent's, with the same cramp of fear and excitement in my breast as I had felt the first time. When I picked up the papers the ink came off on my hands, and the coins slipped in my sweaty fingers. The girl with the pimples gave me another look. She had a curious, smeared sort of gaze, it seemed to pass me by and take me in at the same time. Pre-menstrual, I could tell by her manner, that tensed, excitable air. I turned my back on her and scanned the papers. By now the story had seeped up from the bottom of the front pages like a stain, while reports on the bombing dwindled, the injured having stopped dying off. There was a photograph of the car, looking like a wounded hippo, with a stolid guard standing beside it and a detective in Wellington boots pointing at something. The boys who had found it had been interviewed. Did they remember me, that pallid stranger dreaming on the bench in the deserted station? They did, they gave a description of me: an elderly man with black hair and a bushy beard. The woman at the traffic lights was sure I was in my early twenties, well-dressed, with a moustache and piercing eyes. Then there were the tourists at Whitewater who saw me make off with the painting, and Reck and his ma, of course, and the idiot boy and the woman at the garage where I hired the car: from each of their accounts another and more fantastic version of me emerged, until I became multiplied into a band of moustachioed cut-throats, rushing about glaring and making threatening noises, like a chorus of brigands in an Italian opera. I nearly laughed. And yet I was disappointed. Yes, it's true, I was disappointed. Did I want to be found out, did I hope to see my name splashed in monster type across every front page? I think I did. I think I longed deep down to be made to stand in front of a jury and reveal all my squalid little secrets. Yes, to be found out, to be suddenly pounced upon, beaten, stripped, and set before the howling multitude, that was my deepest, most ardent desire. I hear the court catching its breath in surprise and disbelief. But ah, do you not also long for this, in your hearts, gentlepersons of the jury? To be rumbled. To feel that heavy hand fall upon your shoulder, and hear the booming voice of authority telling you the game is up at last. In short, to be unmasked. Ask yourselves. I confess (I confess!), those days that passed while I waited for them to find me were the most exciting I have ever known, or ever hope to know. Terrible, yes, but exciting too. Never had the world appeared so unstable, or my place in it so thrillingly precarious. I had a raw, lascivious awareness of myself, a big warm damp thing parcelled up in someone else's clothes. At any moment they might catch me, they might be watching me even now, murmuring into their handsets and signalling to the marksmen on the roof. First there would be panic, then pain. And when everything was gone, every shred of dignity and pretence, what freedom there would be, what lightness! No, what am I saying, not lightness, but its opposite: weight, gravity, the sense at last of being firmly grounded. Then finally I would be me, no longer that poor impersonation of myself I had been doing all my life. I would be real. I would be, of all things, human.

I took the bus to town, and got off at a street where I used to live years ago, when I was a student, and walked along by the railings of the park in the warm wind under the seething trees, my heart filled with nostalgia. A man in a cap, with terrible, soiled eyes, stood on the pavement shaking a fist in the air and roaring obscene abuse at the cars passing by. I envied him. I would have liked to stand and shout like that, to pour out all that rage and pain and indignation. I walked on. A trio of light-clad girls came tripping out of a bookshop, laughing, and for a second I was caught up in their midst, my side-teeth bared in a frightful grin, a beast among the graces. In a bright new shop I bought a jacket and trousers, two shirts, some ties, underwear, and, in a flourish of defiance, a handsome but not altogether unostentatious hat. I thought I detected a slight stiffening of attention when I produced Charlie's credit cards – my God, did they know him, did he shop here? – but I turned up my accent to full force and dashed off his signature with aplomb, and everyone relaxed. I was not really worried. In fact, I felt ridiculously excited and happy, like a boy on a birthday spree. (What is it about the mere act of buying things, that it can afford me so much simple pleasure?) I seemed to swim along the street, upright as a sea-horse, breasting the air. I think I must have been feverish still. The people among whom I moved were strange to me, stranger than usual, I mean. I felt I was no longer of their species, that something had happened since I had last encountered a crowd of them together, that an adjustment had occurred in me, a tiny, amazingly swift and momentous evolutionary event. I passed through their midst like a changeling, a sport of nature. They were beyond me, they could not touch me – could they see me, even, or was I now outside the spectrum of their vision? And yet how avidly I observed them, in hunger and wonderment. They surged around me at a sort of stumble, dull-eyed and confused, like refugees. I saw myself, bobbing head and shoulders above them, disguised, solitary, nursing my huge secret. I was their unrecognised and their un-acknowledged dream – I was their Moosbrugger. I came to the river, and dawdled on the bridge, among the beggars and the fruit-sellers and the hawkers of cheap jewellery, admiring the wind-blurred light above the water and tasting the salt air on my lips. The sea! To be away, out there, out over countless fathoms, lost in all that blue!

I went – everything was so simple – I went into a bar and bought a drink. Each sip was like a sliver of metal, chill and smooth. It was a cavernous place, very dark. The light from the street glared whitely in the open doorway. I might have been somewhere in the south, in one of those dank, tired ports I used to know so well. At the back, in a lighted place like a stage, some youths with shaven heads and outsize lace-up boots were playing a game of billiards. The balls whirred and clacked, the young men softly swore. It was like something out of Hogarth, a group of wigless surgeons, say, intent over the dissecting table. The barman, arms folded and mouth open, was watching a horse-race on the television set perched high up on a shelf in a corner above him. A tubercular young man in a black shortie overcoat came in and stood beside me, breathing and fidgeting. I could tell from the tension coming off him that he was working himself up to something, and for a moment I was pleasurably alarmed. He might do anything, anything. But he only spoke. *I've lived here thirty-three years*, he said, in a tone of bitter indignation, *and everyone is afraid*. The barman glanced at him with weary contempt and turned back to the television. Blue horses galloped in silence over bright-green turf. *I* am afraid, the young man said, resentful now. He gave a tremendous twitch, hunching his shoulders and ducking his head and throwing up one arm, as if something had bitten him on the neck. Then he turned and went out hurriedly, clutching his coat around him. I followed, leaving my drink half-finished. It was blindingly bright outside. I spotted him, a good way off already, dodging along through the crowds with his elbows pressed to his sides, taking tight, swift little steps, nimble as a dancer. Nothing could stop him. In the thickest surge of bodies he would find a chink at once, and swivel deftly from the waist up and dive through without altering his pace. What a pair we would have made, if anyone had thought to link us, he in his tight shabby coat and I with my fancy hat and expensive clutch of carrier bags. I could hardly keep up with him, and after a minute or two I was puffing and in a sweat. I had an unaccountable sense of elation. Once he paused, and stood glaring into the window of a chemist's shop. I waited, loitering at a bus-stop, keeping him in the corner of my eye. He was so intent, and seemed to quiver so, that I thought he was going to do something violent, turn and attack someone, maybe, or kick in the window and stamp about among the cameras and the cosmetic displays. But he was only waiting for another shudder to pass through him. This time when he flung up his arm his leg shot up as well, as if elbow and knee were connected by an invisible string, and a second later his heel came down on the pavement with a ringing crack. He cast a quick look around him, to see if anyone had noticed, and gave himself a casual little shake, as if by that he would make the previous spasm appear to have been intentional too, and then he was off again like a whippet. I wanted to catch up with him, I wanted to speak to him. I did not know what I would say. I would not offer him sympathy, certainly not. I did not pity him, I saw nothing in him to merit my pity. No, that's not true, for he was pathetic, a maimed and mad poor creature. Yet I was not sorry for him, my heart did not go out to him in that way. What I felt was, how shall I say, a kind of brotherly regard, a strong, sustaining, almost cheerful sense of oneness with him. It seemed the simplest thing in the world for me to walk up now and put my hand on that thin shoulder and say: *my fellow sufferer, dear friend, compagnon de misères!* And so it was with deep disappointment and chagrin that at the next corner I stopped and looked about me in the jostling crowd and realised that I had lost him. Almost at once, however, I found a substitute, a tall fat girl with big shoulders and a big behind, and big, tubular legs ending in a pair of tiny feet, like a pig's front trotters, wedged into high-heeled white shoes. She had been to the hairdresser's, her hair was cropped in a fashionable, boyish style that was, on her, grotesque. The stubbled back of her neck, with its fold of fat, was still an angry shade of red from the dryer, it seemed to be blushing for her. She was so brave and sad, clumping along in her ugly shoes, and I would have followed her all day, I think, but after a while I lost her, too. Next I took up with a man with a huge strawberry mark on his face, then a tiny woman wheeling a tiny dog in a doll's pram, then a young fellow who marched resolutely along, as if he could see no one, with a visionary's fixed glare, swinging his arms and growling to himself. In a busy pedestrian thoroughfare I was surrounded suddenly by a gang of tinker girls, what my mother would have called *big rawsies*, with red hair and freckles and extraordinary, glass-green eyes, who pushed against me in truculent supplication, plucking at my sleeve and whining. It was like being set upon by a flock of importunate large wild birds. When I tried to shoo them away one of them knocked my hat off, while another deftly snatched out of my hand the carrier bag containing my new jacket. They fled, shoving each other and laughing shrilly, their raw, red heels flying. I laughed too, and picked up my hat from the pavement, ignoring the looks of the passers-by, who appeared to find my merriment unseemly. I did not care about the jacket – in fact, the loss of it chimed in a mysteriously apt way with that of its discarded predecessor – but I would have liked to see where those girls would go. I imagined a lean-to made of rags and bits of galvanised iron on a dusty patch of waste ground, with a starving dog and snot-nosed infants, and a drunken hag crouched over a steaming pot. Or perhaps there was a Fagin somewhere waiting for them, skulking in the shadows in some derelict tenement, where the light of summer fingered the shutters, and dust-motes drifted under lofty ceilings, and the rat's claw in the wainscoting scratched at the silence, scratched, stopped, and scratched again. So I went along happily for a little while, dreaming up other lives, until I spotted a whey-faced giant with rubber legs clomping ahead of me on two sticks, and I set off after him in avid pursuit.

What was I doing, why was I following these people – what enlightenment was I looking for? I did not know, nor care. I was puzzled and happy, like a child who has been allowed to join in an adults' game. I kept at it for hours, criss-crossing the streets and the squares with a drunkard's dazed single-mindedness, as if I were tracing out a huge, intricate sign on the face of the city for someone in the sky to read. I found myself in places I had not known were there, crooked alleyways and sudden, broad, deserted spaces, and dead-end streets under railway bridges where parked cars basked fatly in the evening sun, their toy-coloured roofs agleam. I ate a hamburger in a glass-walled café with moulded plastic chairs and tinfoil ashtrays, where people sat alone and gnawed at their food like frightened children abandoned by their parents. The daylight died slowly, leaving a barred, red and gold sunset smeared on the sky, and as I walked along it was like walking under the surface of a broad, burning river. The evening crowds were out, girls in tight trousers and high heels, and brawny young men with menacing haircuts. In the hot, hazy dusk the streets seemed wider, flattened, somehow, and the cars scudded along, sleek as seals in the sodium glare. I got back late to Charlie's house, footsore, hot and dishevelled, my hat awry, but filled with a mysterious sense of achievement. And that night I dreamed about my father. He was a miniature version of himself, a wizened child with a moustache, dressed in a sailor suit, his pinched little face scrubbed and his hair neatly parted, leading by the hand a great, tall, dark-eyed matron wearing Greek robes and a crown of myrtle, who fixed me with a lewd, forgiving smile.

I HAVE HAD A SHOCK. My counsel has been to see me today, bringing an extraordinary piece of news. Usually I enjoy our little conferences, in a lugubrious sort of way. We sit at a square table in a small airless room with no windows. The walls are painted filing-cabinet grey. Light from a strip of neon tubing above our heads sifts down upon us like a fine-grained mist. The bulb makes a tiny, continuous buzzing. Maolseachlainn at first is full of energy, rooting in his bag, shuffling his papers, muttering. He is like a big, worried bear. He works at finding things to talk to me about, new aspects of the case, obscure points of law he might bring up, the chances of our getting a sympathetic judge, that sort of thing. He speaks too fast, stumbling over his words as if they were so many stones. Gradually the atmosphere of the place gets in at him, like damp, and he falls silent. He takes off his specs and sits and blinks at me. He has a way of squeezing the bridge of his nose between two fingers and a thumb which is peculiarly endearing. I feel sorry for him. I think he truly does like me. This puzzles him, and, I suspect, disturbs him too. He believes he is letting me down when he runs out of steam like this, but really, there is nothing left to say. We both know I will get life. He cannot understand my equanimity in the face of my fate. I tell him I have taken up Buddhism. He smiles carefully, unsure that it is a joke. I divert him with tales of prison life, fleshing them out with impersonations – I do our governor here very convincingly. When Maolseachlainn laughs there is no sound, only a slow heaving of the shoulders and a stretched, shiny grin.

By the way, what an odd formulation that is: to get life. Words so rarely mean what they mean.

Today I saw straight away he was in a state about something. He kept clawing at the collar of his shirt and clearing his throat, and taking off his half-glasses and putting them back on again. Also there was a smeary look in his eye. He hummed and hawed, and mumbled about the concept of justice, and the discretion of the courts, and other such folderol, I hardly listened to him. He was so mournful and ill at ease, shifting his big backside on the prison chair and looking everywhere except at me, that I could hardly keep from laughing. I pricked up my ears, though, when he started to mutter something about the possibility of my making a guilty plea – and this after all the time and effort he expended at the beginning in convincing me I should plead not guilty. Now when I caught him up on it, rather sharply, I confess, he veered off at once, with an alarmed look. I wonder what he's up to? I should have kept at it, and got it out of him. As a diversionary measure he dived into his briefcase and brought out a copy of my mother's will. I had not yet heard the contents, and was, I need hardly say, keenly interested. Maolseachlainn, I noticed, found this subject not much easier than the previous one. He coughed a lot, and frowned, and read out stuff about gifts and covenants and minor bequests, and was a long time getting to the point. I still cannot credit it. The old bitch has left Coolgrange to that stable-girl, what's-her-name, Joanne. There is some money for Daphne, and for Van's schooling, but for me, nothing. I suppose I should not be surprised, but I am. I was not a good son, but I was the only one she had. Maolseachlainn was watching me with compassion. I'm sorry, he said. I smiled and shrugged, though it was not easy. I wished he would go away now. Oh, I said, it's understandable, after all, that she would make a new will. He said nothing. There was a peculiar silence. Then, almost tenderly, he handed me the document, and I looked at the date. The thing was seven, nearly eight years old. She had cut me out long ago, before ever I came back to disgrace her and the family name. I recalled, with shocking clarity, the way she looked at me that day in the kitchen at Coolgrange, and heard again that cackle of raucous laughter. Well, I'm glad she enjoyed her joke. It's a good one. I find a surprising lack of bitterness in my heart. I am smiling, though probably it seems more as if I am wincing. This is her contribution to the long course of lessons I must learn.

Maolseachlainn stood up, assuming his heartiest manner, as always, in an attempt to disguise his relief at the prospect of getting away. I watched him struggle into his navy-blue overcoat and knot his red woollen muffler around his neck. Sometimes, when he first arrives, his clothes give off little wafts and slivers of the air of outdoors, I snuff them up with surreptitious pleasure, as if they were the most precious of perfumes. What's it like, outside? I said now. He paused, and blinked at me in some alarm. I think he thought I was asking him for an overall picture, as if I might have forgotten what the world looked like. The day, I said, the weather. His brow cleared. He shrugged. Oh, he said, grey, just grey, you know. And I saw it at once, with a pang, the late November afternoon, the dull shine on the wet roads, and the children straggling home from school, and rooks tossing and wheeling high up against ragged clouds, and the tarnished glow in the sky off behind bare, blackened branches. These were the times I used to love, the weather's unconsidered moments, when the vast business of the world just goes on quietly by itself, as if there were no one to notice, or care. I see myself as a boy out there, dawdling along that wet road, kicking a stone ahead of me and dreaming the enormous dream of the future. There was a path, I remember, that cut off through the oak wood a mile or so from home, which I knew must lead to Coolgrange eventually. How green the shadows, and deep the track, how restless the silence seemed, that way. Every time I passed by there, coming up from the cross, I said to myself, Next time, next time. But always when the next time came I was in a rush, or the light was fading, or I was just not in the mood to break new ground, and so I kept to the ordinary route, along the road. In the end I never took that secret path, and now, of course, it is too late.

I have been doing calculations in my head — it keeps my mind off other things — and I find to my surprise that I spent no more than ten days in all at Charlie's house, from midsummer day, or night, rather, until the last, momentous day of June. That *is* ten, isn't it? Thirty days hath September, April, June — yes, ten. Or is it nine. It's nine nights, certainly. But where does the day end and the night start, and vice versa? And why do I find the night a more easily quantifiable entity than day? I have never been any good at this kind of thing. The simpler the figures the more they fox me. Anyway. Ten days, thereabouts, more or less, is the length of my stay with Charlie French, whose hospitality and kindness I did not mean to betray. It seemed a longer time than that. It seemed weeks and weeks. I was not unhappy there. That's to say, I was no more unhappy there than I would have been somewhere else. Unhappy! What a word! As the days went on I grew increasingly restless. My nerves seethed, and there was a permanent knot of pain in my guts. I suffered sudden, furious attacks of impatience. Why didn't they come for me, what were they doing? In particular I resented the Behrenses' silence, I was convinced they were playing a cruel game with me. But all the time, behind all these agitations, there was that abiding, dull, flat sensation. I felt disappointed. I felt let down. The least I had expected from the enormities of which I was guilty was that they would change my life, that they would make things happen, however awful, that there would be a constant succession of heart-stopping events, of alarms and sudden frights and hairbreadth escapes. I do not know how I got through the days. I awoke each morning with an anguished start, as if a pure, distilled drop of pain had plopped on my forehead. That big old house with its smells and cobwebs was oppressive. I drank a lot, of course, but not enough to make myself insensible. I tried to achieve oblivion, God knows, I poured in the booze until my lips went numb and my knees would hardly bend, but it was no good, I could not escape myself. I waited with a lover's rapt expectancy for the evenings, when I would put on my hat and my new clothes – my new mask! – and step forth gingerly, a quavering Dr Jekyll, inside whom that other, terrible creature chafed and struggled, lusting for experience. I felt I had never until now looked at the ordinary world around me, the people, places, things. How innocent it all seemed, innocent, and doomed. How can I express the tangle of emotions that thrashed inside me as I prowled the city streets, letting my monstrous heart feed its fill on the sights and sounds of the commonplace? The feeling of power, for instance, how can I communicate that? It sprang not from what I had done, but from the fact that I had done it and *no one knew*. It was the secret, the secret itself, *that* was what set me above the dull-eyed ones among whom I moved as the long day died, and the streetlights came on, and the traffic slid away homeward, leaving a blue haze hanging like the smoke of gunfire in the darkening air. And then there was that constant, hot excitement, like a fever in the blood, that was half the fear of being unmasked and half the longing for it. Somewhere, I knew, in dayrooms and in smoke-filled, shabby offices, faceless men were even now painstakingly assembling the evidence against me. I thought about them at night, as I lay in Charlie's mother's big lumpy bed. It was strange to be the object of so much meticulous attention, strange, and not entirely unpleasant. Does that seem perverse? But I was in another country now, where the old rules did not apply.

It was hard to sleep, of course. I suppose I did not want to sleep, afraid of what I would encounter in my dreams. At best I would manage a fitful hour or two in the darkness before dawn, and wake up exhausted, with an ache in my chest and my eyes scalding. Charlie too was sleepless, I would hear at all hours his creaking step on the stair, the rattle of the teapot in the kitchen, the laborious, spasmodic tinkle as he emptied his old man's bladder in the bathroom. We saw little of each other. The house was big enough for us both to be in it at the same time and yet feel we were alone. Since that first, drunken night he had been avoiding me. He seemed to have no friends. The phone never rang, no one came to the house. I was surprised, then, and horribly alarmed, to come back early one evening from my rambles in town and find three big black cars parked on the road, and a uniformed guard loitering in the company of two watchful men in anoraks at the harbour wall. I made myself walk past slowly, an honest citizen out for a stroll at end of day, though my heart was hammering and my palms were damp, and then skipped around the back way and got in through the mews. Halfway up the jungly garden I tripped and fell, and tore my left hand on a rose-bush that had run wild. I crouched in the long grass, listening. Smell of loam, smell of leaves, the thick feel of blood on my wounded hand. The yellow light in the kitchen window turned the dusk around me to tenderest blue. There was a strange woman inside, in a white apron, working at the stove. When I opened the back door she turned quickly and gave a little shriek. Holy God, she said, who are you? She was an elderly person with a henna wig and ill-fitting dentures and a scattered air. Her name, as we shall discover presently, was Madge. They're all upstairs, she said, dismissing me, and turned back to her steaming saucepans.

There were five of them, or six, counting Charlie, though at first it seemed to me there must be twice that number. They were in the big, gaunt drawing-room on the first floor, standing under the windows with drinks in their hands, ducking and bobbing at each other like nervous storks and chattering as if their lives depended on it. Behind them the lights of the harbour glimmered, and in the far sky a huge bank of slate-blue cloud was shutting down like a lid on the last, smouldering streak of sunset fire. At my entrance the chattering stopped. Only one of them was a woman, tall, thin, with foxy red hair and an extraordinary stark white face. Charlie, who was standing with his back to me, saw me first reflected in their swivelling glances. He turned with a pained smile. Ah, he said, there you are. His winged hair gleamed like a polished helm. He was wearing a bow-tie. Well, I heard myself saying to him, in a tone of cheery truculence, well, you might have told me! My hands were trembling. There was a moment of uncertain silence, then the talk abruptly started up again. The woman went on watching me. Her pale colouring and vivid hair and long, slender neck gave her a permanently startled look, as if at some time in the past she had been told a shocking secret and had never quite absorbed it. Charlie, mumbling apologetically, had put a shaky old hand under my elbow and was gently but firmly steering me backwards out of the room. The fear I had felt earlier had turned into annoyance. I felt like giving him a clout, and putting a dent in that ridiculous praetorian helmet of hair. Tell Madge, he was saying, tell Madge to give you something to eat, and I'll be down presently. He was so worried I thought he was going to weep. He stood on the top step and watched me make my way downstairs, as if he were afraid I would come scampering back up again if he took his eye off me, and only when I had safely reached the bottom and was heading for the kitchen did he turn back to the drawing-room and his guests.

The kitchen was filled with steam, and Madge, her wig awry, looked even hotter and more harassed than before. This place, she said bitterly, honest to God! She was, as she picturesquely put it, Mr French's occasional woman, and came in when there were dinner parties, and that. This was interesting. Dinner parties, indeed! I helped her by opening the wine, and sat down at the table with a bottle for myself. I had drunk half of it when there was a loud knock at the front door that set my heart thumping again. I went into the hall, but Charlie was already rattling hurriedly down the stairs. When he opened the door I could see the two anoraks outside, guarding the way for a burly

man and a tall, sleek woman, as they advanced at a
regal pace into the hall. Ah, Max, Charlie said, and stepped
forward with clumsy eagerness. The woman he ignored.
Max shook hands with him briefly, and then took back his
hand and ran it upwards quickly over his low, truculent
brow. Christ, he said, you're far enough out, I thought we
were never going to get here. They moved towards the
stairs, Charlie and Max in front and the woman behind
them. She wore an ugly blue gown and a triple rope of
pearls. She glanced along the hall and caught my eye, and
held it until I looked away. Madge had come out of the
kitchen, and hovered at my shoulder. There's his nibs, she
whispered, and the missus too.

I waited a while after they had gone up, and when
Madge returned to her cooking I followed them, and
slipped into the drawing-room again. Charlie and Max and
Mrs Max were standing at one of the windows admiring
the view, while the others bobbed and clucked and tried
not to stare too openly in their direction. I seized an armful
of bottles from the mantelpiece and passed among them,
topping up their glasses. The men had a scrubbed, eager,
slightly anxious air, like that of big, blue-suited schoolboys
on their first adult outing, except for one old chap with a
nose like a blood-orange and stains down the front of his
waistcoat, who stood to one side all on his own, glazed and
dejected. The others carefully looked through me, but he
brightened up at once, and was ready for a chat. What do
you think, anyway, he said loudly, will we win, will we? I
understood it to be a rhetorical question. We will, I said
stoutly, and gave him a broad wink. He raised his
eyebrows and stepped back a pace, however, peering at me
doubtfully. By God, he said, I don't know, now. I
shrugged, and passed on blandly. Charlie had caught sight
of me, and was smiling fixedly in alarm. Mine was a

vodka, Mrs Max said coldly when I offered her gin. My attention was on her husband. He had a raw, scrubbed look to him, as if he had been exposed for a long time to some far rougher form of light and weather than the others in the room had ever known. His movements, too, the way he held himself, the slow, deliberate way he turned his glance or lifted his hand to his brow, all these bore a unique stamp, and were weighted with a kind of theatrical awareness. His voice was slow and guttural, and he had a violent manner of speaking that was impressive, and even, in an odd way, seductive. It was the voice of a man moving inexorably forward through a forest of small obstacles. I imagined him carelessly crunching things underfoot, flowers, or snails, or the insteps of his enemies. Well, Charlie, he was saying, still buying cheap and selling dear? Charlie blushed, and glanced at me. That's right, Mrs Max said, embarrass everyone. She spoke loudly, with a dull emphasis, and did not look at him. It was as if she were lobbing remarks past his shoulder at a sardonic ally listening there. Nor did he look at her, it might have been a disembodied voice that had spoken. He laughed harshly. Have you acquired that Dutch job for me yet? he said. Charlie, grinning in anguish, shook his head, speechless. His left eyelid began to flutter, as if a moth had suddenly come to life under it. I proffered the whiskey bottle but he put a hand quickly over his glass. Max also waved me away. The woman with the foxy hair had come up behind me. Your hand, she said, you've cut it. For a moment we all stood in silence, Max and his missus, and Charlie and Foxy and me, contemplating the beaded scratch across my knuckles. Yes, I said, I fell over a rose-bush. I laughed. That half-bottle of wine had gone straight to my head. Charlie was shifting stealthily from foot to foot, afraid, I suppose, that I was about to do something outrageous. It struck me for the first time how frightened

177

of me he was. Poor Charlie. A lighted yacht was gliding silently across the inky harbour. Lovely view, Max said grimly.

In the dining-room the stuffed owl looked out of its bell-jar at the company with an expression of surprise and some dismay. By now Patch, I mean Madge, was in a state of panic. I carried plates for her, and serving-dishes, and plonked them down on the table with extravagant waiterly flourishes. I confess, I was enjoying myself. I was light-headed, brimming with manic glee, like a child in a dressing-up game. I seemed to move as if under a magic spell, I do not know how it worked, but for a while, for an hour or two, posing as Charlie's factotum, I was released from myself and the terrors that had been pursuing me relentlessly for days. I even invented a history for myself as I went along, I mean I – how shall I express it – I fell into a certain manner that was not my own and that yet seemed, even to me, no less authentic, or plausible, at least, than my real self. (My real self!) I became Frederick the Indispensable, Mr French's famous man, without whom that crusty, moneyed old bachelor would not be able to survive. He had rescued me from uncongenial circumstances when I was a young man – tending the bar, say, in some sleazy downtown pub – and now I was devoted to him, and loyal to the point of ferocity. I bullied him too, of course, and could be a terror when he had people in. (Jealousy? Acquaintances did sometimes speculate among themselves, but no, they decided, Charlie was not that way inclined: remember that horsy woman down the country, the lost love of his life?) Really, we were like father and son, except that no son would be so steadfast, and no father so forgiving of my little ways. At times it was hard to tell which was master and which the man. Tonight, for instance, when the main course was finished, I sat myself down among the guests and poured a glass of wine as if it were the most natural thing in the world. A silence fell, and Charlie frowned, and rolled a breadcrumb about on the tablecloth, pretending he was thinking about something else, and Max stared balefully out the window at the harbour lights while his henchmen around him fidgeted and glanced at each other nervously, and at last I took up my glass, and rose and said, Well! I suppose us ladies better withdraw, and fairly flounced out of the room. In the hall, of course, I leaned against the wall and laughed. All the same, my hands were shaking. Stage fright, I suppose. What an actor the world has lost in me!

Now what shall I do?

I went upstairs to the drawing-room. No, I went into the kitchen. Madge: wig, false teeth, white apron, I have done all that. Out again. In the hall I found Foxy. She had wandered out of the dining-room. Under the stairs was a dark place, there we met. I could see her face in the gloom, her eyes watching me, so solemn and fearful. Why are you sad? I said, and for a moment she did not know what to do with her hands, then she put them behind her back, and flexed one knee and briefly swayed her shoulders and her hips, like a schoolgirl playing the coquette. Who says I'm sad? she said. I'm not sad. And I thought she was going to cry. Did she see it in me, the terror and the shame, had she seen it from the first? For she had sought me out, I knew that. I reached behind her and opened a door, and we stepped suddenly on to bare floorboards in an empty room. There was a smell, dry and oniony, that was the smell of a certain attic room at Coolgrange. A parallelogram of moonlight was propped against one wall like a broken mirror. I am still holding these damned plates. I put them on the floor at our feet, and while I was still bending she touched my shoulder and said something which I did not catch. She laughed softly, in surprise, it seemed, as if the sound of her own voice were unexpected. Nothing, she said, nothing. She shook in my arms. She was all teeth, breath, clutching fingers. She held my head between her hands as if she would crush it. She had kicked off her shoes, they clattered where they fell. She raised one foot behind her and pressed it against the door, pressed, and pressed. Her thighs were cold. She wept, her tears fell on my hands. I bit her throat. We were like – I don't know. We were like two messengers, meeting in the dark to exchange our terrible news. O God, she said, O God. She put her forehead against my shoulder. Our hands were smeared with each other. The room came back, the moonlight, the oniony smell. No thought, except: her white face, her hair. Forgive me, I said. I don't know why I laughed. Anyway, it wasn't really a laugh.

How peaceful the days are now, here at the dead end of the year. Sitting in the fastness of this grey room I sometimes imagine I am utterly alone, that there is no one around me for miles and miles. It is like being in the deep hold of a great grey ship. The air is heavy and still, it presses in my ears, on my eyes, on the base of my skull. A trial date has been fixed at last. I know this should concentrate my mind, give me a purpose and so on, make me excited, or afraid, but it does not. Something has happened to my sense of time, I think in aeons now. The days, the weeks of this banal little courtroom drama will register as no more than a pinprick. I have become a lifer.

Again today Maolseachlainn brought up the topic of how I should plead. I let him maunder on for a while, then I got fed up and told him I would dispense with his services if he did not come straight out and say whatever it was he had on his mind. This was disingenuous of me, for I had realised, of course, since his last visit, that he was hinting at the possibility of an arrangement – I understand, from the conversations I have had in here, that there is hardly a sentence handed down that has not been pre-arranged among counsel. I was curious to know what the court could want from me. Now, as I watched poor old Mac squirm and sweat, I thought I had it: Charlie, of course, they were trying to salvage something of Charlie's reputation. (How could I have imagined they would care a fig for Charlie, or his reputation?) I would do all I could for him, that went without saying, though it seemed to me a bit late now. All right, Mac, I said, holding up a hand, I'll plead guilty – and what then? He gave me one of his over-the-spectacles looks. Then it'll be an open-and-shut case, won't it? he said. This, I realised after a moment, was intended as a witticism. He grinned dolefully. What he meant was that the trial would open, I would deny the charges as stated, plead guilty to manslaughter or something, the judge would pass sentence, with a bit lopped off in return for my co-operation, and then, presto, it would all be over, the hearing would end, the case would be closed. He could guarantee nothing, he said, but he had a duty to his client to try to secure the best judgement that was possible within the law. He is very charming when he waxes pompous like this. What's the point, I said, what's the trick? He shrugged. The trick is that no evidence will be heard. Simple as that. For a moment we were silent. And will that work, I said, will that save him? He frowned in puzzlement, and at once I saw I had been wrong, that Charlie and his embarrassment were not the subject here. I laughed. I've said it before, sometimes I think I am hopelessly innocent. Maolseachlainn glanced over his shoulder – he did, he really did – and

181

leaned across the table conspiratorially. No one is worrying about Charlie French, he said, no one is worrying about *him*.

Your honour, I do not like this, I do not like this at all. I'll plead guilty, of course – haven't I done so all along? – but I do not like it that I may not give evidence, no, that I don't like. It's not fair. Even a dog such as I must have his day. I have always seen myself in the witness box, gazing straight ahead, quite calm, and wearing casual clothes, as the newspapers will have it. And then that authoritative voice, telling my side of things, in my own words. Now I am to be denied my moment of drama, the last such, surely, that I'll know in this life. No, it's not right.

Look, the fact is I hardly remember that evening at Charlie French's. I mean, I remember the evening, but not the people, not with any clarity. I see far more vividly the lights on the water outside, and the last streak of sunset and the dark bank of cloud, than I do the faces of those hearty boy-men. Even Max Molyneaux is not much more, in my recollection, than an expensive suit and a certain sleek brutishness. What do I care for him and his ilk, for God's sake? Let them keep their reputations, it's nothing to me, one way or the other, I have no interest in stirring up scandal. The occasion passed before me in a glassy blur, like so much else over those ten days. Why, even poor Foxy was hardly more substantial to me in my frantic condition than a prop in a wet dream. No, wait, I take that back. However much they may hoot in ribald laughter, I must declare that I remember her clearly, with tenderness and compassion. She is, and will most likely remain, the last woman I made love to. Love? Can I call it that? What else can I call it. She trusted me. She smelled the blood and the horror and did not recoil, but opened herself like a flower and let me rest in her for a moment, my heart shaking, as we exchanged our wordless secret. Yes, I remember her. I was falling, and she caught me, my Gretchen.

In fact, her name was Marian. Not that it matters.

They stayed very late, all except Mrs Max, who left directly dinner was over. I watched as she was driven away, sitting up very straight in the back of one of the black limousines, a ravaged Nefertiti. Max and his pals went upstairs again, and caroused until the dawn was breaking. I spent the night in the kitchen playing cards with Madge. Where was Marian? I don't know – I got blotto, as usual. Anyway, our moment was over, if we were to encounter each other now we would only be embarrassed. Yet I think I must have gone to look for her, for I recall blundering about upstairs, in the bedrooms, and falling over repeatedly in the dark. I remember, too, standing at a wide-open window, very high up, listening to the strains of music outside on the air, a mysterious belling and blaring, that seemed to move, to fade, as if a clamorous cavalcade were departing into the night. I suppose it came from some dancehall, or some nightclub on the harbour. I think of it, however, as the noise of the god and his retinue, abandoning me.

NEXT DAY THE WEATHER BROKE. At mid-morning, when my hangover and I got up, the sun was shining as gaily and as heartlessly as it had all week, and the houses along the coast shimmered in a pale-blue haze, as if the sky had crumbled into airy geometry there. I stood at the window in my drawers, scratching and yawning. It struck me that I had become almost accustomed to this strange way of life. It was as if I were adapting to an illness, after the initial phase of frights and fevers. A churchbell was ringing. Sunday. The strollers were out already, with their dogs and children. Across the road, at the harbour wall, a man in a raincoat stood with his hands clasped behind his back, gazing out to sea. I could hear voices downstairs. Madge was in the kitchen doing last night's washing-up. She gave me a peculiar glance. I was wearing Charlie's dressing-gown. How is it, I wonder, that I did not catch it then, that new, speculative note in her voice, which should have alerted me? She had a helper with her this morning, her niece, a dim-looking child of twelve or so with – with what, what does it matter what she had, what she was like. All these minor witnesses, none of whom will ever be called now. I sat at the table drinking tea and watched them as they worked. The child I could see was frightened of me. Fe fi fo fum. He's gone out, you know, Madge said, her arms plunged in suds, Mr French, he went out as I was coming in. Her tone was unaccountably accusing, as if Charlie had fled the house because of me. But then, he had.

In the afternoon a huge cloud grew up on the horizon, grey and grainy, like a deposit of silt, and the sea swarmed, a blackish blue flecked with white. I watched an undulant curtain of rain sweep in slowly from the east. The man at the harbour wall buttoned his raincoat. The Sunday morning crowd was long gone, but he, *he* was still there.

Strange how it felt, now that it was here at last. I had expected terror, panic, cold sweat, the shakes, but there was none of that. Instead, a kind of wild-eyed euphoria took hold of me. I strode about the house like the drunken captain of a storm-tossed ship. All sorts of mad ideas came into my head. I would barricade the doors and windows. I would take Madge and her niece hostage, and barter them for a helicopter to freedom. I would wait until Charlie came back, and use him as a human shield, marching him out ahead of me with a knife at his throat — I even went down to the kitchen to find a blade for the purpose. Madge had finished the washing-up, and was sitting at the table with a pot of tea and a Sunday tabloid. She watched me apprehensively as I rummaged in the cutlery drawer. She asked if I would be wanting my lunch, or would I wait for Mr French. I laughed wildly. Lunch! The niece laughed too, a little parrot squawk, her top lip curling up to reveal a half-inch of whitish, glistening gum. When I looked at her she shut her mouth abruptly, it was like a blind coming down. Jacintha, Madge said to her sharply, you go home. Stay where you are! I cried. They both flinched, and Jacintha's chin trembled and her eyes filled up with tears. I abandoned the search for a knife, and plunged off upstairs again. The man in the mackintosh was gone. I gave a great gasp of relief, as if I had been holding my breath all this time, and slumped against the window-frame. The rain teemed, big drops dancing on the road and making the surface of the water in the harbour seethe. I heard the front door open and bang shut, and Madge and the girl appeared below me and scampered away up the street with their coats over their heads. I laughed to see them go, the child leaping the puddles and Madge wallowing in her wake. Then I spotted the car, parked a little way up the road, on the other side, with two dim, large, motionless figures seated in the front, their faces blurred behind the streaming windscreen.

I sat in a chair in the drawing-room, gazing before me, my hands gripping the armrests and my feet placed squarely side by side on the floor. I do not know how long I stayed like that, in that glimmering, grey space. I have an impression of hours passing, but surely that cannot be. There was a smell of cigarettes and stale drink left over from last night. The rain made a soothing noise. I sank into a kind of trance, a waking sleep. I saw myself, as a boy, walking across a wooded hill near Coolgrange. It was in March, I think, one of those blustery, Dutch days with china-blue sky and tumbling, cindery clouds. The trees above me swayed and groaned in the wind. Suddenly there was a great quick rushing noise, and the air darkened, and something like a bird's vast wing crashed down around me, thrashing and whipping. It was a branch that had fallen. I was not hurt, yet I could not move, and stood as if stunned, aghast and shaking. The force and swiftness of the thing had appalled me. It was not fright I felt, but a profound sense of shock at how little my presence had mattered. I might have been no more than a flaw in the air. Ground, branch, wind, sky, world, all these were the precise and necessary co-ordinates of the event. Only I was misplaced, only I had no part to play. And nothing cared. If I had been killed I would have fallen there, face down in the dead leaves, and the day would have gone on as before, as if nothing had happened. For what would have happened would have been nothing, or nothing extraordinary, anyway. Adjustments would have been made. Things would have had to squirm out from under me. A stray ant, perhaps, would explore the bloody chamber of my ear. But the light would have been the same, and the wind would have blown as it had blown, and time's arrow would not have faltered for an instant in its flight. I was amazed. I never forgot that moment. And now another branch was about to fall, I could hear that same rushing noise above me, and feel that same dark wing descending.

The telephone rang, with a sound like glass breaking. There was a hubbub of static on the line. Someone seemed to be asking for Charlie. No, I shouted, no, he's not here! and threw down the receiver. Almost at once the thing began to shrill again. Wait, wait, don't hang up, the voice said, this *is* Charlie. I laughed, of course. I'm down the road, he said, just down the road. I was still laughing. Then there was a silence. The guards are here, Freddie, he said, they want to speak to you, there's been some sort of misunderstanding. I closed my eyes. Part of me, I realised, had been hoping against hope, unable quite to believe that the game was up. The hum in the wires seemed the very sound of Charlie's anxiety and embarrassment. Charlie, I said, Charlie, Charlie, why are you hiding in a phone-box, what did you think I would do to you? I hung up before he could answer.

I was hungry. I went down to the kitchen and made an enormous omelette, and devoured half a loaf of bread and drank a pint of milk. I sat hunched over the table with my elbows planted on either side of the plate and my head hanging, stuffing the food into myself with animal indifference. The rain-light made a kind of dusk in the room. I heard Charlie as soon as he entered the house – he never was very good at negotiating his way around the furniture of life. He put his head in at the kitchen door and essayed a smile, without much success. I motioned to the chair opposite me and he sat down gingerly. I had started on the cold remains of last night's boiled potatoes. I was ravenous, I could not get enough to eat. Charles, I said, you look terrible. He did. He was grey and shrunken, with livid hollows under his eyes. The collar of his shirt was buttoned though he wore no tie. He ran a hand over his jaw and I heard the bristles scrape. He had been up early, he said, they had got him up and asked him to go to the station. For a second I did not understand, I thought he meant the train station. He kept his eyes on my plate, the mess of spuds there. Something had happened to the silence around us. I realised that the rain had stopped. God almighty, Freddie, he said softly, what have you done? He seemed more bemused than shocked. I fetched another, half-full bottle of milk from the back of the fridge. Remember, Charlie, I said, those treats you used to stand me in Jammet's and the Paradiso? He shrugged. It was not clear if he was listening. The milk had turned. I drank it anyway. I enjoyed them, you know, those occasions, I said, even if I didn't always show it. I frowned. Something wrong there, something off, like the milk. Mendacity always makes my voice sound curiously dull, a flat blaring at the back of the throat. And why resurrect now an ancient, unimportant lie? Was I just keeping my hand in, getting a bit of practice for the big tourney that lay ahead? No, that's too hard. I was trying to apologise, I mean in general, and how was I supposed to do that without lying? He looked so old, sitting slumped there with his head drooping on its stringy neck and his mouth all down at one side and his bleared eyes fixed vaguely before him. Oh, fuck it, Charlie, I said. I'm sorry.

Was it coincidence, I wonder, that the policeman made his move just at that moment, or had he been listening outside the door? In films, I have noticed, the chap with the gun always waits in the corridor, back pressed to the wall, the whites of his eyes gleaming, until the people inside have had their say. And this one was, I suspect, a keen student of the cinema. He had a hatchet face and lank black hair and wore a sort of padded military jacket. The sub-machinegun he was holding, a blunt squarish model with only about an inch of barrel, looked remarkably like a toy. Of the three of us he seemed the most surprised. I could not help admiring the deft way he had kicked in the back door. It hung quivering on its hinges, the broken latch lolling like a hound's tongue. Charlie stood up. It's all right, officer, he said. The policeman advanced into the doorway. He was glaring at me. You're fucking under arrest, you are, he said. Behind him, in the yard, the sun came out suddenly, and everything shone and glittered wetly.

More policemen came in then by the front way, there seemed to be a large crowd of them, though they were in fact only four. One of them was the fellow I had seen standing at the harbour wall that morning, I recognised the raincoat. All were carrying guns, of assorted shapes and sizes. I was impressed. They ranged themselves around the walls, looking at me with a kind of bridling curiosity. The door to the hall stood open. Charlie made a move in that direction and one of the policemen in a flat voice said: Hang on. There was silence except for the faint, metallic nattering of police radios outside. We might have been awaiting the entrance of a sovereign. The person who came in at last was a surprise. He was a slight, boyish man of thirty or so, with sandy hair and transparent blue eyes. I noticed at once his hands and feet, which were small, almost dainty. He approached me at an angle somehow, looking at the floor with a peculiar little smile. His name, he said, was Haslet, Detective Inspector Haslet. (Hello, Gerry, hope you don't mind my mentioning your dainty hands – it's true, you know, they are.) The oddness of his manner – that smile, the oblique glance – was due, I realised, to shyness. A shy policeman! It was not what I had expected. He looked about him. There was a moment of awkwardness. No one seemed to know quite what to do next. He turned his downcast eyes in my direction again. Well, he said to no one in particular, are we right? Then all was briskness suddenly. The one with the machine-gun – Sergeant Hogg, let's call him – stepped forward and, laying his weapon down on the table, deftly clapped a pair of handcuffs on my wrists. (By the way, they are not as uncomfortable as they might seem – in fact, there was something about being manacled that I found almost soothing, as if it were a more natural state than that of untrammelled freedom.) Charlie frowned. Is that necessary, Inspector? he said. It was such a grand old line, and so splendidly delivered, with just the right degree of solemn hauteur, that for a second I thought it might elicit a small round of applause. I looked at him with renewed admiration. He had thrown off that infirm air of a minute or two ago, and looked, really, quite impressive there in his dark suit and silver wings of hair. Even his unshaven cheeks and tieless collar only served to give him the appearance of a statesman roused from his bed to deal with some grave crisis in the affairs of the nation. Believe me, I am sincere when I say I admire his expertise as a quick-change artist. To place all faith in the mask, that seems to me now the true stamp of refined humanity. Did I say that, or someone else? No matter. I caught his eye, to show him my appreciation, and to ask him – oh, to ask some sort of pardon, I suppose. Afterwards I worried that my glance might have seemed to him more derisive than apologetic, for I think I must have worn a smirk throughout that grotesque kitchen comedy. His mouth was set grimly, and a nerve was twitching in his jaw – he had every right to be furious – but in his eyes all I could see was a sort of dreamy sadness. Then Hogg prodded me in the back, and I was marched quickly down the hall and out into the dazzling light of afternoon.

There was a moment of confusion as the policemen milled on the pavement, craning their stumpy necks and peering sharply this way and that about the harbour. What did they expect, a rescue party? I noticed that they all wore running shoes, except Haslet, the good country boy, in his stout brown brogues. One of his men bumped into him. Too many cops spoil the capture, I said brightly. No one laughed, and Haslet pretended he had not heard. I thought it was awfully witty, of course. I was still in that mood of mad elation, I cannot explain it. I seemed not to walk but bound along, brimful of tigerish energy. Everything sparkled in the rinsed sea-air. The sunlight had a flickering, hallucinatory quality, and I felt I was seeing somehow into the very process of it, catching the photons themselves in flight. We crossed the road. The car I had seen from the upstairs window was still there, the windscreen stippled with raindrops. The two figures sitting in the front watched us with cautious curiosity as we went past. I laughed – they were not police, but a large man and his large missus, out for a Sunday spin. The woman, chewing slowly on a sweet, goggled at the handcuffs, and I raised my wrists to her in a friendly salute. Hogg poked me again between the shoulder-blades, and I almost stumbled. I could see I was going to have trouble with him.

There were two cars, unmarked and nondescript, a blue one and a black. The comedy of car-doors opening, like beetles' wings. I was put into the back seat with Sergeant Hogg on one side of me and a big, baby-faced bruiser with red hair on the other. Haslet leaned on the door. Did you caution him? he enquired mildly. There was silence. The two detectives in the front seat went very still, as if afraid to stir for fear of laughing. Hogg stared grimly before him, his mouth set in a thin line. Haslet sighed and walked away. The driver carefully started up the engine. You have the right to remain silent blah blah blah, Hogg said venomously, without looking at me. Thank you, Sergeant, I said. I thought this another splendid bit of repartee. We took off from the kerb with a squeal, leaving a puff of tyre-smoke behind us on the air. I wondered if Charlie was watching from the window. I did not look back.

I pause to record that Helmut Behrens has died. Heart. Dear me, this is turning into the Book of the Dead.

How well I remember that journey. I had never travelled so fast in a car. We fairly flew along, weaving through the sluggish Sunday traffic, roaring down the inside lanes, taking corners on two wheels. It was very hot, with all the windows shut, and there was a musky, animal stink. The atmosphere bristled. I was entranced, filled with terror and

192

a kind of glee, hurtling along like this, packed in with these big, sweating, silent men, who sat staring at the road ahead with their arms tightly folded, clasping to them their excitement and their pent-up rage. I could feel them breathing. Speed soothed them: speed was violence. The sun shone in our eyes, a great, dense glare. I knew that at the slightest provocation they would set on me and beat me half to death, they were just waiting for the chance. Even this knowledge, though, was bracing. I had never in my life been so entirely the centre of attention. From now on I would be watched over, I would be tended and fed and listened to, like a big, dangerous babe. No more running, no more hiding and waiting, no more decisions. I snuggled down between my captors, enjoying the hot chafe of metal on my wrists. Yet all the while another part of my mind was registering another version of things — was thinking, for instance, of all that I was losing. I looked at the streets, the buildings, the people, as if for the last time. I, who am a countryman at heart — yes, yes, it's true — and never really knew or cared for the city, even when I lived here, had come to love it now. Love? That is not a word I use very often. Perhaps I mean something else. It was the loss, yes, the imminent loss of — of what, I don't know. I was going to say, *of the community of men*, something solemn and grand like that, but when was I ever a part of *that* gathering? All the same, as we travelled along, some deep cavern of my heart was filling up with the grief of renunciation and departure. I recall especially a spot, near the river, where we were held up for a minute by a faulty traffic light. It was a street of little houses wedged between grey, featureless buildings, warehouses and the like. An old man sat on a window-sill, an infant played in the gutter with a grimy pup. Lines of brilliant washing were strung like bunting across an alleyway. All was still. The light stayed red. And then, as if a secret lever somewhere had been pressed, the whole rackety little scene came slowly, shyly to life. First a green train passed over a red metal bridge. Then two doors in two houses opened at once, and two girls in their Sunday best stepped out into the sunlight. The infant crowed, the pup yapped. A plane flew overhead, and an instant later its shadow skimmed the street. The old man hopped off the window-sill with surprising sprightliness. There was a pause, as if for effect, and then, with a thrilling foghorn blast, there glided into view above the rooftops the white bridge and black smokestack of an enormous, stately ship. It was all so quaint, so innocent and eager, like an illustration from the cover of a child's geography book, that I wanted to laugh out loud, though if I had, I think what would have come out would have sounded more like a sob. The driver swore then, and drove on through the red light, and I turned my head quickly and saw the whole thing swirling away, bright girls and ship, child and dog, old man, that red bridge, swirling away, into the past.

The police station was a kind of mock-Renaissance palace with a high, grey, many-windowed stone front and an archway leading into a grim little yard where surely once there had been a gibbet. I was hauled brusquely out of the car and led through low doorways and along dim corridors. There was a Sunday-afternoon air of lethargy about the place, and a boarding-school smell. I confess I had expected that the building would be agog at my arrival, that there would be clerks and secretaries and policemen in their braces crowding the hallways to get a look at me, but hardly a soul was about, and the few who passed me by hardly looked at me, and I could not help feeling a little offended. We stopped in a gaunt, unpleasant room, and had to wait some minutes for Inspector Haslet to arrive. Two tall windows, extremely grimy, their lower panes reinforced with wire mesh, gave on to the yard. There was a scarred desk, and a number of wooden chairs. No one sat. We shuffled our feet and looked at the ceiling. Someone cleared his throat. An elderly guard in shirt-sleeves came in. He was bald, and had a sweet, almost childlike smile. I noticed he was wearing a pair of thick black boots, tightly laced and buffed to a high shine. They were a comforting sight, those boots. In the coming days I was to measure my captors by their footwear. Brogues and boots I felt I could trust, running shoes were sinister. Inspector Haslet's car arrived in the yard. Once again we stood about awaiting his entrance. He came in as before, with the same diffident half-smile. I stood in front of the desk while he read out the charges. It was an oddly formal little ceremony. I was reminded of my wedding day, and had to suppress a grin. The bald old guard typed out the charge sheet on an ancient upright black machine, as if he were laboriously picking out a tune on a piano, the tip of his tongue wedged into a corner of his mouth. When Inspector Haslet asked if I had anything to say I shook my head. I would not have known where to begin. Then the ritual was over. There was a kind of general relaxing, and the other detectives, except Hogg, shuffled out. It was like the end of Mass. Hogg produced cigarettes, and offered the grinning packet to Haslet and the guard at the typewriter, and even, after a brief hesitation, to me. I felt I could not refuse. I tried not to cough. Tell me, I said to Haslet, how did you find me? He shrugged. He had the air of a schoolboy who has scored an embarrassingly high mark in his exams. The girl in the paper shop, he said. You never read only the one story, every day. Ah, I said, yes, of course. It struck me, however, as not at all convincing. Was he covering up for Binkie Behrens, for Anna, even?

(He wasn't. They kept silent, to the end.) We smoked for a while, companionably. Twin shafts of sunlight leaned in the windows. A radio was squawking somewhere. I was suddenly, profoundly bored.

Listen, Hogg said, tell us, why did you do it?

I stared at him, startled, and at a loss. It was the one thing I had never asked myself, not with such simple, unavoidable force. Do you know, sergeant, I said, that's a very good question. His expression did not change, indeed he seemed not to move at all, except that his lank forelock lifted and fell, and for an instant I thought I had suffered a seizure, that something inside me, my liver, or a kidney, had burst of its own accord. More than anything else I felt amazement – that, and a curious, perverse satisfaction. I sank to my knees in a hot mist. I could not breathe. The elderly guard came from behind the desk and hauled me to my feet – did he say Oops-a-daisy, surely I imagine it? – and led me, stumbling, through a door and down a corridor and shoved me into a noisome, cramped lavatory. I knelt over the bowl and puked up lumps of egg and greasy spuds and a string of curdled milk. The ache in my innards was extraordinary, I could not believe it, I, who should have known all about such things. When there was nothing left to vomit I lay down with my arms clasped around my knees. Ah yes, I thought, this is more like it, this is more what I expected, writhing on the floor in a filthy jakes with my guts on fire. The guard knocked on the door and wanted to know was I done. He helped me to my feet again and walked me slowly back along the corridor. Always the same, he said, in a chatty tone, stuff comes up that you think you never ate.

Hogg was standing at the window with his hands in his pockets, looking out at the yard. He glanced at me over his shoulder. Better now? he said. Inspector Haslet sat in front of the desk, wearing a faraway frown and drumming his fingers on a jumble of papers. He indicated the chair beside him. I sat down gingerly. When he turned sideways to face me our knees were almost touching. He studied a far corner of the ceiling. Well, he said, do you want to talk to me? Oh, I did, I did, I wanted to talk and talk, to confide in him, to pour out all my poor secrets. But what could I say? What secrets? The bald guard was at his typewriter again, blunt fingers poised over the keys, his eyes fixed on my lips in lively expectation. Hogg too was waiting, standing by the window and jingling the coins in his trouser pocket. I would not have cared what I said to them, they meant nothing to me. The inspector was a different matter. He kept reminding me of someone I might have known at school, one of those modest, inarticulate heroes who were not only good at sport but at maths as well, yet who shrugged off praise, made shy by their own success and popularity. I had not the heart to confess to him that there was nothing to confess, that there had been no plan worthy of the name, that I had acted almost without thinking from the start. So I made up a rigmarole about having intended to make the robbery seem the work of terrorists, and a lot of other stuff that I am ashamed to repeat here. And then the girl, I said, the woman – for a second I could not think of her name! – and then *Josie*, I said, had ruined everything by trying to stop me taking the picture, by attacking me, by threatening to to to – I ran out of words, and sat and peered at him helplessly, wringing my hands. I so much wanted him to believe me. At that moment his credence seemed to me almost as desirable as forgiveness. There was a silence. He was still considering the corner of the ceiling. He might not have been listening to me at all. Jesus, Hogg said

197

quietly, with no particular emphasis, and the guard behind the desk cleared his throat. Then Haslet stood up, wincing a little and flexing one knee, and ambled out of the room, and shut the door softly behind him. I could hear him walk away along the corridor at the same leisurely pace. There were voices faintly, his and others. Hogg was looking at me over his shoulder in disgust. You're a right joker, aren't you, he said. I thought of answering him, but decided on prudence instead. Time passed. Someone laughed in a nearby room. A motorcycle started up in the yard. I studied a yellowed notice on the wall dealing with the threat of rabies. I smiled, Mad-dog Montgomery, captured at last.

Inspector Haslet came back then, and held open the door and ushered in a large, red-faced, sweating man in a striped shirt, and another, younger, dangerous-looking fellow, one of Hogg's breed. They gathered round and looked at me, leaning forward intently, breathing, their hands flat on the desk. I told my story again, trying to remember the details so as not to contradict myself. It sounded even more improbable this time. When I finished there was another silence. I was becoming accustomed already to these interrogative and, as it seemed to me, deeply sceptical pauses. The red-faced man, a person of large authority, I surmised, appeared to be in a rage which he was controlling only with great difficulty. His name will be – Barker. He looked at me hard for a long moment. Come on, Freddie, he said, why did you kill her? I stared back at him. I did not like his contemptuously familiar tone – *Freddie*, indeed! – but decided to let it go. I recognised in him one of my own kind, the big, short-tempered, heavy-breathing people of this world. And anyway, I was getting tired of all this. I killed her because I could, I said, what more can I say? We were all startled by that, I as much as they. The younger one, Hickey – no, Kickham, gave a sort of laugh. He had a thin, piping, almost musical voice that was peculiarly at odds with his menacing look and manner. What's-his-name, he said, he's a queer, is he? I looked at him helplessly. I did not know what he was talking about. Pardon? I said. French, he said impatiently, is he a fairy? I laughed, I could not help it. I did not know whether it was more comic or preposterous, the idea of Charlie prancing into Wally's and pinching the bottoms of his boys. (It appears that Wally's creature, Sonny of the emerald hues, had been telling scurrilous lies about poor Charlie's predilections. Truly, what a wicked world this is.) Oh no, I said, no – he has an occasional woman. It was just nervousness and surprise that made me say it, I had not meant to attempt a joke. No one laughed. They all just went on looking at me, while the silence tightened and tightened like something being screwed shut, and then, as if at a signal, they turned on their heels and trooped out and the door slammed behind them, and I was left alone with the elderly guard, who smiled his sweet smile at me and shrugged. I told him I was feeling nauseous again, and he went off and fetched me a mug of sticky-sweet tea and a lump of bread. Why is it that tea, just the look of it, always makes me feel miserable, like an abandoned waif? And how lost and lonely everything seemed, this stale room, and the vague noises of people elsewhere going about their lives, and the sunlight in the yard, that same thick steady light that shines across the years out of farthest childhood. All the euphoria I had felt earlier was gone now.

Haslet returned, alone this time, and sat down beside me at the desk as before. He had removed his jacket and tie and rolled up his sleeves. His hair was tousled. He looked more boyish than ever. He too had a mug of tea, the mug looking enormous in that small, white hand. I had an image of him as a child, out on some bog in the wastes of the midlands, stacking turf with his da: quake of water in the cuttings, smell of smoke and roasting spuds, and the flat distances the colour of a hare's pelt, and then the enormous, vertical sky stacked with luminous bundles of cloud.

Now, he said, let's start again.

We went on for hours. I was almost happy, sitting there with him, pouring out my life-story, as the shafts of sunlight in the windows lengthened and the day waned. He was infinitely patient. There seemed to be nothing, no detail, however minute or enigmatic, that did not interest him. No, that's not quite it. It was as if he were not really interested at all. He greeted everything, every strand and knot of my story, with the same passive air of toleration and that same, faint, bemused little smile. I told him about knowing Anna Behrens, and about her father, about his diamond mines and his companies and his priceless art collection. I watched him carefully, trying to judge how much of this was new to him, but it was no good, he gave nothing away. Yet he must have spoken to them, must have taken statements and all the rest of it. Surely they would have told him about me, surely they were not protecting me still. He rubbed his cheek, and gazed again into the corner of the ceiling. Self-made man, is he, he said, this Behrens? Oh Inspector, I said, aren't we all? At that he gave me a peculiar look, and stood up. I noticed again that brief grimace of pain. Bad knee. Footballer. Sunday afternoons, the shouts muffled in grey air, the flat thud of leather on leather. Now what, I said, what happens now? I did not want him to leave me yet. What would I do when the darkness came? He said I should give the guard my solicitor's name, so he could be told I was here. I nodded. I had no solicitor, of course, but I felt I could not say so – everything was so relaxed and chummy, and I did not want to create any awkwardnesses. Anyway, I was fully intending to conduct my own defence, and already saw myself making brilliant and impassioned speeches from the dock. Is there anything else I should do, I said, frowning up at him seriously, is there anyone else I should tell? (Oh, I was so good, so compliant, what a warm thrill of agreeableness I felt, deferring like this to this good chap!) He gave me that peculiar look again, there was irritation and impatience in it, but a certain ironic amusement too, and even a hint of complicity. What you can do, he said, is get your story straight, without the frills and fancy bits. What do you mean, I said, what do you mean? I was dismayed. Bob Cherry had suddenly turned harsh, had almost for a moment become Mr Quelch. You know very well what I mean, he said. Then he went off, and Hogg came back, and he and the elderly guard – oh, call him something, for God's sake – he and Cunningham, old Cunningham the desk sergeant, took me down to the cells.

Am I still handcuffed?

I do not know why I say they took me *down* (well, I do, of course) for we simply walked a little way along a corridor, past the lavatory, and through a steel gate. I confess I felt a qualm of fear, but that was quickly replaced by surprise: it was all just as I expected! There really are bars, there really is a bucket, and a pallet with a striped, lumpy mattress, and graffiti on the scarred walls. There was even a stubbled old-timer, standing white-knuckled at the door of his cell, who peered out at me in wordless, angry derision. I was given a piece of soap and a tiny towel and three pieces of shiny toilet-paper. In return I surrendered my belt and shoelaces. I saw at once the importance of this ritual. Cowering there, with the tongues of my shoes hanging out, clutching in one hand the waistband of my trousers and holding in the other, for all to see, the fundamental aids to my most private functions, I was no longer wholly human. I hasten to say this seemed to me quite proper, to be, indeed, a kind of setting to rights, an official and outward definition of what had been the case, in my case, all along. I had achieved my apotheosis. Even old Cunningham, even Sergeant Hogg seemed to recognise it, for they treated me now, brusquely, with a sort of truculent, abstracted regard, as if they were not my jailers, but my keepers, rather. I might have been a sick old toothless lion. Hogg put his hands in his pockets and went off whistling. I sat down on the side of the cot. Time passed. It was very quiet. The old boy in the other cell asked me my name. I did not answer him. Well fuck you, then, he said. Dusk came on. I have always loved that hour of the day, when that soft, muslin light seeps upward, as if out of the earth itself, and everything seems to grow thoughtful and turn away. It was almost dark when Sergeant Hogg came back, and handed me a grubby sheet of foolscap. He had been eating chips, I could smell them on his breath. I peered in bafflement at the ill-typed page. That's your confession, Hogg said. Feel like signing it? The lag next door cackled grimly. What are you talking about? I said. These are not my words. He shrugged, and belched into his fist. Suit yourself, he said, you'll be going down for life anyway. Then he went off again. I sat down and examined this strange document. Oh, well-named Cunningham! Behind the mask of the bald old codger a fiendish artist had been at work, the kind of artist I could never be, direct yet subtle, a master of the spare style, of the art that conceals art. I marvelled at how he had turned everything to his purpose, mis-spellings, clumsy syntax, even the atrocious typing. Such humility, such deference, such ruthless suppression of the ego for the sake of the text. He had taken my story, with all its – what was it Haslet said? – with all its frills and fancy bits, and pared it down to stark essentials. It was an account of my crime I hardly recognised, and yet I believed it. He had made a murderer of me. I would have signed it there and then, but I had nothing to write with. I even searched my clothing for something sharp, a pin or something, with which to stick myself, and scrawl my signature in blood. But what matter, it did not require my endorsement. Reverently I folded the page in four and placed it under the mattress at the end where my head would be. Then I undressed and lay down naked in the shadows and folded my hands on my breast, like a marble knight on a tomb, and closed my eyes. I was no longer myself. I can't explain it, but it's true. I was no longer myself.

That first night in captivity was turbulent. I slept fitfully, it was not really sleep, but a helpless tossing and sliding on the surface of a dark sea. I could sense the deeps beneath me, the black, boundless deeps. The hour before dawn was, as always, the worst. I masturbated repeatedly – forgive these squalid details – not for pleasure, really, but to exhaust myself. What a motley little band of manikins I conjured up to join me in these melancholy frottings. Daphne was there, of course, and Anna Behrens, amused and faintly shocked at the things I was making her do, and poor Foxy as well, who wept again in my arms, as I, silent and stealthy about my felon's work, pressed her and pressed her against that door in the empty, moonlit room of my imagination. But there were others, too, whom I would not have expected: Madge's niece, for instance –

remember Madge's niece? – and the big girl with the red neck I had followed through the city streets – remember *her*? – and even, God forgive me, my mother and the stable-girl. And in the end, when they all had come and gone, and I lay empty on my prison bed, there rose up out of me again, like the spectre of an onerous and ineluctable task, the picture of that mysterious, dark doorway, and the invisible presence in it, yearning to appear, to be there. To live.

MONDAY MORNING. Ah, Monday morning. The ashen light, the noise, the sense of pointless but compulsory haste. I think it will be Monday morning when I am received in Hell. I was wakened early by a policeman bearing another mug of tea and lump of bread. I had been dozing, it was like being held fast in the embrace of a large, hot, rank-smelling animal. I knew at once exactly where I was, there was no mistaking the place. The policeman was young, an enormous boy with a tiny head, when I opened my eyes first and looked up at him he seemed to tower above me almost to the ceiling. He said something incomprehensible and went away. I sat on the edge of the cot and held my head in my hands. My mouth was foul, and there was an ache behind my eyes and a wobbly sensation in the region of my diaphragm. I wondered if this nausea would be with me for the rest of my life. Wan sunlight fell at a slant through the bars of my cage. I was cold. I draped a blanket around my shoulders and squatted over the bucket, my knees trembling. I would not have been surprised if a crowd had gathered in the corridor to laugh at me. I kept thinking, yes, this is it, this is how it will be from now on. It was almost gratifying, in a horrible sort of way.

Sergeant Cunningham came to fetch me for the first of that day's inquisitions. I had washed as best I could at the filthy sink in the corner. I asked him if I might borrow a razor. He laughed, shaking his head at the idea, the richness of it. He thought I really was a card. I admired his good humour: he had been here all night, his shift was only ending now. I shuffled after him along the corridor, clutching my trousers to keep them from falling down. The dayroom was filled with a kind of surly pandemonium. Typewriters clacked, and short-wave radios snivelled in adenoidal bursts, and people strode in and out of doorways, talking over their shoulders, or crouched at desks and shouted into telephones. A hush fell when I came through – no, not a hush, exactly, but a downward modulation in the noise. Word, obviously, had spread. They did not stare at me, I suppose that would have been unprofessional, but they took me in, all the same. I saw myself in their eyes, a big, confused creature, like a dancing bear, shambling along at the steel-tipped heels of Cunningham's friendly boots. He opened a door and motioned me into a square, grey room. There was a plastic-topped table and two chairs. Well, he said, I'll be seeing you, and he winked and withdrew his head and shut the door. I sat down carefully, placing my hands flat before me on the table. Time passed. I was surprised how calmly I could sit, just waiting. It was as if I were not fully there, as if I had become detached somehow from my physical self. The room was like the inside of a skull. The hubbub in the dayroom might have been coming to me from another planet.

Barker and Kickham were the first to arrive. Barker today wore a blue suit which had been cut in great broad swathes, as if it were intended not for wearing, but to house a collection of things, boxes, perhaps. He was red-faced and in a sweat already. Kickham had on the same leather jacket and dark shirt that he was wearing yesterday – he did not strike me as a man much given to changing his clothes. They wanted to know why I had not signed the confession. I had forgotten about it, and left it under the mattress, but I said, I don't know why, that I had torn it up. There was another of those brief, stentorian silences, while they stood over me, clenching their fists and breathing heavily down their nostrils. The air rippled with suppressed violence. Then they trooped out and I was left alone again. Next to appear was an elderly chap in cavalry twill and a natty little hat, and a narrow-eyed, brawny young man who looked like the older one's disgruntled son. They stood just inside the door and studied me carefully for a long moment, as if measuring me for something. Then Detective Twill advanced and sat down opposite me, and crossed his legs, and took off his hat, revealing a flattish bald head, waxen and peculiarly pitted, like that of an ailing baby. He produced a pipe and lighted it with grave deliberation, then recrossed his legs and settled himself more comfortably, and began to ask me a series of cryptic questions, which after some time I realised were aimed at discovering what I might know about Charlie French and his acquaintances. I answered as circumspectly as I could, not knowing what it was they wanted to know – I suspect they didn't, either. I kept smiling at them both, to show how willing I was, how compliant. The younger one, still standing by the door, took notes. Or at least he went through the motions of writing in a notebook, for I had an odd feeling that the whole thing was a sham, intended to distract or intimidate me. All that happened, however, was that I grew bored – I could not take them seriously – and got muddled, and began to contradict myself. After a while they too seemed to grow discouraged, and eventually left. Then my chum

Inspector Haslet came sidling in with his shy smile and averted glance. My God, I said, who were they? Branch, he said. He sat down, looked at the floor, drummed his fingers on the table. Listen, I said, I'm worried, my wife, I – He wasn't listening, wasn't interested. He brought up the matter of my confession. Why hadn't I signed it? He spoke quietly, he might have been talking about the weather. Save a lot of trouble, you know, he said. Suddenly I flew into a rage, I don't know what came over me, I banged my fist on the table and jumped up and shouted at him that I would do nothing, sign nothing, until I got some answers. I really did say that: *until I get some answers!* At once, of course, the anger evaporated, and I sat down again sheepishly, biting on a knuckle. The ruffled air subsided. Your wife, Haslet said mildly, is getting on a plane – he consulted his watch – just about now. I stared at him. Oh, I said. I was relieved, of course, but not really surprised. I knew all along Señor what's-his-name would be too much of a gentleman not to let her go.

It was noon when Maolseachlainn arrived, though he had the rumpled air of having just got out of bed. He always looks like that, it is another of his endearing characteristics. The first thing that struck me was how alike we were in build, two big soft broad heavy men. The table groaned between us when we leaned forward over it, the chairs gave out little squeaks of alarm under our ponderous behinds. I liked him at once. He said I must be wondering who had engaged him on my behalf. I nodded vigorously, though in truth no such thought had entered my head. He grew shifty then, and mumbled something about my mother, and some work he claimed to have done for her in some unspecified period of the past. It was to be a long time before I would discover, to my surprise and no little dismay, that in fact it was Charlie French who arranged it all, who called my mother that Sunday evening and broke the news to her of my arrest, and told her to contact straight away his good friend Maolseachlainn Mac Giolla Gunna, the famous counsel. It was Charles too who paid, and is paying still, Mac's not inconsiderable fees. He puts the money through the bank, and my mother, or it must be that stable-girl, now, I suppose, sends it on as if it were coming from Coolgrange. (Sorry to have kept this bit from you, Mac, but it's what Charlie wanted.) You made some sort of confession, Maolseachlainn was saying, is that right? I told him about Cunningham's marvellous document. I must have grown excited in the telling, for his brow darkened, and he closed his eyes behind his half-glasses as if in pain and held up a hand to silence me. You'll sign nothing, he said, nothing — are you mad? I hung my head. But I'm guilty, I said quietly, I *am* guilty. This he pretended not to hear. Listen to me, he said, listen. You will sign nothing, say nothing, do nothing. You will enter a plea of not guilty. I opened my mouth to protest, but he was not to be interrupted. You will plead not guilty, he said, and when I judge the moment opportune you will change your submission, and plead guilty to manslaughter. Do you understand? He was looking at me coldly over his glasses. (This was early days, before he had become my friend.) I shook my head. It doesn't seem right, I said. He gave a sort of laugh. Right! he said, and did not add: that's rich, coming from you. We were silent for a moment. My stomach made a pinging sound. I felt sick and hungry at the same time. By the way, I said, have you spoken to my mother, is she coming to see me? He pretended not to hear. He put away his papers, and took off his glasses and squeezed the bridge of his nose. Was there anything I wanted? Now it was my turn to snicker. I mean is there anything I can have them get for you, he said, in a primly disapproving tone. A razor, I said, and they could give me back my belt, I'm not going to hang myself. He stood up to leave. Suddenly I wanted to detain him. Thank you, I said, so fervently that he paused and stared at me owlishly. I meant to kill her, you know, I said, I have no explanation, and no excuse. He just sighed.

I was brought to court in the afternoon. Inspector Haslet and two uniformed guards accompanied me. My hand where I had caught it on the rose-bush had become infected. O Frederick, thou art sick. I have a strangely hazy recollection of that first appearance. I had expected the courtroom to be rather grand, something like a small church, with oaken pews and a carved ceiling and an air of pomp and seriousness, and I was disappointed when it turned out to be little more than a shabby office, the kind of place where obscure permits are issued by incompetent clerks. When I was led in, there was a sort of irritable flurry of activity which I took to be a general making-ready, but which was, as I discovered to my surprise, the hearing itself. It cannot have lasted more than a minute or two. The judge, who wore an ordinary business suit, was a jolly old boy with whiskers and a red nose. He must have had a reputation as a wit, for when he fixed me with a merry eye and said, Ah, Mr Montgomery, the whole place fairly rocked with amusement. I smiled politely, to show him I could take a joke, even if I did not get it. A guard prodded me in the back, I stood up, sat down, stood up again, then it was over. I looked about me in surprise. I felt I must have missed something. Maolseachlainn was asking for bail. Judge Fielding gently shook his head, as if he were reproving a forward child. Ah no, he said, I think not, sir. That provoked another tremor of merriment in the court. Well, I was glad they were all having such a good time. The guard behind me was saying something, but I could not concentrate, for there was a horrible, hollow sensation in my chest, and I realised that I was about to weep. I felt like a child, or a very old man. Maolseachlainn touched my arm. I turned away helplessly. Come on now, the guard said, not unkindly, and I blundered after him. Everything swam. Haslet was behind me, I knew his step by now. In the street a little crowd had gathered. How did they know who I was, which court I would be in, the time at which I would appear? When they caught sight of me they gave a cry, a sort of ululant wail of awe and execration that made my skin prickle. I was so confused and frightened I forgot myself and waved – I waved to them! God knows what I thought I was doing. I suppose it was meant as a placatory gesture, an animal sign of submission and retreat. It only made them more furious, of course. They shook their fists, they howled. One or two of them seemed about to break from the rest and fly at me. A woman spat, and called me a dirty bastard. I just stood there, nodding and waving like a clockwork man, with a terrified grin fixed on my face. That was when I realised, for the first time, it was *one of theirs* I had killed. It had rained while I was inside, and now the sun was shining again. I remember the glare of the wet road, and a cloud stealthily disappearing over the rooftops, and a dog skirting the angry crowd with a worried look in its eye. Always the incidental things, you see, the little things. Then the blanket was thrown over me and I was pushed head-first into the police car and we sped away, the tyres hissing. Hee-haw, hee-haw. In the hot, woolly darkness I wept my fill.

*

Prison. This place. I have described it already.

My first visitor was a surprise. When they told me it was a woman I expected Daphne, straight from the airport, or else my mother, and at first when I came into the visiting-room I did not recognise her. She seemed younger than ever, in her shapeless pullover and plaid skirt and sensible shoes. She had the unformed, palely freckled look of a schoolgirl, the dullard of the class, who cries in the dorm at night and is mad on ponies. Only her marvellous, flame-coloured hair proclaimed her a woman. Jenny! I said, and she blushed. I took her hands in mine. I was absurdly pleased to see her. I did not know then that she would soon prove my usurper. Joanne, actually, she mumbled, and bit her lip. I laughed in embarrassment. Joanne, I said, of course, forgive me, I'm so confused just now. We sat down. I beamed and beamed. I felt light-hearted, almost skittish. I might have been the visitor, an old bachelor friend of the family, come to see the poor duckling on the school open day. She had brought my bag from Coolgrange. It looked strange to me, familiar and yet alien, as if it had been on an immense, transfiguring voyage, to another planet, another galaxy, since I had seen it last. I enquired after my mother. I was tactful enough not to ask why she had not come. Tell her I'm sorry, I said. It sounded ridiculous, as if I were apologising for a broken appointment, and we looked away from each other furtively and were silent for a long, awkward moment. I have a nickname in here already, I said, they call me Monty, of course. She smiled, and I was pleased. When she smiles, biting her lip like that, she is more than ever like a child. I cannot believe she is a schemer. I suspect she was as surprised as I when the will was read. I find it hard to see her as the mistress of Coolgrange. Perhaps that is what my mother intended – after *her*, the drip. Ah, that is unworthy of me, my new seriousness. I do not hate her for disinheriting me. I think that in her way she was trying to teach me something, to make me look more closely at things, perhaps, to pay more attention to people, such as this poor clumsy girl, with her freckles and her timid smile and her almost invisible eyebrows. I am remembering what Daphne said to me only yesterday, through her tears, it has lodged in my mind like a thorn: *You knew nothing about us, nothing!* She's right, of course. She was talking about America, about her and Anna Behrens and all that, but it's true in general – I know nothing. Yet I am trying. I watch, and listen, and brood. Now and then I am afforded a glimpse into what seems a new world, but which I realise has been there all along, without my noticing. In these explorations my friend Billy is a valuable guide. I have not mentioned Billy before, have I? He attached himself to me early on, I think he is a little in love with me. He's nineteen – muscles, oiled black hair, a killer's shapely hands, like mine. Our trials are due to open on the same day, he takes this as a lucky omen. He is charged with murder and multiple rape. He insists on his innocence, but cannot suppress a guilty little smile. I believe he is secretly proud of his crimes. Yet a kind of innocence shines out of him, as if there is something inside, some tiny, precious part, that nothing can besmirch. When I consider Billy I can almost believe in the existence of the soul. He has been in and out of custody since he was a child, and is a repository of prison lore. He tells me of the various ingenious methods of smuggling in dope. For instance, before the glass screens were put up, wives and girlfriends used to hide in their mouths little plastic bags of heroin, which were passed across during lingering kisses, swallowed, and sicked-up later, in the latrines. I was greatly taken with the idea, it affected me deeply. Such need, such passion, such charity and daring – when have I ever known the like?

What was I saying. I am becoming so vague. It happens to all of us in here. It is a kind of defence, this creeping absent-mindedness, this torpor, which allows us to drop off instantly, anywhere, at any time, into brief, numb stretches of sleep.

Joanne. She came to see me, brought me my bag. I was glad to have it. They had confiscated most of what was in it, the prison authorities, but there were some shirts, a bar of soap – the scented smell of it struck me like a blow – a pair of shoes, my books. I clutched these things, these icons, to my heart, and grieved for the dead past.

But grief, that kind of grief is the great danger, in here. It saps the will. Those who give way to it grow helpless, a wasting lethargy comes over them. They are like mourners for whom the period of mourning will not end. I saw this danger, and determined to avoid it. I would work, I would study. The theme was there, ready-made. I had Daphne bring me big thick books on Dutch painting, not only the history but the techniques, the secrets of the masters. I studied accounts of the methods of grinding colours, of the trade in oils and dyes, of the flax industry in Flanders. I read the lives of the painters and their patrons. I became a minor expert on the Dutch republic in the seventeenth century. But in the end it was no good: all this learning, this information, merely built up and petrified, like coral encrusting a sunken wreck. How could mere facts compare with the amazing knowledge that had flared out at me as I stood and stared at the painting lying on its edge in the ditch where I dropped it that last time? That knowledge, that knowingness, I could not have lived with. I look at the reproduction, pinned to the wall above me here, but something is dead in it. Something is dead.

It was in the same spirit of busy exploration that I pored for long hours over the newspaper files in the prison library. I read every word devoted to my case, read and re-read them, chewed them over until they turned to flavourless mush in my mind. I learned of Josie Bell's childhood, of her schooldays – pitifully brief – of her family and friends. Neighbours spoke well of her. She was a quiet girl. She had almost married once, but something had gone wrong, her fiancé went to England and did not return. First she worked in her own village, as a shopgirl. Then, before going to Whitewater, she was in Dublin for a while, where she was a chambermaid in the Southern Star Hotel. The Southern Star! – my God, I could have gone there when I was at Charlie's, could have taken a room, could have slept in a bed that she had once made! I laughed at myself. What would I have learned? There would have been no more of her there, for me, than there was in the newspaper stories, than there had been that day when I turned and saw her for the first time, standing in the open french window with the blue and gold of summer at her back, than there was when she crouched in the car and I hit her again and again and her blood spattered the window. This is the worst, the essential sin, I think, the one for which there will be no forgiveness: that I never imagined her vividly enough, that I never made her be there sufficiently, that I did not make her live. Yes, that failure of imagination is my real crime, the one that made the others possible. What I told that policeman is true – I killed her because I could kill her, and I could kill her because for me she was not alive. And so my task now is to bring her back to life. I am not sure what that means, but it strikes me with the force of an unavoidable imperative. How am I to make it come about, this act of parturition? Must I imagine her from the start, from infancy? I am puzzled, and not a little fearful, and yet there is something stirring in me, and I am strangely excited. I seem to have taken on a new weight and density. I feel gay and at the same time wonderfully serious. I am big with possibilities. I am living for two.

I have decided: I will not be swayed: I will plead guilty to murder in the first degree. I think it is the right thing to do. Daphne, when I told her, burst into tears at once. I was astonished, astonished and appalled. What about *me*, she cried, what about the child? I said, as mildly as I could, that I thought I had already destroyed their lives, and that the best thing I could do was to stay away from them for as long as possible – forever, even – so that she might have the chance to start afresh. This, it seems, was not tactful. She just cried and cried, sitting there beyond the glass, clutching a sodden tissue in her fist, her shoulders shaking. Then it all came out, the rage and the shame, I could not make out the half of it through her sobs. She went back over the years. What I had done, and not done. How little I knew, how little I understood. I sat and gazed at her, aghast, my mouth open. I could not speak. How was it possible, that I could have been so wrong about her, all this time? How could I not have seen that behind her reticence there was all this passion, this pain? I was thinking about a pub I had passed by late on one of my night rambles through the city in that week before I was captured. It was in, I don't know, Stoney Batter, somewhere like that, a working-class pub with protective steel mesh covering the windows and old vomit-stains around the doorway. As I went past, a drunk stumbled out, and for a second, before the door swung shut again, I had a glimpse inside. I walked on without pausing, carrying the scene in my head. It was like something by Jan Steen: the smoky light, the crush of red-faced drinkers, the old boys propping up the bar, the fat woman singing, displaying a mouthful of broken teeth. A kind of slow amazement came over me, a kind of bafflement and grief, at how firmly I felt myself excluded from that simple, ugly, roistering world. That is how I seem to have spent my life, walking by open, noisy doorways, and passing on, into the darkness. – And yet there are moments too that allow me to think I am not wholly lost. The other day, for instance, on the way to yet one more remand hearing, I shared the police van with an ancient wino who had been arrested the night before, so he told me, for killing his friend. I could not imagine him having a friend, much less killing one. He talked to me at length as we bowled along, though most of what he said was gibberish. He had a bloodied eye, and an enormous, weeping sore on his mouth. I looked out the barred window at the city streets going past, doing my best to ignore him. Then, when we were rounding a sharp bend, he fell off his seat on top of me, and I found myself holding the old brute in my arms. The smell was appalling, of course, and the rags he wore had a slippery feel to them that made me clench my teeth, but still I held him, and would not let him fall to the floor, and I even – surely I am embroidering – I think I may even have clasped him to me for a moment, in a gesture of, I don't know, of sympathy, of comradeship, of solidarity, something like that. Yes, an explorer, that's what I am, glimpsing a new continent from the prow of a sinking ship. And don't mistake me, I don't imagine for a second that such incidents as

217

this, such forays into the new world, will abate my guilt one whit. But maybe they signify something for the future.

Should I destroy that last paragraph? No, what does it matter, let it stand.

Daphne brought me one of Van's drawings. I have pinned it up on the wall here. It is a portrait of me, she says. One huge, club foot, sausage fingers, a strangely calm, cyclopean eye. Quite a good likeness, really, when I think about it. She also brought me a startling piece of news. Joanne has invited her and the child to come and live at Coolgrange. They are going to set up house together, my wife and the stable-girl. (How quaintly things contrive to make what seems an ending!) I am not displeased, which surprises me. Apparently I am to live there also, when I get out. Oh, I can just see myself, in Wellingtons and a hat, mucking out the stables. But I said nothing. Poor Daphne, if only – ah yes, if only.

Maolseachlainn too was horrified when I told him of my decision. Don't worry, I said, I'll plead guilty, but I don't want any concessions. He could not understand it, and I had not the energy to explain. It's what I want, that's all. It's what I must do. Apollo's ship has sailed for Delos, the stern crowned with laurel, and I must serve my term. By the way, Mac, I said, I owe a plate to Charlie French. He did not get the joke, but he smiled anyway. She wasn't dead, you know, when I left her, I said. I wasn't man enough to finish her off. I'd have done as much for a dog. (It's true – is there no end to the things I must confess?) He nodded, trying not to show his disgust, or perhaps it was just shock he was hiding. Hardy people, he said, they don't die easily. Then he gathered up his papers and turned to go. We shook hands. The occasion seemed to require that small formality.

*

Oh, by the way, the plot: it almost slipped my mind. Charlie French bought my mother's pictures cheap and sold them dear to Binkie Behrens, then bought them cheap from Binkie and sold them on to Max Molyneaux. Something like that. Does it matter? Dark deeds, dark deeds. Enough.

Time passes. I eat time. I imagine myself a kind of grub, calmly and methodically consuming the future, what the world outside calls the future. I must be careful not to give in to despair, to that aboulia which has been a threat always to everything I tried to do. I have looked for so long into the abyss, I feel sometimes it is the abyss that is looking into me. I have my good days, and my bad. I think of the monsters on whose side my crime has put me, the killers, the torturers, the dirty little beasts who stand by and watch it happen, and I wonder if it would not be better simply to stop. But I have my task, my term. Today, in the workshop, I caught her smell, faint, sharp, metallic, unmistakable. It is the smell of metal-polish — she must have been doing the silver that day. I was so happy when I identified it! Anything seemed possible. It even seemed that someday I might wake up and see, coming forward from the darkened room into the frame of that doorway which is always in my mind now, a child, a girl, one whom I will recognise at once, without the shadow of a doubt.

It is spring. Even in here we feel it, the quickening in the air. I have some plants in my window, I like to watch them, feeding on the light. The trial takes place next month. It will be a quick affair. The newspapers will be disappointed. I thought of trying to publish this, my testimony. But no. I have asked Inspector Haslet to put it into my file, with the other, official fictions. He came to see me today, here in my cell. He picked up the pages, hefted them in his hand. It was to be my defence, I said. He gave me a wry look. Did you put in about being a scientist, he said, and knowing the Behrens woman, and owing money, all that stuff? I smiled. It's my story, I said, and I'm sticking to it. He laughed at that. Come on, Freddie, he said, how much of it is true? It was the first time he had called me by my name. True, Inspector? I said. All of it. None of it. Only the shame.